I0545980

KATHRYN'S BEACH

NADINE LAMAN

Arizona USA

KATHRYN'S BEACH

25th Anniversary Edition

Copyright © 2024 by NADINE LAMAN
Copyrights enforced.

First Edition.

ALL RIGHTS RESERVED BY THE AUTHOR. No part of this book may be reproduced or transmitted in any format or by any means, including scanning into a database, or used by artificial intelligence without written permission of the author or the author's heirs – with a witnessed signature in ink, NOT a digital signature. Rights use requests are logged. Purchasers of this book do not purchase any rights of use other than to read for their own enjoyment and cannot assign any rights. Libraries may only lend, not scan this book. NO ONE may scan this book in full or in part. Contact information for permission to use requests: Nadine@CactusRainPublishing.com.

This is a work of fiction. Names, characters, places, and incidents are fictitious or are used fictitiously. Any perceived resemblance to actual persons, living or dead, business establishments, events, or locales is false. A few family and friends wanted cameo roles in this adventure or to name characters, they have read and given approval of those items.

Cover Design by Nadine Laman
Cover Photo Seal Beach, California, USA by Nadine Laman

ISBN 978-1-947646-16-2

Published by Cactus Rain Publishing, San Tan Valley, Arizona, USA
Published December 5, 2024
Originally Printed in the United States of America

~ Dedication ~

To Charley Lawrence Laman
and our sons,
Sean Russell James Laman,
Maitiu Ioseph Lawrence Laman,
Tomas Andrew Lambert Laman

~~~

To my mentors:
Dr. Lois Johnson, Ilene Shrimplin Wood,
Jeannine Garsee, Janice Laman Zitek,
Judith McKee, and Ellen Lyon.

~~~

In affectionate memory of:
Julia Marquis, Governor Joan Finney,
Jean M. Flynn, G. Irene Unruh,
Irene Watson, and Karen Stewart.

~~~

A humble "thank you" to
Gladys Knight and Rhonda Holman,
two women who inspired me
and touched my heart and soul.

~~~

To those who have profoundly come into my life,
you know who you are.

~~~

Other books by Nadine Laman

High Tide
Storm Surge
The Trilogy

Kathryn's Beach

It isn't how long one lives,
it is how wide that really matters.

~ CHAPTER 1 ~

Enigma

"And you?" he asks. "What about you?"

"Oh, I don't know. Someone called me an enigma once."

Quickly, I pour a highball, hoping to appear disinterested in the conversation.

He stirs on his barstool, turning to look directly at me and squints his small middle-aged eyes through the bar's dim light.

"Enigma?" he queries with a tone of renewed curiosity.

Smoke from his cigarette curls above his head, then floats lazily into the light hanging from the ceiling. Carelessly he flicks his ashes in the direction of the ashtray. He doesn't notice or doesn't care that the ashes miss their mark and fall on the bar. It's a lazy kind of evening with no real purpose, like most of the nights before it and those in the foreseeable future.

The smoke works its way toward the light a second time. I watch it as I wonder why I have given him such a truthful answer. Silently, I admonish myself for letting my guard slip with this man who ordinarily wouldn't be an intellectual match for me.

"Yeah." I smile with a slight laugh to cover my previously mistaken honesty. "I had to look it up, then still wasn't sure it was a compliment."

I laugh again, take a step back, adding some distance between us. Moving away from him is only a symbolic gesture, but I make it anyway. It's a reminder to keep my wits about me. It seems I need reminders more often these days, and even then, he slipped by my defenses. Before I noticed, we were into the wrong conversation.

To escape further, I plunge the last two dirty beer glasses, one in each hand, up and down on the glass brushes at the bottom of the sink. The activity and renewed frothy beer-scented suds tranquilize my mind.

He watches me work as he swirls the last of the drink in his glass. "Well, was it?" He shoots back the question with a serious tone. While drinking most of the amber liquid in one large swallow, he eyes me for an answer.

As I take another step back my heel catches on the rubber mat. Why am I so clumsy? Once, long ago, I was a model of confidence in and out of the courtroom, but not now.

On the floor near the sink a stowaway lime wedge catches my attention. Thankfully, to cover my clumsiness with the mat, I scoop up the exiled garnish and smoothly deposit it in the trash bin.

Still not sure of the answer, I wipe the counter, weighing the best reply. I need an answer that isn't too serious and certainly not too revealing. Quickly, I sort through possible responses while continuing my distancing act. Think, think, I pressure myself. Turning away, I wipe the back bar with a bar towel. I don't want to get engaged in a personal conversation with him, or anyone else.

Slowly turning, I say in a matter-of-fact tone, "Yes. Yes, it was a compliment."

Briefly, I look straight into his eyes, then attend to wiping the beer taps one more time.

A lie? No, it's true. It is a compliment, but it wasn't meant to be when it was said.

Shrugging off the memory, I continue to work. As I wash the last of the bar utensils, my thoughts hurl me back in time. I remember the moment I was called an enigma. I remember being hurt by the tone of the word. I remember feeling my face grow hot and my eyes water with the sting of the insult. I was younger then and had hoped to please, though now, I wonder why conforming had been so important.

He finishes the last half-swallow of his drink and sets the glass on the bar with the tenor of finality. The sound hangs in the thick air. He stirs, hesitates, then slides off his barstool. He pulls out three or four wadded bills from the front pocket of his jeans, sorts through them, then tosses a crumpled bill next to his empty glass.

"Catch you later," he says.

Glancing toward the door, then back to me, he slips on his coat and ball cap with a seed company logo on it. After a final adjustment of his cap to secure it against the wind, he opens the door and goes out.

Dropping my towel on the bar, I hurry to lock the door behind him. Finally! I draw a deep breath and sigh with relief to be alone.

This is an odd little town. It's stuck in the time of post-WWII days. Very little has changed and isn't likely to change any time soon. To look at it, the town is charming. Ancient oak and elm trees line the sidewalks with their branches touching above the street to create a green, shady archway.

Autumn blazes with color, then blows into piles behind the shed. In the winter everything has a covering of snow that shimmers in the sunlight. Spring comes, goes, then comes again to stay, but is gone all too soon to be replaced by summer's waves of heat. Then the cycle repeats to mark yet another year's passing like the rings inside a tree, and we become a year older.

There are stately stone mansions that were built after the Civil War by those who came to town with carpetbags full of money. Most of the other houses are white wooden structures with black-trimmed windows and a modest porch, all remnants of the railroad town it was originally. The railroad and the interstate highway bypassed the town two generations ago. A tree grows through the window of the abandoned train station as a reminder that those days will never return.

The town is picture-postcard pretty. But the people aren't pretty. Life has been especially hard for them through the years of the Dust Bowl and the droughts. It shows on their faces and in their walk. Farming isn't easy, but they love it. When the winter wheat sprouts, everyone drives slower simply to admire the wonder of it and hope for a good covering of snow.

The only other thing they love is gossip. They accept it as they accept thunderstorms and tornadoes. They know its sting, but seek a fix every chance they get. Like every other addiction, it cuts deep into relationships and scars them for all time.

Moving to a small, rural town is a careful, dangerous dance. Soon after my arrival, I observed firsthand gossip's sting. The townspeople usually didn't keep the facts straight even when they did know the truth. In time, I made the extra effort to remain uninteresting. They could, and would (and often did) say what they wanted to say about me, an outsider.

Even years later outsiders are still only outsiders. They can never be elevated to the status of being one of the locals; they are never quite allowed to belong in this place. Besides gossip there isn't much entertainment in this town of 1,523 people—gossip is about all they have.

Despite the summer heat, they congregate on the bleachers down at the ballpark, gossiping while watching the games or on front porches along the railing, the steps, and the porch swing—gossiping.

In the winter the people gather in Rex's Diner on Main Street for breakfast, and here, Ruthie's Bar, later in the day to talk about each other, about the absent locals, and especially about the outsiders.

Occasionally the gossip is innocent, but usually it's just plain mean. Sometimes it seems the meaner the better. The face of the informant lights up with a surge of power they hold over the listeners. It's a fleeting moment until their face hardens with the spirit of their hurtful words. Then their audience tries to outdo them with their own moment in the spotlight.

Expertly, I have managed to keep my private life private. I stay out of political arguments. There is little discussion of religion since there are only two churches in town. I never mentioned that I am Catholic because everyone here is either Baptist or Methodist. I drive to the next county to attend Mass.

Just last Easter a bunch of Methodists became Baptists overnight when the Methodist Bishop sent a woman minister into their midst. As it turns out, she is a nice person—but no matter, they will run her out of town before next Easter.

My best defense became turning the conversation away from me and on to farming. They didn't know where I was from, but they knew I needed educated on farming. I could write a book about what I have heard from my side of the bar. It would be a bestseller, with the gossip.

With an approving nod I compliment myself that I have escaped once more. Luckily, I timed my response to his question just right, avoiding a conversation about me.

"Besides," I say aloud, "bartenders listen to people talk about their lives, not the other way around."

Kathryn's Beach

I shake my head, thinking about this place. It's becoming more difficult to maintain my reclusive lifestyle. I long for friendships and maybe even a romance. Real relationships elude me, leaving the re-emerging desires for intimate connections unanswered.

Of all the choices of places to go, I am not certain why I came here. At the time, where didn't matter. I came to escape from life, my life. Like the corporate executives who started cottage industries in Vermont to escape their rat race, I am taking a break from the real world.

On rare instances, I admit being amused by my introduction to rural living. There is a strange wholesomeness about rural America. Nevertheless, this is an odd refuge, an unlikely choice considering who I once was and who these people are. My observations of how they treat each other only prove that we have nothing in common and I don't belong here. I'm becoming lonely—terribly, terribly lonely.

Straightening the barstools and restocking the liquor, I'm deep in thought about what I left behind in Los Angeles: my work, my friends and family, my beach, and my comfortable life. Memories play like a movie trailer in my mind. The scenes hook me and I want more. I want to experience the story and escape into it, buttered popcorn and all.

Despite the overwhelming flood of emotions churning inside me, I return to the nightly ritual of closing the bar. After removing his ashtray and wiping the ring of ashes left on the counter, all that remains is to close the cash register tape and count the money.

Tonight my mind won't allow idle thoughts; it continues to demand an awakening of memories I abandoned five years ago. I had driven aimlessly for days. When I arrived here, I simply couldn't go any farther. I was emotionally exhausted. By the time I stopped driving, I was a shell of my former self.

Suddenly, five years seems like a long time. I am urgently restless. Why have I stayed so long?

"Okay, Katey. It's time to go home," I say aloud, as I adjust the thermostat for the night, and walk around the room shutting off the lights. Standing by the door, ready to shut off the last light

I look back at the buzzing neon beer advertisements dimly lighting the pool table. Decisively I admit, "It is time to go back to the world where I belong; back to my real life."

Securing the door, the deadbolt clicks sluggishly from the cold. Slipping the key in my pocket, I pull up my coat collar, and tighten the scarf around my neck and across my face to keep the cutting cold from burning my skin and taking my breath away. My gloves barely make a difference. The cold sneaks up my sleeve before I can put my hands in my pockets.

With the wind chill below zero again tonight, I feel tired of winter. The ambient temperature has not been above freezing for more than three weeks, and the wind chill makes it all the more inhospitable. A blast of night-wind cuts through my scarf with a stinging that burns my cheeks. It makes me eager to get home, to my real home in L.A.

After snowing all day, the previously shoveled sidewalk is covered with six inches of new snow. The bar is only two blocks from my apartment and it is easier to walk than to drive in this weather, especially after the ice storm we had yesterday.

Tonight's walk home is different. For five years my routine has never varied. I had no plan to my days except to work at the bar. Now my mind is planning the trip home. It's strangely refreshing to plan something meaningful, especially like being where I belong.

I carefully ascend the icy incline toward my apartment. The street I live on is up the first block of the hill, then right for half a block, and walk up the alley. It is a slow ascent. My steps are unreliable when the unanchored snow gives way from the ice beneath it. Racing thoughts deep inside me add to the difficulty to concentrate. I grab for the metal railing along the sidewalk.

Pausing at the corner I turn and look down the street behind me. The snow goes over my shoes and sticks to the top of my socks. Distracted for a minute by the wet cold soaking my ankles as the warmth of my body melts the snow, I shake the snow from my shoes—wishing I had taken my bigger boots to work this afternoon. It's a mute thought now.

Looking into the night, there is an eerie quiet. Even the wind isn't making the sounds one would expect. I look back at the bar at the foot of the hill, down on Main Street. It looks alone in the cold dark—if a building can look any particular way.

"Lonely buildings? I have lost all sense of reality. Reality, Katey! Reality? Now there is a concept foreign to my life."

With that, I resume inching the slope toward my apartment. The fat snowflakes fall lazily from the dark heaven. Stopping midway across the street, I look around in the crisp night air. The Christmas-movie snow reflects the moonlight, making it easy to see well, while increasing the sharp contrast between the snow and the night shadows.

Considering my feelings toward the meanness of these gossiping people, it is still a pretty town. My glance settles on an old house someone is restoring to the Grand Old Victorian era. It has dentil and gingerbread trim. It's painted like a paint store advertisement. Painted Ladies are what they call the bright mix of contrasting colors. It looks out of place next to the plain white houses up and down the street. As with many of the things here, it is all a façade.

It is obvious by the architecture (little balconies outside of each bedroom's window) this house was originally a bordello. I surprise myself when I laugh out loud. It is so quiet this time of night that my laugh echoes against the buildings along the empty street. It embarrasses me that I have made such a noise.

Stepping up the curb to the sidewalk, I grasp the railing to steady my step. The incline is steeper on this side of the street. My knit glove sticks to the frosty metal handrail.

"It's cold out here, quit being so smug and go home," I admonish myself under my breath and begin to walk more deliberately. Pay attention, Katey, or you will roll down this icy hill.

My focus doesn't last. It would be quite a sight when they chisel me out of the ice at the bottom of the hill. I laugh again visualizing the American Gothic people cutting me out of a block of frozen snow and ice. Wait, no! They would leave me, discussing my situation, but not wanting to get involved.

Despite the pity I feel toward these people and their petty ways, they do amuse me. The few of us who are outsiders probably amuse them with our other-world ways.

"Katey, you're talking to yourself entirely too much." The realization startles me. "Oh, Katey!" I sigh. "Go home!"

I carefully walk up the ice-crusted wooden stairs to my two-room apartment above the garage. In an effort to regain control of them, I begin to organize my thoughts. Go to bed. Tomorrow, start packing.

Heaped with blankets, I lay listening to the snowflakes, now frozen into ice crystals, softly pelting against the window. It feels good to make a decision. In reality, I haven't put much thought into the decision to go home, though now I grasp it firmly. I desperately own it.

There is no escape from the daunting presence of the memories. What do I hope to gain by going home? I don't know. But, then again, there is nothing to gain by staying here.

The rafters creak when the wind gusts. The steady sound of the wind driving the sleet against the window eventually lulls me to sleep.

~~~

In the morning, I lay in bed listening to the sound of ice cracking and falling through the frozen tree limbs, crashing to the hard ground below. Obviously, the sun has been up for hours, for the ice on the higher limbs of the trees to begin to melt. There is no real hurry to get out of bed, so I snuggle deeper under the blankets and listen to the winter sounds until I am fully awake. Slowly I realize I had the best night's sleep I have had for a very long time. No nightmares.

The next few days my mind is remembering more and more about the home I left, thoughts that I haven't had for years. I miss the pleasant weather, the familiar freeways, my friends, and the comforting sense of belonging—at the beach and with my family.

The bar provides a constant supply of boxes. Selectively, I watch for good ones to take home. The few cooking pans I have go into the thrift store box along with other less-used kitchen items. I didn't bring many things with me when I came, only what I tossed into my car. Perhaps I brought too much emotional baggage. But I will deal with that later.

~~~

The only thing left for me to do before I leave is work through the holidays while Ruthie visits her grandchildren in St. Louis. I have no holiday plans, so I'll wait to go home in January.

The patrons' activities at the bar never change from day-to-day. But Ruthie takes on an alternate personality during the holidays. Beginning before Thanksgiving, each time she leaves the bar to run an errand, she returns with her arms full of bags of Christmas decorations.

Even though Ruthie does this every year, it never ceases to amaze me. Her decorations multiply exponentially. They're everywhere, from the oddly shaped Santa on the inside of the front door that erupts into an off-pitch electronic version of eight different Christmas songs every time the door opens to the plastic snowman lights hanging precariously from the light fixture above the pool table.

I have never known any one person to own so many Christmas lights. She has the usual blinking lights, chasing lights, icicle lights, in addition to red chili pepper lights, tiny angel lights, and plastic reindeer lights that insist on hanging upside down no matter what Ruthie does to right them. Lights are strung on the juke box, the walls, around the beer glass shelves, the pool cue rack, the restroom doors, and beyond. By Christmas the bar looks like the Las Vegas Strip. She even found a battery-operated blinking bow tie for me to wear on New Year's Eve. Oh, lovely.

Amidst the chaos of Ruthie's all-out eclectic version of Christmas decorating, my packing goes quickly and effortlessly. Most of the things I acquired during my time here land in the thrift store boxes. There are only a few boxes to ship home to my cousin Ilene. Shortly, I can give away my winter clothes.

I hate winter.

~~~

After New Year's Day I ship my boxes to California, purchase an airline ticket home, and arrange to sell my car with the delivery date set for the morning I leave. Perhaps for a little post-holiday cash I can convince someone to take me to the airport in Lincoln. Everything is settled. Soon I will be on my way home. I've been here entirely too long.

As usual, it takes the whole first week and a half of January to get Ruthie's lights down and packed in boxes. When Raymond came into the bar Ruthie talked him into helping move the boxes to the attic. While he was in the mood to be helpful, I asked him to if he would give me a ride to the airport. Actually, it took more cash than talk to get the ride, but there is no shuttle service out here—so I pay up.

Finally, the day to leave arrives. As a traveling companion, Raymond isn't the best choice. His conversation is anything but stimulating. In addition to the periods of silence from my driver, he has the radio tuned to the monotone AM station's farm report.

The news of hog futures and wheat prices fade into the background noise of my mind while I think of the life waiting in L.A. The five-hour car ride to the airport seems to last for days. We get behind a slow-moving farm vehicle with a huge round bale of alfalfa completely filling the bed of the truck. We can't see around nor go around him since the two-lane road has only three ruts in the hard-packed snow.

For months the snow plows have piled the snow at the sides of the road until the endless mound is above the top of our pickup cab. In essence, we are driving 35 mph through a topless white tunnel, staring at the butt-end of a bale of alfalfa. At the "T" in the road, the truck ahead turns right while we skid left toward the next one-horse town, then eventually to the interstate leading to Lincoln.

~~~

In contrast to the road trip, the airline seat caresses me. There are no farm reports to be heard, and for that I am thankful. I have never felt more relieved than I feel now. Committed. Ready.

After the usual delays, the air rushes out the little spout above my head, the engine sounds accelerate, followed by a backwards lurch as the tow vehicle begins to push the plane from the gate. Taxi, another wait, then the rush down the runway pavement, incremented by expansion joints, and the anticipated leap into the sky. With it, my spirit leaps.

It isn't long before we are flying west over the Platte River. This is where the cranes nest? I didn't get around to seeing the annual migration. But now I am on my own migration, I whisper to myself, as I look out of the oval window at the wide river basin below. Just like the birds, I am driven by instinct to go home.

As the plane makes its final approach to the new Denver airport, the dim silhouette of the city appears far in the distance and the snow-covered mountains rise in the west beyond the city. The snow is falling thicker as we approach the ground. The sun's descent behind the Rockies is beautiful. A few hours past those mountains and I will be home. There is only a short delay scheduled as we change planes for the next leg of the journey.

Unfortunately, just as we prepare to board our connecting flight to Los Angeles, we are told it's canceled. The planes can't de-ice fast enough to get airborne. As a matter of fact, the snow plows can't keep up with the windblown snowdrifts across the runways—the airport is now closed.

"What! Closed?" I ask the person beside me in line to make sure I understood correctly.

Several other travelers with a deer-in-the-headlights stare nod affirmatively to my question.

The information seems true. Flights in or out of the Denver airport are canceled. Furthermore, all of the hotels near the airport have been full for hours, reports an airline spokesperson. It hardly seems worth the long bus trip to Denver for a short night's stay.

Some stranded travelers are visibly frustrated, and a few spew their anger at the gate staff. Certainly, it must be true, the staff caused the storm as part of a conspiracy against the passengers. I smile to myself at the thought of such reasoning.

Like many of the other passengers, I decide to stay in the terminal and sleep across several seats near the gate until we can get airborne.

~~~

In the morning, as the terminal comes to life, I wake with an airline blanket covering me. Someone must have come during the night and laid one over each of us.

Sitting up, I look around wondering if the person who had been so thoughtful is still nearby. No one seems to be watching us for a sign of appreciation for their deed. It leaves me with an uneasy feeling—I don't like being in debt. Not to anyone. Not ever.

Watching people come and go, I sit at the gate for a long time thinking about going home. These past five years my world has been narrow and solitary. It's a defense mechanism, no doubt, but in L.A. all of that will have to change.

Maybe the layover in Denver has been good. I needed this time. My thoughts overwhelm me. I feel frustrated. A sense of panic rushes over me and I begin to wish for the security of a plan—a definite, concrete plan. I desperately wish for a traveling companion to tell me everything will be all right.

Grandmother's words come to the forefront of my thoughts. In the way only grandmothers can, mine would smile, tilt her head and say, "If wishes were horses, beggars would ride; if turnips were watches, I'd have one by my side..."

Irish women of her vintage were on a first-name basis with hardship. The memory of her words is enough to stop my whining. I straighten in my chair, searching for new resolve.

The wind and snow subsided during the night, allowing the snow plows to liberate the runways. In a language distinctive to airport public address systems, a voice not meant for such purposes announces our plane is ready for departure.

"My plane," I whisper while joining the line forming at the jetway entrance. Despite any uncertainty about going home, I am relieved to be on my way. I vow never to leave again. I am tired of being an outsider, especially with no hope of acceptance.

As the plane lifts from the runway and climbs, it lurches in response to turbulent weather above us. Another winter storm is brewing over the Rockies. The land disappears below, and I am glad to see the snow and ice go out of sight.

We jerk in our seats with each bout of turbulence. There's a loud, sudden thud, then metallic crash from the galley as a soda can hits the floor and rolls against the cabinet. Startled outbursts and excited half-whispers from passengers follow the decidedly abrupt "bump in the road" as the plane lifts straight up.

A terrified baby cries, followed by whimpering, then sucking sounds. A young female voice from behind me hums softly, soothingly. Soon the sucking sound becomes more rhythmic and less desperate. Within minutes the baby takes a deep breath and begins to breathe as if it is asleep.

~~~

I don't mind the storm. I am determined to ignore the pain from my body jerking against the seat belt across my lap. This is nothing compared to what I have been through. I can take turbulence.

Rising into the clouds, the sky disappears from view. Glued to the window, I stare at the wings, watching the pattern the moisture makes as it rushes over them. It's good to see moisture rather than ice on the wings, but I am not sure I would care about ice as long as we continue to fly west.

The plane breaks through to the top of the clouds where the sun is bright above us. To crowd out the chill of winter, I lean toward the window and soak in every ray of sunlight.

By the time our plane reaches L.A. I am beginning to thaw. But there is still a deeper chill in my bones.

~~~

~ CHAPTER 2 ~

Home, Sweet Home

Among the crowd waiting for our luggage at LAX, reality is a lot different from my imagining of how this would play out once the plane landed. I don't know what I was thinking, but my plan only went as far as getting here. Beyond that, well, I simply couldn't imagine beyond that.

None of the luggage inching down the conveyor looks familiar. Is this some kind of hidden camera joke? Next time I'll have to remember that everyone has black luggage and put a strap or something on mine. But there will be no next time. No point in it, is there? With my luggage in tow, I make the customary pilgrimage to the rental car counter.

With unexpected certainty, I pull into the traffic and decide to stop by my old office. It isn't exactly on the way home, but most of my friends are there. They are part of the importance of coming home.

Heading downtown, the mass of humanity on the freeway catches me off guard. I am glad to see the rushing, reckless traffic, but I am dangerously out of practice driving in it.

Driving someone else's car doesn't help, but at least I know my way around the area. Soon the familiar surroundings inspire my confidence and I accelerate into the fast lane. This is going to be easy, I decide, as I realize the speed with which I eased back into city traffic.

~~~

Outside the towering building, I pause to get the feel of being home. I think about my friends and wonder how many of them still work here. Maybe it is a mistake to come. I hope not. Standing in front of the door is a bad time to second-guess my decision.

With the draw of a deep breath, I pull open the heavy glass door. The comfort of familiar surroundings wraps its arms around me as I walk back into my former life. It is almost as if I am returning from a day at court rather than having been away for five years.

Things look much as I remember, typical government office decor. It is funny how something like this makes me feel good to be back. I breathe easier.

After the routine security check, the lobby receptionist waves me to her desk. She greets me enthusiastically, dispelling more of my doubts about the visit. Reaching for the phone, she winks, and motions me toward the stairs. "I'll tell them you're coming."

My step gains confidence as I start up the stairs to the inner sanctuary. In the time it takes to walk the three flights, I nearly delude myself into thinking the last five years were a bad dream and I am coming back to the office from an investigation.

At the top of the stairs I recognize three police officers in the corridor that joins our buildings, police department and welfare department. Seeing them completes my delusion that I haven't been away long.

It feels good not to be an outsider, even though it has only been slightly over two hours since the plane landed at LAX. Coming home was long overdue. I was foolish to leave, and more foolish to remain away.

The corridor opens into the large room that is the heart of the work area. The least inconsequential thing brings comforting memories of the time I spent in this room, first as a student, then as the resident expert.

I scan the room, enjoying the solace of familiarity. Groups of desks are crowded around the perimeter. The desks are situated in sets of two, facing each other to optimize the space. My old desk is among those perpendicular to the coveted wall of large, arched windows, molded with wide, dark 1920s woodwork.

Most of the people I worked with are still here. Former colleagues congregate around me. Ever so slowly, I notice how different everyone seems. It is more than their new hairstyles and five years' worth of aging. The reality of how long I have been gone creeps into my thoughts. I wonder how they see me after all this time. How much have I changed in their eyes?

In a brief time, everyone filters back to their desks. It feels awkward with no desk of my own. I should have left before the last person walked away. I wish for a dignified means of escape. It would be perfect timing if Keith walked through the corridor from the police station. I'd exit in the pretense of a conversation. Keith is the detective who was my counterpart from the other building. He was my mentor, my partner.

Unfortunately, Keith doesn't come to rescue me from the awkwardness of standing alone while everyone else is engaged in work. Still, I glance in the direction of the hallway with the hope he will come, he always had before.

Feeling lost, I look around one more time for the missing co-worker I most wanted to see. Her desk next to mine, the one that was mine, is empty. Disappointed with her absence, I turn toward the door to leave.

Barely catching my peripheral vision, Maggie enters at the back of the room. She stops at the coffee machine, notices me, and raises a cup in my direction as if she half expected me.

Relieved to see her, I walk toward her and whisper excitedly, "Coffee?"

She pours a cup for each of us and we slip down the back stairs to our old spot on the patio at a table away from everyone where we can talk privately.

After the leafless dreariness of a Midwest winter, it's good to see green plants. The sun is soft in the winter sky. A slight breeze moves the branches of the palm trees. Just like the old days, I'm content sipping the industrial-strength coffee with Maggie.

It's good to see her. It's entirely my fault that we haven't kept in touch. Under the influence of the coffee aroma, I study her.

We met in undergraduate school, then attended grad school together. We became closer when a forced transfer brought her to our department because her department never fully recovered from Reaganomics' cuts decades before.

We reconnected our college friendship once we were working in the same department. Our paths had paralleled so many times that it was either our destiny or just plain luck that we became close friends. It was this friendship that proved priceless to me five years ago as we worked on what became my last child abuse investigation.

It's comfortable to sit in our spot, together again, after my self-imposed exile. Maggie looks really good. Her dark shoulder-length hair is in a new and very flattering style that suits her quite well. I hope I look good too, though that might be expecting too much after the overnight stop in the Denver airport.

Putting down my cup, I study her again, watching for the Maggie I knew. There! I see something familiar in her eyes. Her green eyes can go from ornery to intelligent with the tilt of her head.

It's reassuring to see my old friend again. Taking another sip of coffee, I think about our shared history. Quietly, I reminisce fondly about this place and these people, my friends. The memories are calming. Relaxed, tentative music begins to meander in my mind, soothing the five years of forced silence.

"It wasn't your fault, Kate." Maggie jumps right into the conversation.

Startled, I look up for an indication of her intent. Five years doesn't mean anything to her. Damn! She's good.

Maggie doesn't mention my abrupt departure or my sudden reappearance. She looks at me intensely as she speaks, pausing only slightly to catch a breath between sentences —leaving no chance for a response from me.

"It was a clean investigation." Maggie continues confidently, "I reread the case file. We chipped in and ordered the transcript of the trial, even Karen."

"Maybe so—" my voice trails off, still not processing that Karen had contributed.

The entire case springs to the forefront of my memory with the bitter taste of day-old coffee.

"It was all there, Kate. No one could have done better," she says in a soft, reassuring voice that echoes within me.

She's taken aim and shot right to the heart of things. I can't sidestep her volley. Court transcripts aren't cheap. Maggie hasn't given me time to process that Karen, a keen fiscal manager, had ordered it.

I'm obligated to the conversation now. There is no getting out of it.

I set my cup down and wrap my fingers around it for the warmth it provides.

"But it didn't save her," I counter.

"It was Judge Jones' ruling that was in error, not anything you did or didn't do." Her tone dares me to disagree.

"He didn't see it. He let that sick bastard go!"

My voice betrays me with its mixed tone of anger and hurt. I feel the flood of emotions rushing over me and I'm not ready to deal with the memories. Struggling to process what she is saying and wrestling with my emotions is getting the best of me.

Maggie pushes straight on.

"The night before the murder trial, Judge Jones was dead."

"Dead?" I whisper, stunned. I lean forward at the shock of it, resting my arms against the edge of the table to brace myself. I had wished him dead when he sent her home to her abuser, essentially ruling a death sentence for the little girl in my case. I didn't mean it, not literally anyway.

I don't know if it is intentional or not, but Maggie is moving too fast. I had hoped to ease back into my L.A. life, not be tossed into the deep without warning.

"He shot himself in chambers," she continues with the matter-of-fact tone of someone who has seen too much violence for her age.

"Keith said, it looked like he was reading the grand jury indictment on the murder charges against the perp in your case. Maybe he saw the horrible thing he did. Maybe he knew it would come out in the murder trial." She finally pauses. The silence hangs in the thick city air.

It's all very complicated. I don't believe for one minute he admitted his culpability—even to himself. He might have feared that I would testify, and he should have, if he didn't. I am an excellent witness. The words of my testimony would have pointed at him with benign contempt and delivered him at the feet of Lady Justice.

The only flaw in that scheme is no one knew where I was. Even if they did, the subpoena wouldn't reach that distance. They could ask, but not compel me to return. If he was afraid of me, he killed himself for nothing.

My coffee tastes bitter.

Maggie stops playing with the undissolved sugar at the bottom of her cup, "And Kate, Judge Jones wrote a letter to you."

She sets her cup down and looks at me, seeming to search for an indication to the letter's content.

There are no clues for her to discover. I can't imagine why he would write to me. Maybe later I will be amused, wondering if Maggie thought there had been some sort of scandalous relationship between the Judge and me. But for now I am just as surprised about the letter as she must have been when it arrived.

Looking directly into my eyes, she continues a little softer, "Keith brought the letter by the office, hoping I knew where you were."

I make no response. She isn't going to guilt information out of me. If she wants to know about the last five years, she will have to ask outright.

But she doesn't ask. "We didn't open it. Keith said the suicide note was all the police needed."

I cock my head to the side, studying her, listening.

Maggie looks at her cup again as if trying to coax more coffee to appear. "I have it at home. We thought you should be the first to read it."

First? I catch her meaning and make a mental note she expects the letter to be shared with her. "Why would he write to me? It doesn't make sense."

Maggie looks straight into my eyes—I can't escape her gaze. I am trying to put it together as fast as she is handing out the information. I can't keep up with her. Struggling deep in thought, I realize she is saying something about dinner at her apartment.

"Oh, thanks. I can't tonight," I lie. Actually, dinner sounds good, but I am not up to more of her direct ways, at least not today.

I should have kept in touch with Maggie while I was gone, but it is too late to change that now. I'll just have to sort things out the best I can.

"Then come, and pick up the letter." Maggie can still read when I have reached my limit. "We'll have dinner some other time." She reaches for our cups, saying something about time to call it a day, then smiles.

At last this conversation is over. Knowing Maggie, I am sure this is only a temporary reprieve. When she has something to say, she will wait for her moment, then say it perfectly timed. There is never a permanent escape from her.

Maybe it had been a mistake to come to the office. No. No, it is good to see Maggie and the others. At one time Maggie, Keith, and I had been quite the team. No one in the state came near our record of closed cases or favorable court dispositions. We made sure the facts were clear and correct before we submitted the case to Karen to be sent to the District Attorney's office.

I have missed Maggie. Seeing her again is a significant part of why I came home. I was correct, I had to come here first. No other way would have felt right.

I would have liked to have seen Karen. It will be harder to come back the next time. In the end, my instincts have served me well. I had to come here before I can think about anything else.

When I reach the stairs to leave, Karen is coming up them. I quietly study her as she comes closer. She has lost about ten pounds and her hair color is a little different. Karen looks good. She is taller than I, with beautiful hazel eyes, an engaging smile, and short, dark brown hair.

There is something solid about her. She was always very classy, charming, and bright. I never wanted to be friends with Karen, I was perfectly happy with the distance afforded by our roles within the department, nothing more.

It surprises me that Karen chipped in for the transcript. It has nothing to do with money, but seems different from how I remember her.

As Karen nears the top of the stairs, she looks up. When she sees me, she smiles.

"Into my office, Kathryn," Karen says without breaking stride as she walks past me—not looking back.

Some things don't change. I smile, thinking about how natural it is to be summoned to her office.

It is good to be home.

Out of instinct I almost reply, "Yes, ma'am," as I follow her. I spent more than my share of time being reprimanded in this office. At least this time she won't lecture me to move a case along before I'm satisfied I have all of the facts. This time, she isn't my boss. This time—

"Yes, ma'am," I say for the pure enjoyment of it just as Karen shuts the wooden door. The latch, sluggish, causes the frosted glass to rattle in the dried-out putty.

She sets her briefcase and armload of files on her desk, positioning the files in stacks.

I stand back and wait near the door, perhaps poised for escape, then ease toward the chair in front of her desk.

Karen is always in command of her environment. It has been a long time since I felt a sense of command over my world. Life seems uncertain ever since that horrible last case. I've been lost a long time. I don't know what the rules are anymore. Someone changed them, and I didn't get the memo.

She startles me when she turns and gives me a motherly hug. It seems to fit the moment, though it wasn't her usual way. Neither of us is the hugging type—certainly not with each other.

Ours was an antagonistic relationship, to put it nicely. I was the problem employee. I never crossed the line in the process, but I wasn't afraid to come toe-to-toe with it. I questioned everything. I wanted to see all sides of the case. Most of all I didn't want to follow along mindlessly with the masses. Doing what everyone else did was the worst reason to do anything. I never bowed to pressure to close a case prematurely, not that she would have asked. But others did, and she'd hear about my mouthy reply. Usually they'd fail to mention their role in the exchange.

Until five years ago, social work was my life. I lived and breathed social work. Almost nothing else mattered, nothing except my family and the beach. I was good at my job, very good, in fact. However, I was unconventional, and that resulted in many summons to Karen's office.

Only my skill kept me from being transferred out of the department, or worse. Most of the time the results paid off and I was given absolution for my transgressions.

That was a long time ago. The hug feels good on my weary shoulders. I hope to remember this unprecedented moment, and the brief feeling of a sense of security.

"Kathryn, how are you?" she asks in a warm maternal tone unfamiliar to me. She continues before I can answer the first question. "Are you ready to get back to work?"

I can't help being amused. Is it me or are these people behaving strangely about my return?

Apparently I was more surprised with the decision to come home than they are with my arrival. I press my lips together just enough to conceal the grin that I'd rather not explain.

In the past I irreverently referred to Karen as a "Mother Superior." She was always commanding and unwavering in her opinions, only yielding to irrefutable empirical evidence. After the headaches I gave her, Karen is brave to invite me back to the department.

"I'm not sure." I hadn't expected her reception or the offer of a job. I'm not sure what I expected, but this certainly isn't it.

"Maggie told me about Judge Jones' letter," she says as she looks up from sorting her papers. She still sounds maternal, though she is busy unpacking her briefcase.

Again with the letter? The letter is nearly five years old. How could it possibly matter now?

When I think I have people figured out, they rewrite their script, and it's a whole new scene. Maybe I still have jet lag. It seems that, that—I don't know how it seems. It's confusing.

"When you are ready to read it, if you like, you can call me." She looks up and smiles, "We hated to see you leave." Without missing an opportunity, she says softly, "Kathryn, we couldn't all run away. Now that you're back we need to finish this."

Something is different now. Her ultimatums are not annoying me the way they did when she was my supervisor. I know she is right. She was always right.

"All right," I acquiesce, a bit unsure of entering into an agreement with her. Karen takes a business card from the card holder on her desk, writes on the back, then hands it to me.

She has written her personal phone number. It's a bit odd, but odd seems to be today's theme.

In the moment it takes for me to glance at the card and slip it into my jacket pocket, she starts packing the reports she is taking home to read over the weekend.

I know her weekend habit. I have seen her on the beach reading reports a million times. I went to the beach to get away from work and to clear my mind. It seemed she went there to get work done. We had nothing in common, not how cases should be managed or how to spend time on the beach.

In retrospect, she is probably a better social worker than I had given her credit. I don't know much about her, only that she left her private practice as a child psychologist in San Francisco to take the governor's appointment to head our troubled department with the mandate to straighten it out.

I know she has a master's degree in social work, as well as a Ph.D. in psychology. Somewhere I heard she graduated with honors, I don't remember the context of the conversation.

When Karen came on board with the department it was rumored that she had received numerous prestigious awards in both fields. If they exist, they are not on display in her office. It occurs to me now that other than her excessive work habits, I really don't know her after all the years of working for her.

~~~

~ CHAPTER 3 ~

Lullaby Litany

Speeding along the freeway after leaving the office, I come alive in the fast pace of the traffic. Moving across the lanes, it feels good to be unleashed again after all the time away from the city.

I love it here. I feel less confined surrounded by millions of strangers in the second largest city in the country than in a small town in the wide-open plains.

"These are my kind of trees, my gray-hazy skies, my buildings," I announce aloud, chanting to myself as the freeway loops. One last time, I look back toward the towering buildings glistening in the late afternoon sun, for a final glimpse before the interchange that sends me speeding south toward the beach.

"I love the Pacific." The litany suddenly stops.

Why was it that I left? I desperately ask myself. What did I think I could find somewhere else that I couldn't find here? And worse yet, why did I stay away so long?

The questions continue, even though I really don't want to know the answers, especially after the intensity of the visit to the office. My mind doesn't care what I want. My thoughts continue to taunt me. "What had I been thinking?" I say aloud.

That is just it. Five years ago there had been too many things to think about—all of them competing for attention. The torrents of emotion were overwhelming after years of child abuse investigations. I couldn't take it any longer. I couldn't reconcile the senseless death of an innocent child simply because the system didn't work as it should.

There was more to the emotions than a case of burnout that sent me running from the place I love. That last case was one too many. It focused all humanities' ugliness on one small child, a child I could not save.

It frightened me when I couldn't make the system work as it was meant to work. For the first time, being a good social worker was not good enough. A child died a horrible death. If my skills weren't enough, I didn't know what to do for the next child that was sure to come. The system was a lie. It was a horrible lie. I was hopelessly powerless. I left. It was that simple. I drove until I couldn't drive any more.

~~~

My thoughts ricochet back and forth between the past and the present. I am lost in thought when the sign for the off-ramp leading to Maggie's condo catches my sight. Mindlessly, out of habit, I ease onto the ramp.

At the first traffic light I realize what I have done. "Katey, I guess you are going to pick up that letter whether you planned to do it tonight or not."

I can see in some ways being back in L.A. is going to be easy. I am being swept along by instinct even after all the time away.

Reality strikes in waves washing over me. Obviously, that case is still on Karen and Maggie's minds too. Karen is right. Our lives can't move forward until we move past that horrible death. Me running away trapped part of each of us in a fragmented past. We have to see this to the end, whatever that might be. It is my hope we each find peace, and that my little client found a better place than this world was for the short time she was here.

Sigh. The air is heavy to breathe. Guilt and feelings of responsibility for failing to save that little girl begin choking me into overwhelming restlessness. The tightness in my chest forces me to gasp for air. No inhaler, no source of oxygen can cure this. I break my thoughts away from the case and my emotions. I struggle to think benign thoughts.

Amazed, I wonder how long my friends would have waited for me to come back before someone opened the judge's letter. If I never came back would they have eventually opened it? I try to focus on that thought to block out the more demanding thought, thoughts that really matter. It's a draining struggle, but, for the time being, I am winning.

~~~

When she opens the door, Maggie must sense I'm not ready to continue our earlier conversation. At least not on the terms she exacts. Apparently sensing that I'm not staying, she hands me the manila envelope, then politely guides me to the door and out into the early evening light.

Back in the rental car, I open the envelope only to see another smaller, sealed envelope inside. It isn't worth playing his game. I shudder and toss both envelopes onto the passenger seat.

As I accelerate down the on-ramp of the 405 freeway, I can see the traffic thinning to a fluid flow toward Orange County and beyond. Rush hour has passed, a definite indication that it is time to find lodging for the night.

I wonder whether instinct will find me a place to sleep. "No time to worry about dead judges." I'm talking to myself too much.

Out of sheer desperation, my mind recalls an inn near the ocean. The owners were in their late fifties, as I remember. We saw each other on the beach during the tourists' off-season, when they had the time to enjoy the ocean. We never spoke at length, but acknowledged each other—as beach people do —with a smile and a nod while walking on the beach. "They might have a room. And it's close to the beach," I whisper with relief for an easy answer.

With new confidence I continue south, moving parallel to the coast. As I approach the exit that leads to Pacific Coast Highway, the ocean smell begins to soothe my frayed emotions. Highway One: One—the beginning. I am coming back to the beginning. Is this instinct or is that just how things have to be, some law of physics, the natural order of things? I have the strangest sense of security here, near where I lived when I last felt vital, whole.

~~~

The sounds of the seagulls and smells of the ocean bring a wave of comfort. Waiting for a few minutes before going inside, I want, maybe need, to inhale every moment of this safe feeling before it passes. It's a sweet, secure, comforting mother's-milk feeling. It's like a towel, still warm from the dryer, after coming inside from a sudden and unexpected downpour. My eyes close and everything slows to a pleasant quiet for the first time since I arrived home this afternoon. A breeze blows in the window, trying to coax me to move.

Even after I am absolutely certain the calm has passed and is not returning, I sit completely still. All of the nagging questions in my head are silent. My doubts and uncertainties are quiet. I could be content to sit here all night if there was a promise the comfort would linger.

I glance at the Ocean Shores Inn sign above the 1940s-style building and decide to chance stirring, with the hope that I have the strength to dare to move.

Once inside the office, I am struck with the decor that hasn't been updated since the 1960s. The woman behind the counter has her face tilted downward, writing a letter on tie-dye-designed stationary. Her blonde hair is long, mid-back long, with bangs covering her eyebrows. Pink, orange, and lime green plastic bangles rest on her wrist. She is wearing a peasant blouse and love beads, and, I suspect, her usual peasant skirt and leather sandals, as she did in the past.

"May I help you?" the woman asks without looking up.

"Yes. Do you have a room?" I ask, fairly confident there is at least one available this time of year. There were only two cars in the parking lot. How busy could they be?

"How many people?"

"One," I reply, slightly curious whether she will recognize me when she finally looks up.

"Fill out the registration form. There's a pen on the counter."

She hasn't aged as much as I expected. She still looks about the age I thought she was five years ago.

Finally she looks at me when I put the pen down and hand the small clipboard and attached registration form toward her.

For a moment she looks as though she is trying to figure where she has seen me. I can almost see her straining to place me somewhere within her daily routine. Maybe a store clerk, a bank teller? What the heck, I'll save her the trouble of guessing.

"Hi. I used to see you walking the beach when I lived here."

She smiles with one of those sure-I-remember-now smiles and gives me a room key. I haul my luggage to the room. The decor is 1960s too. It isn't a retro decorating, it's original.

The ocean isn't visible from the window, but it doesn't matter. I plan to spend my first morning home on the beach, my beach. Since I won't be in this room more than a week or two, the view can wait until I have a place of my own.

I'm tired from the travel and the intensity of the day. I don't know what I had expected, but the reality was more than I wanted. A couple pieces of fruit and the mint from the pillow is all I eat before I fall into bed too tired to be hungry. Home.

~~~

Reluctantly waking to the sounds of the surf muffled through the walls of my room, I turn over to go back to sleep. The dream of the ocean is too good to waste by getting up. After a moment more my mind realizes that it isn't a dream. I am in California.

It is perfect to wake up at home. In a very short while I'm out of bed, pulling on jeans and a hooded sweatshirt, and out the door to the beach. The bakery down the street provides me with a muffin and two cups of coffee to go: one for now, the other for right after "now."

My pace increases as I near the water's edge. It is an unseasonably cool Saturday morning. It could have been a blizzard and still I would have come to the beach today. My beach. Kathryn's Beach.

Winter is the best time of year to spend on the beach. Only real beach people are out on a day like this. A few surfers and kids with boogie boards are dressed in wet suits and booties. The water is always cold. It's the ocean currents swirling down from the Aleutians that make the California Pacific so cold.

I have never quite trusted the Pacific since she nearly swept me out to sea when I was seven. I was caught in the undertow at Morro Bay, a place famous for such dangers. It is a memory vivid in my mind.

On the other hand, the beach has always been a comforting, healing place for me, especially during the long gray winter. I hope to find the beach healing and nurturing again today. God knows I need it.

The earthy smell of the water, the dampness in the air, the sand, all of it, is consoling. And the sounds: wave sounds, crashing on the beach before rushing out to collide into the next incoming wave; bird sounds, operatic, excited screeching of distant birds pursuing fishing boats as they chug out to sea, and those nearby; and boat sounds, motors, signal horns and an occasional human voice carried across the water. I breathe it all in. The beach delights my senses, much as the sight of a lover would. I have been away far too long.

An innate urge to feel the sand beneath my shoes pushes me to walk a half mile along the shore, just out of reach of the cool, gritty spray. The ocean-water smell begins to clear my head.

Even before the sun comes fully up, I find a place in the dry sand to rest out of reach of the incoming spray. I had expected walking would keep the chill away, but I had walked too slowly to feel the effect of exercise. The breeze coming off the water is chilly, but I shiver for a different reason.

The waves crash onto the breakwater to the left, farther down the beach. Dampness awakens me to the core in a way that I have not been awake for the last five years.

Perhaps later, I will walk to the jetty for a second helping of this treat. Aware that I am tired, but not necessarily from the walk, I begin to feel a sense of focus awaken as I sit quietly, running my fingers through the silky dry sand. This awakening feels similar to the clarity I felt when I decided to come home.

It was an oddly decisive moment in the bar that resulted in a clear decision to return to L.A. Again, today, born out of my defenseless fatigue, I'm aware of its emerging again. I welcome the sensation of renewed awareness, while I watch the waves break and rush forward into tan froth on the wet sand not far away.

Mimicking the receding waves, the awareness slips back into the deep waters of my consciousness. Closing my eyes to shut out everything, except for the sounds and smells of the beach, I try to hold on to the retreating feeling of well-being.

Despite my best effort to capture and internalize it, the feeling fades completely. I wonder what will come to fill the void, and hope it isn't tormented memories.

After the clarity is gone, I release my barrette, shake my head, unleashing my long auburn hair to fly wildly free in the morning breeze. Perhaps removing the barrette is symbolic, but now isn't the time to analyze my behavior. I am free.

The rising sun reveals a greenish cast to the water and the glitter in the wet sand. I lean back on my elbows to take it all in.

My lungs respond with a deep, slow breath, a breath that brings a sigh of relief as it leaves. The essence of safety remains as an undefined melody in my mind. It's a timid score, but it is growing stronger.

Seagulls screech, claiming ownership of the morsels left behind by the retreating tide. The sandpipers play a hurried game of tag with the tan foam at the waves' edge as it advances and retreats. The endless sound of the waves coming and going, and the occasional sound of a boat motor revving to pull away from the pier are familiar and comfortable sounds. The surf soothes my thoughts into idleness.

The last of the commercial fishing boats begin to come in with their morning catch. They pass into the channel leading to port. The boats are near enough to see the swarm of seagulls following them to the wharf beyond my view.

It is a relief to sit and enjoy the knowledge that I am where I belong. The familiarity of the sights, sounds, and smells wrap around me in a maternal embrace. There seems to be nothing in the world except this corner of the Earth. I belong here. Comfort wraps its arms around me and holds me securely.

The day drifts by on the unpeopled January beach. I imagine the weather deliberately turned cool, so I can have the beach to myself. It's a harmless fantasy.

The mindless musing doesn't hold my attention. My mind begins to sift through Maggie's unexpected information from yesterday. It reminds me of a jigsaw puzzle without a picture on the box, maybe one without a box. A few pieces fit together here and there. But I can't tell what to make of it. Something does not feel quite right about the Judge's letter.

Hunger moves me to the present. I've been too preoccupied to think of eating. Now the sun has crested and is beginning to make its descent. It must be 2:00 or 3:00 o'clock, judging by the sun's westward placement.

Walking back to my room, I stop to purchase a fish taco and vanilla shake from a beachfront restaurant. Pulling a chair from across the room, I sit with my feet propped on the bed and my drink set within reach on the TV stand. After dinner and a shower, contentedly I crawl onto the bed on this, my first full day home. The last thing I remember as I drift off to sleep is thinking it is good to be here.

~~~

Early Sunday morning, I return to watch the water, to feel the sand between my fingers as I rake through the soft grains and bits of shell, and feel the ocean breeze in my hair. The borrowed beach bag is laden with an ample supply of steaming coffee, the complimentary Sunday paper, and a beach blanket on loan from the Inn. It is a bit unbelievable that I am home and about to spend a second day on the beach.

I watch the horizon for the sunrise, and the water's edge for the next wave, alternating my gaze between the two. A satisfied sigh slips from my lips, followed by a smile. A genuine smile, not the bartender variety.

"Listen to the calm rhythm of the waves, Katey." I lean back on my blanket, shut my eyes, and reach to touch the sand with my fingertips. Until now I hadn't realized the full impact of being away. The morning slips by under the influence of caffeine and the intoxicating setting.

With my container of coffee empty, I turn my attention to the Sunday paper. Reality in the form of caffeine surges through my veins motivating me to look for a job, an apartment, and a car of my own, but not necessarily in that order.

I love the freedom of having my own car—it's an L.A. thing—but shopping for a vehicle is of little interest to me. Knowing this, I promise myself to return the rental car by the end of the week. Deadline or goal? It doesn't matter, it's a start.

For employment. It seems peculiar that Karen offered me a job in the department that I abandoned without notice five years ago. On the other hand, the fact is that I am very good at my job. It takes a certain breed of social worker to do child abuse investigations day in and day out, and to do them well. Child Protective Services doesn't exactly have social workers fighting for the positions, for obvious reasons there's always a vacancy in the department.

Now that I think of it, the job offer is quite practical from her standpoint. If Karen rehires me, she saves training time needed to get a social worker ready to carry a full caseload. She knows what I can do, and that I know how to deliver what she expects. It might work.

The only thing is that the nature of the work is physically and emotionally demanding. Unfortunately, society requires that someone does it and, until five years ago, I was one of the social workers who did.

When I was a student, a career in Child Protection was the last thing I wanted. At the beginning of my junior year, I was assigned to the department for the mandatory internship. I was told to do necessary non-social work tasks that bogged down the real social workers' schedules. For the department, my internship was purely a staff utilization decision.

The attitude in the department was unbearable, worse toward students. I was determined to complete the internship even if it killed me. The next year wasn't any better until Karen arrived at midterm, and students were given useful experience. After graduation I was eligible for a real social work position. Consequently, I have worked in Child Protection since then. (The job at the bar doesn't count.)

Outside of CPS, I'm not sure what else I could do or would want to do. On the other hand, what I am most uncertain about is not whether I want to return to Child Protection, but if I can handle it again. It was all-consuming. It consumed my energy. It consumed my soul.

Unfortunately, today's classifieds don't offer employment in my field. Fortunately, there are more strategic ways to find employment than the want ads. I'll worry about employment after I find a place to live.

Systematically, I scan the real estate ads for a feel of the real-world prices with hopes of a beach house to sublet. Actually, what I want is my old apartment back. I wonder if there are any apartments available in my former complex. Is that an attempt to recreate the past? The familiarity draws me, but I am concerned about the danger of picking up where I left off. I know that sounds like approach-avoidance, and it probably is. The urge to follow my instincts is strong.

The questions about what course to take for an apartment and employment, in addition to all of the trivial details of living, continue to dominate my thoughts the rest of the afternoon. Am I trying to recreate the life I left, the life that I couldn't live? Or have I come back to release the past, setting each of us free, so we can allow that thread of time to intertwine with the present? Why exactly did I run away, and what is driving me now?

The beach sounds and smells recede into the background of my thoughts. I am restless. The waves of questions catch me off guard. The answers don't follow. Only the questions fill my mind. I can think of nothing else as I walk along the beach back to my room.

I can't say what I had for dinner or exactly when sleep overtook my thoughts. It was a hard sleep, a deadman sleep.

~~~

~ CHAPTER 4 ~

Sweet Dreams

Restlessness enters my dreams. There is someone in my room. I can't tell if the presence is a danger, but I feel alerted to run.

"Kate? Kate. Kate! Wake up!" Maggie shakes me—saving me from the certain peril looming in my sleep.

My eyes aren't willing to open, but I can smell the coffee she brought. Slowly, I awake from the unconsciousness of the night. Finally, but only slightly, I open my eyes. I am groggy, but not so much that I don't remember I am back in California. At least, that isn't a dream.

"Good morning, sleepyhead," Maggie teases cheerfully.

I smile and pull myself up on one elbow. It is good to see her. I have missed her more than I realized.

"Sleepyhead? Aren't you late for work?" I tease back with an invented serious expression.

"It's a holiday. I'm not on call," she replies in a mischievous tone. She hands me a Styrofoam cup—tempting me to complete wakefulness with the steaming brew.

"Holiday?" I ask, and inhale the steam rising from the cup.

"Martin Luther King," she says, concentrating on removing the plastic lid from her coffee without getting burned.

I hadn't kept track of the date. Of course, it's Monday and mid-January. There is no particular reason to be mindful of the actual date until I am employed.

"Thank you," I say before taking a sip. I pause, savoring its taste. "It's good to see you," I add warmly, still amazed at her ability to figure out where I'm staying, but not willing to ask her.

After all, she had the weekend to find me. I know I would have been able to track her down, as well. The two of us had the most investigative experience in the department and the best professional records in the state. Things are back to normal.

"And what do you have planned for your holiday?" I ask, wondering what sleight-handed adventure she has in mind.

"Besides bribing the housekeeper to let me in here?" She grins before taking a full drink. "I thought we would go apartment hunting," Maggie replies without hesitation. "I'll drive, if," she smiles widely, "if you can get dressed before noon."

"You know I'm a night owl." I fire back a grin, throw back the covers, crawl out of bed, and begin searching through my suitcase something to wear. Besides, it is nowhere near noon. I have plenty of time.

"It's because of the nightmares, Kate. You aren't fooling me." Maggie becomes serious, but smiles when I wheel around to look at her.

The only way Maggie could know about the nightmares is if she has them too. She isn't going to trick me into an admission of what neither of us want to confess. Ignoring where she is taking the conversation, I move back to safer ground.

"So the plan is?" I ask, looking for my other shoe.

"I thought we would go by your old apartment and see if they have any apartments available, then go from there." Maggie pauses for a drink before resuming, "Unless you'd rather not."

My apartment? I quietly mouth her words, glancing at my friend through the doorway of the dressing area, to see if I can detect whether or not she is serious.

I lean against the vanity to tie my shoes, but really I am absorbing the reassurance that Maggie thinks there is nothing terribly wrong with moving back into my old neighborhood. I worry about things like the sanity of returning to my past. Nevertheless, there is a certain security in being back in my old neighborhood. I'm glad Maggie came.

I brush my teeth and wash my face. I have no intention of arguing the case about whether there is sanity involved in any of this. Certainly, I'm not going to mention concerns regarding sanity to Maggie, of all people.

~~~

With noticeable confidence, Maggie steers into the freeway traffic. Meanwhile, I settle back and enjoy her company. We chat about nothing, the way people do when they can't find the words to say what needs to be said. Or can't find the courage to say them.

My former apartment and one a floor below are available. They just finished painting both. They said that I can have the pick between them and move in immediately. It takes only a moment's hesitation, I choose the lower- level apartment. It seems right to have a new view of the Pacific this time around.

Maggie approves the choice, though she doesn't say why. I don't ask. I know better than to ask Maggie for a rationale when she doesn't volunteer one. Besides, I don't care what she thinks. I'm home. Nothing else matters.

~~~

The next weekend, Maggie, her brother, Frank, and a couple of his friends help to move my things out of storage, and into my apartment.

After the guys leave, Maggie stays to help set up the kitchen, which begins with making a pot of freshly ground coffee. We look through the boxes to find the coffee cups. There are a few detours along the way, but we find the cups by the time the coffee sputters to a stop.

The truth is, we move to the sofa to catch up with each other and never really get back to unpacking.

The next day, Frank helps me find a suitable used car. Suitable to me means a 5-speed, something with a tight suspension for corners, and a sweet clutch for getting through the gears when the traffic will allow it. Frank's primary task is to check the mechanical integrity. I have been known to blow a head gasket or two in the past, but never a clutch. I don't really speed, but I do get to the speed limit quite efficiently—keep the RPM's up. Having my own vehicle liberates me.

After a quick walk on the beach, I unpack until I am tired of it. Then I shop for towels and different accent pillows for the sofa. It's a relaxing activity. Additional items will come once I get a paycheck coming again.

Maggie returns the next weekend to help me finish the unpacking. Of course, there is a certain amount of good-natured ribbing that goes along with her assistance. She jokes about my collection of movie sound tracks. Each time the CD changes she moans. I applaud her dramatics, but she is quite bad at acting. I taunt her to guess which movie the songs are from, at least she is good at that.

~~~

With the unpacking nearly finished, I start settling into a routine. Piece by piece, I am constructing a life again. My hair is cut short and styled. It takes a few weeks to complete enough continuing education hours to get my license current. I rework my résumé. Things are falling into place.

My cousin Nick meets me at the pier for some catch-up time. We are only two months apart in age, so we have always been close. Before I left, we would get together for lunch on the pier, then head to the ballpark. Our all-time favorite activity was to attend Dodgers games when they were in town. He doesn't seem to mind that I left without saying a word. Unlike my friends, he asks if I want to talk about why I left and my return.

After brief consideration, I tell him, "Not now. Thanks for asking. Maybe some other time."

He understands my confession that I am not sure I can put it into words just yet.

After lunch we take our time walking up the pier toward town, stopping to look over the railing at the water below.

"You still surf?" I ask, curious whether he still enters surfing contests, and amazed at his bravery since he can't swim. It would seem that he would have learned by now. I wouldn't take that kind of risk.

"I'm back to making custom bats. I'm making practice bats for the Dodgers." He raises his eyebrows in emphasis.

"Thank God it's not the Angels!" I tease.

"Yeah, how 'bout them Dodgers! Lookin' good," he jokes playfully and nods his head.

"It must be the bats."

"Must be." He smiles sheepishly.

We stop again to lean on the guardrail overlooking the waves breaking below. Spending the day with Nick reminds me of how much I have missed him.

~~~

The search for employment continues, but only half-heartedly. I still haven't decided about Karen's offer to return to the department. Getting the job would be easy. Doing the job, with no end of little victims in sight, is never easy. I remember the last case.

I haven't worked up the energy to face Karen, and make the hard decision about child abuse investigations. Perhaps it is because I can't envision myself doing anything else, even though I desperately need to do something else.

In the meantime, I am getting back into shape walking the beach twice a day. Walking in the soft, dry sand nearly killed my calf muscles the first few days. My muscles still ache terribly, but my head is beginning to clear and the distant winter's chill inside of me is thawing.

Occasionally, I experience a sense of clarity, but most of the time I am operating on instinct. So far it serves me well.

~~~

Many of my old neighbors still live in the apartments. Mr. Goldstein, who reminds me of an older version of Ben Kingsley, stops in every couple of days to check my progress with the last of the unpacking.

It seems like it's taking forever to unpack, but I haven't seen this stuff for five years. The hours slip by as I get lost in old photo albums. I hardly remember the person in the pictures of me. She looks strong, confident, and alive. I gently touch the image with my fingertips while tears well in my eyes at the loss of that person.

~~~

While I make lunch for us, Mr. Goldstein inquires about the pile of photos I've left out. Solely to satisfy his curiosity, I invite him to the sofa after we eat and look through the photos.

These are the photos I laid aside to look through a second time: photos from my childhood at the beach with my parents; old black-and-white photos of my parents before I was born; photos of me with my first bike, wavy hair flowing behind; prom photos; graduation; Mother and her friend, Amelia; Mother and her sisters and brothers; but none of Father's family.

Mr. Goldstein listens to the narratives and studies each photo in depth. He asks thoughtful questions. I freely answer them. While he is learning about me, I am rediscovering myself.

Thinking about it now, I realize I have been afraid that I would never find myself again. Maybe that is why I stayed away for so long. Maybe that is why I left in the first place. In the end, being lost among strangers was far worse than facing my lost self on home ground.

The afternoon drifts on lazily. Before Mr. Goldstein leaves for his rest, he offers unsolicited advice about the arrangement of my framed movie posters and helps me hang the biggest ones. The chair isn't quite rightly placed in the room. He tests it several times before he is satisfied with its final location. The view of the ocean has to be perfect. The more he visits, the more I discover that I want him in my life in a way that no one else seems to fit.

I watch Mr. Goldstein climb the stairs to his apartment. His wife died while I was away. I would have liked to have seen her again. The two of them were inseparable. I can't imagine him living alone.

He is frail without a companion. It is obvious he hasn't been very active, and he probably doesn't eat right, either. For the most part, he seems to do all right. I'm sorry I had not kept in touch with them. I've made a lot of mistakes.

Throughout my career, being the quintessential social worker was my identity. In the end I couldn't accept failure or separate my career from me as a person. Failure was personal, an unacceptable weakness. I couldn't take any more tragedy, especially murder—a preventable murder. So I left it all. I see now in doing so, I left everything that defined me.

Trying to figure out things alone was another horrible failure. Coming home was my only option to be alive again. At last I can admit I need people to complete my life in a way that being alone left it incomplete. Yet, I need to become comfortable with myself before I can allow anyone to see my vulnerabilities. I have not mastered that quite yet. But there is hope.

There are fleeting moments when I feel focused and determined, moments when it's more than innate instinct driving me. Unfortunately, the focus comes and leaves on its own volition. It encourages me that I am allowing Mr. Goldstein inside the perimeter of my defenses, a widening of my inner circle.

Mr. Goldstein returns unexpectedly as I am preparing to leave for my evening walk on the beach. He wants to walk too. I accept his desire for companionship and acknowledge my need for the same.

Since he doesn't have athletic shoes, he is wearing his everyday street shoes. With his shoulders back and his chest swelled, he looks proud in his new warm-up outfit, complete with price tag still dangling from his armpit. With a quick snip, the price tag is removed and we are officially walking buddies.

On this first walk, Mr. Goldstein makes it across the street and to the edge of the sand. Technically, we are on the beach, but at least a hundred yards from the last high tide mark. It is obvious this is as far as we are walking today.

He's frail from age and limited activity. Now that we are in the sand, I am not sure he can make it back across the street on his own. Apparently, neither is he. He slides his arm desperately around my waist, while I slip mine around his back to steady him. I hope this is enough support for his weak, spindly legs. The urgency in his grasp doesn't boost my confidence in this endeavor. It seems the spirit is willing, but the flesh is weak.

He has an odd quick-step gait that is hard to match. His pace throws me slightly off balance, causing us to be even more out of step with each other. We stop to rest several times before we make it home where we are safe.

I think we were both scared he wouldn't make it back, but neither of us mention it. We breathe a sigh of relief when I finally ease him into a chair to rest before going upstairs to his apartment.

~~~

Mr. Goldstein becomes stronger as the days pass. We walk a little farther each time. By the end of two weeks he is walking to the water's edge with ease and has bought shoes better suited to the task.

During our walks, we begin to talk about things people with a two-generation age difference talk about with each other. They are comfortable, non-intrusive conversations. Still, a deeper warmth is developing between us. I love the easy way we laugh together. It is always preceded by a slow grin on Mr. Goldstein's lips, and a twinkle in his eyes.

Today's conversation is more personal. Without warning, he talks about losing his babies in the war. He confides, in detail, how frightening the death camps were for Mrs. Goldstein and for him, and the others. Without hesitation he describes the things they did to survive and to help each other to survive. His honesty makes listening to the details of his experiences difficult. I don't interrupt.

He seems extraordinarily accepting of the people around him who responded differently to the same situation, even if becoming lackeys when survival required it. He makes no excuse for their behavior, nor passes judgment on them.

"Those were terrible days, Katerina. No one could be blamed how they survived the camp." He confides in a soft steady voice that some gave in to their fears and ended it all. There was little to account for why any of them lived through it.

There is nothing I can say in response to what he tells me. No comment is worthy of this story. Nothing, nothing justifies the death camps. Nothing can be said to heal what he went through. I don't understand this kind of hate, nor how so many people found it acceptable. I wonder whether any of those people later had regrets for what they did to people, including children.

We walk in silence for a long time. Suddenly he stops, looks at the evening sky, then he looks at me in an intense moment. All he says is, "We should go now," and turns for home. And that is that. We go.

~~~

The following day Mr. Goldstein returns for what has become our daily ritual: an evening walk on the beach. Since California is the only place Mr. Goldstein has lived in the U.S., he asks questions about life on the prairie.

I tell of the combines cutting wide swaths around the wheat field until it circles down to the final pass of the equipment.

"There is haze in the air from the machines churning out the chaff to remove the grain from the heads of the plants."

I explain that only the most essential activities occur during harvest. It was always a race with the weather and crop prices. Nothing else mattered until the wheat was in, until harvest was finished.

Twelve-year-old children, women, and old men drove two-ton grain trucks. Some trucks were so old they looked like a parade of vintage vehicles creeping down Main Street. Some farmers had several matching new grain trucks that were bought on the gamble it would be a good crop this year.

I describe the long lines of trucks at the elevator waiting to weigh and dump their load of grain. I tell him how the drivers got out of their trucks to stand under shade trees along the road, waiting for their turn at the scales and worrying about their grain's moisture content. Sometimes two or three drivers would gather near the lead truck, visiting with each other while watching the activities across the yard at the Double Circle Co-Op elevator until it was their turn.

Mr. Goldstein listens to my stories with interest and has many questions.

During those first few weeks home, Maggie and I see each other every few days. I suspect her of helping me readjust to city life as if I am a stray in need of adoption.

Sometimes Maggie and I get together for lunch with several of the staff from work. There has always been a standing lunch invitation at the office. At times, I almost imagine being part of the team again.

Most often Maggie and I eat alone in one of the sandwich shops we frequented when we worked together. Maggie can be so frustrating with her direct ways. Yesterday, for example, she took advantage of the privacy to talk seriously. She smoothly eased the conversation into making her point.

"Kate, you are a one-woman world. You haven't always been that way. You think instinct brought you home. I think it was courage. It's easier to run away and keep running than to come home and face something you consider a failure. I think you have courage," Maggie spoke softly, hauntingly.

Why in the world did I confide my feelings to her? I admit, she makes me think about things, especially things I am avoiding. But I don't have to admit it to her—only to myself.

~~~

Today when I come to the office looking for Maggie for an impromptu lunch date, Karen is with the receptionist. I was so preoccupied with having lunch that it catches me by surprise to see her. She looks pleasantly surprised to see me, which still seems odd.

"Hello, Kathryn. Do you have a minute?"

This might seem strange, but I'm sure she said, "Into my office, Kathryn!" Though I know that she didn't, I fight the temptation to respond with my usual, "Yes, ma'am," as we walk toward the elevator to her office.

Once inside, Karen shuts the door and the glass window in it rattles.

I smile to myself.

Karen goes straight to her desk to unload her cargo. I watch her dispatch her briefcase and the armload of case files. It occurs to me that she wants my answer about the position. I don't think I can handle the horrors the investigations reveal, then repeat them in court under the strong objections of the defense attorney. I can't risk having another client murdered because I can't make the system work as it should. I miss my work and my friends, but I don't think I can do this again—at least not yet.

Karen seems to detect my thoughts. It makes me uneasy to be transparent in her gaze. She occupies her attention with shuffling the stacks of files on her desk to make room for more. But I can tell she is thinking in the background of the activity.

After a minute of awkward silence Karen looks up and asks, "How have you been, Kathryn?" in that new-to-me motherly tone she has acquired.

"I've been unpacking and working on my résumé." I catch the implications of saying, résumé.

Karen looks at me intensely. To my surprise, she seems to understand my offhand reply, though I haven't really answered her question.

"You've decided to leave Child Protection."

"Yes. Yes, I guess that I have." She makes me realize working on my résumé indicates I am headed elsewhere in social work. I haven't made much progress. However, if I was returning to the department, I wouldn't need an updated résumé. They have my HR file. We both know that I am moving on. A new beginning.

"I just returned from a meeting with the director of a new program. It's a program for homeless families. You might like it.

It'll be a change of pace for you." Karen adds after a brief pause, "As of an hour ago she was still hiring staff."

By her expression, it's obvious Karen is providing me with an alternative to working in her department again. I see through her manipulation, but I let it pass. She must think it is a good agency or she wouldn't have mentioned the job.

Karen writes down a phone number and a name, "Sister Elizabeth," on the back of one of her business cards and hands it to me. We pause.

Obviously, we are both reminded of the last time she gave me her business card with her home phone number.

The pause makes me uncomfortable. I look away from her gaze, busying myself with putting the card in my purse.

Karen hesitates a minute, then returns to arranging papers from her briefcase into piles on her desk, but she stops again.

"I was waiting for you to call," she says as she studies me.

I feel terrible. "I'm sorry. I hadn't realized I wasn't coming back to the department until now." I am embarrassed that I have been thoughtless about her need to fill the position.

Maggie told me that Karen had placed me on extended leave of absence. Of course, she hadn't kept my slot open for five years. It just worked out that she has a social work position coming open soon. However, the workload demands that she get the position filled as soon as possible. I feel very selfish for not giving her an answer sooner.

"I know," she says in an understanding tone. "But I'm referring to the Judge's letter," she says softly.

Karen speaks in a hurt tone, one I have never heard her use before. "I would like to know what the man who tore apart my department had to say." Quickly she tempers her tone, her anger isn't directed at me. Karen turns toward me and continues in a softer voice. "If you need to talk about the murder, I'm available."

"I haven't opened his letter, but—" I take one of her cards from the card holder on her desk, and write my address and phone number on the back. "It is Friday. We can order Chinese takeout and open the letter, if you don't have other plans."

"As it turns out, I don't have plans, and I will bring dinner."

Karen picks up the phone as I leave her office.

This seems a little too easy. Is she calling to cancel her plans or is she really free tonight? And the letter, who cares about the damn letter? It won't change anything. It can't bring back that little girl. It won't bring back the last five years or my career.

"I hate him and his stupid letter!" I say under my breath, repulsed with the memory of Judge Jones.

Before leaving the building, I slip to Maggie's desk to use her phone and call Sister Elizabeth. Sister asks me to email my résumé to her and sets an interview appointment for Monday morning. I'm being biased with my surprise about her use of email. This computerized nun intrigues me. Even better, I have a job interview—as easy as that.

~~~

Red enameled chopsticks laid across my mother's hand-painted Chinese dishes are the perfect accents to Mother's black-and-yellow muslin tablecloth. On second thought I add a fork to Karen's place.

The table setting is simple, but ideal for Chinese takeout. The shades are raised, revealing the evening sun glistening on the waves across the street.

Standing back to inspect the room one last time before my guest arrives, I nod approval. I am pleased with my apartment. It's comfortable and cosmopolitan—an absolute contrast to my sparse two rooms above the garage just months ago.

My plan is to eat first, then open the letter from Judge Jones—a simple, but efficient agenda.

By the time Karen appears at the door the tea is brewed and the air filled with its aroma. She comments that I live close to her beach. I smile about her sense of ownership of *my* beach.

We are nimble with our chopsticks, which is something newly discovered that we have in common. To my relief, dinner moves along nicely. The food and conversation are a comfortable fit.

It occurs to me now that when I worked for Karen we never had a conversation that wasn't work related. After all the years at odds with her, I am slowly realizing Karen is a warm and interesting person.

We finish eating just about the time the sun sizzled into the Pacific and the residential lights came on. Glancing at the letter on the coffee table where it has been for the past six weeks, I wonder what the "almighty" Judge Jones had to say. I haven't given the letter as much thought as everyone else seems to have. Honestly, I didn't care for Judge Jones then, and I don't care for him now that he's dead. A letter from him seems inconsequential after what he did in his courtroom. I'm sorry he committed suicide, but I don't miss him. The man was an arrogant ass, and he flexed his power too irresponsibly for my taste. I found it hard to even respect the robe with him in it. I don't know how anyone could respect him.

Something is odd about him writing to me. How can I give much credence when Maggie and Karen weren't curious enough to open it for nearly five years, so why bother with it at all? What could it possibly say that would make any difference?

Was he going to try to explain his ruling? Was he apologizing for letting that deranged man continue to sexually abuse his daughter—leading to her murder? Perhaps he blamed me? No, Maggie said the transcript disputed his ruling. None of it matters. Nothing he wrote will bring the little girl back from the dead.

Karen moves our tea to the living room, then comes to help finish clearing the table.

"Before you open the letter, let's talk," she requests as we move back to the sofa when we finish. "Kathryn, whatever is in the letter, it's collateral to the main issue."

Apparently getting together to read the letter was an excuse to pin me down and make me face that case. It is true the Judge's letter is only a small part of a bigger picture, certainly less important than the children. Even less important than us.

However, after the first year passed without knowing where I was, I would have opened it or tossed it in the trash had I been them. Truthfully, I would have tossed it in the trash when it arrived. It wasn't important to the police, and it wouldn't have been important to me. It still isn't.

A letter from Judge Jones doesn't make sense, and it is likely a moot issue after all of this time has passed. I am slightly disappointed that we aren't opening the letter—only because I would like to be done with it and put it with the garbage bin, and have it hauled away.

Her hazel eyes are unable to hide the pain reflected in her tone of voice. There is a sense of urgency about Karen that I hadn't expected. Maybe she thinks there will not be another opportunity to resolve the past, maybe she thinks that I will slip away again. We were never friends, and having dinner together once doesn't mean we will become friends. "Now" may be all we have. In many ways, all we ever have is "this moment."

I'd rather not have a conversation about the past or Judge Jones. I follow her lead. This pending conversation seems important to her. I suspect it is only a temporary truce between us. We'll see what happens after I've been home for a while. That will be the real test whether things will be different or not. Or even whether we see each other again.

"Everyone was angry when Judge Jones made that horrid ruling." Her voice is clear and controlled. "It was always hard to get a good ruling out of his court." She pauses briefly. "I was angry too," Karen confesses more softly than before, making direct eye contact as she speaks.

Her near-whisper catches my attention. I study her and sit more upright. She is direct. It is definitely similar to Maggie's approach the day I returned. The way she sits forward hints there is an underlying emotion that is still unclear to me.

Karen continues, unaware that I am trying to listen beyond her words. "I knew for a long time that Judge Jones set serious abusers free on petty technicalities, and it was destroying my staff's credibility with other judges."

She pauses for a thoughtful sip of her tea. "Not to mention the children," she almost whispers breathlessly. "He betrayed their trust. I don't know how the man slept at night."

The thought of what Judge Jones did to the children, to us, and eventually to himself—his actions make us both shudder. We look at each other but say nothing. We only sip our tea in silence for a minute or two. My mind adds Karen's words to the memories I possess.

Five years ago I hadn't thought about the rest of the staff. There wasn't a bigger picture in my perception, there was just one small, vulnerable child. She was excited about life and about learning to read.

In the end, I took his ruling as a personal defeat. I hated not being able to protect that little girl. I hated feeling helpless. I hadn't seen that it was more than my case. It was our case.

"I didn't know—" my words are lost.

"Kathryn, I was wrong."

"What?" I whisper. Stunned, I meet her gaze without retreat.

This time her eyes don't betray her, she has gained control over them. Looking past the coffee table between us and directly at me, she continues, "You had a solid case. I wanted you and Keith to prevail for both departments' sake. I wanted this to be the case that beat Judge Jones. You both did everything right. I want you to understand that what happened in court was not your fault."

Keith and I were the lead investigators on the case. Keith was a seasoned police detective. Kevin, a younger officer, was assisting him. Maggie had been assigned to work with me. Ordinarily, there wasn't the staff allocation to double-team the case assignments. I had thought it odd, but didn't question it.

Now I understand why Karen read the file daily. Back then I interpreted her involvement as excessive supervision, nearing micro-management. In reality, she was making sure we could avoid any legal technicalities that would give cause to Judge Jones' dismissal of the case. At the very least, she was maneuvering for a request to the District Attorney to file an appeal.

"Is that why you ordered the transcript?" I ask, now knowing she was preparing for an appeal.

"You know?"

"Maggie told me."

"I could have taken the money out of the budget, but we needed to own it with our own money. This work is difficult enough without judges undermining the system. That case killed a part of everyone involved in it." Then she nearly whispers, "It murdered the little girl."

Karen falls silent.

When she stirs again her voice is more measured. "Keith and I went over every detail of the transcript. I hired a criminal lawyer to review a redacted copy for procedural flaws."

With ease she makes the transition to invoke her motherly tone, "Kathryn, there were no problems with the evidence or the testimony. The 'problem' was Judge Jones."

Clearly, Karen is offering me absolution, that was her agenda for this evening. Her face shows the stress of her job. If only we had known five years ago what we know now, things might have been different.

Emotion wells up inside me as I watch her remember the past. I feel ashamed that I left the way that I had. I have not earned her absolution.

Karen interrupts my regret when she begins to tell what transpired after I left. "Everyone had the opportunity to read the transcript, and almost everyone did. We wanted, no, we needed answers to our questions about Judge Jones' unconscionable rulings." She hesitates, then nearly whispers again, "But there was nothing there. There was nothing we could have done differently then or changed for the next time."

She catches me off guard. The breath I had been holding now slips free, "Nothing?" I lean forward in my chair, slightly closing the distance between us. "There was nothing there?"

Still, I feel there should have been a way to protect my client. There must have been something extra I could have done to protect her from her father and Judge Jones.

The image of her little sweet face, when the Judge made his ruling, flashes in my mind. She was barely old enough to read, but she knew exactly what he had done to her.

Judge Jones sat perched on his bench in his pompous self-righteous smugness. Everyone else in the courtroom was completely stunned. The court reporter's hands hovered over her machine, shaking, and horror showed on her face. The silent slumped bodies of the attorneys standing behind their tables with their heads hung down were an eerie sight.

I can hear her little girl voice plead with the Judge, then each of us. But I was the one she called by name, pleading with me to save her. I wanted to kidnap her and run far away.

The memory is vivid. I feel my throat tighten and my eyes burn with tears threatening. The images are raw even after all of this time has passed. It's as if it happened yesterday.

When I close my eyes at night I still hear her horrifying scream echo throughout the marble and granite courtroom. I see her eyes plead with each of us as she looks around the room from one face to the next. She calls my name. Then it begins again, the scream, the horrifying scream that left a deafening silence when it finally ended. I wake yelling, "Run! Run away!" That was the last day I saw her.

It was less than a week when she was found dead. Homicide notified Keith when her name brought up a red flag in the system. Keith came to tell Karen what had happened. Karen called me to her office.

I thought it was just one more of the seemingly million times I was to be summoned to her office. I expected to be fired for something. Karen and I seemed to be in constant conflict over how to handle my cases. En route to her office I wondered what I had done this time.

Keith was there when I entered Karen's office. I halted. They both looked pale. I was filled with an unimaginable rage when Karen told me my client was dead. I looked at Karen as if it was somehow her fault that I had failed to save the little girl.

When I could finally speak I told her I needed time off. Without waiting for her reply, I slammed the door, hoping that annoying glass would shatter.

It didn't break, but I nearly did. Grief and anger consumed me in the days that followed her funeral. I wandered the beach until I was tired enough to sleep, hoping it would be without hearing her screams just as I am hearing them now.

A shudder travels through my body in response to the memories, forcing me back into the present. I look up to see Karen's face pale. She looks like she is reliving all of it too.

"I am so sorry," I repent for my role in all of this.

She ignores my apology. "I had grad students review our court cases for the twelve months prior to yours." She takes a long breath. "The results showed we had no convictions in Judge Jones' court, none. Our next worse record was Judge Lawrence's court. There we had a 68-percent conviction rate." She pauses to sigh. "Judge Jones had been dead almost a month by the time we had the stats compiled and verified, and the report written. I know he was aware we were checking out court files from the Clerk of the Court. He had to figure out what we were doing." Her voice sounds like she thinks that it might be her fault he killed himself or that she, too, thought she had missed something pivotal in the little girl's case.

"I don't think that had anything to do with his suicide," I assure her the best a strong person can be reassured.

I remember fuming for days, then alternating between self-pity and horrifying anger. I was angry with Judge Jones and the justice system. Justice? That wasn't justice. I couldn't find a way to deal with it. Thinking about it repulsed me, but I could think of nothing else. I had to leave.

I hadn't given Karen time to react the afternoon I walked into her office and tossed my keys and pager on her desk. I had to get away from all of the craziness, the dysfunctional people, and the dysfunctional system.

Karen tried to maneuver her department around Judge Jones. She depended on this case to give her the leverage to serve him notice that justice would prevail. Now I know I had been wrong about everything. None of it had been about me. While I ran away, Karen and Keith stayed and did a retrospective investigation of the system. They didn't run.

"Homicide threw its resources into the investigation. In two months the murder case went to the grand jury."

She looks up and catches my gaze, "Within a week after the grand jury issued an indictment, Judge Jones shot himself." Karen's voice is strong and unemotional. "Eventually our stats convinced the DA's office to request a judicial review of Judge Jones' cases—many of his rulings have been overturned."

"Oh, good." I wonder, but don't ask, about the ones he dismissed. They can't be retried because of double jeopardy.

"Yes. It was a lot of work, but I think it was worth it." She looks past me as she speaks. "The mistrials were retried de novo." She looks tired.

"I didn't know—" I am still apologizing. It must have been difficult retrying my cases without me on the stand. My throat tightens, making it difficult to breathe normally. Inside me is a profound sense of sadness.

I should have been here to help sort through this mess. It was my case. Besides, I am very good at statistics. I tutored it all through college. Karen could have used my help.

"We didn't know where you were," she says in an unaccusing voice.

"I was tending bar in a little town in Nebraska."

Karen laughs, "NEBRASKA?" Her laughter breaks the solemn mood hanging over us.

~~~

The hours pass unnoticed as we move through the shared memories. We need to sort through this ourselves, before we can deliver any sense of resolution to the other people involved in this tragic case.

Perhaps everything can't be resolved in one night, but there seems to be a sense of urgency in Karen to resolve as much as possible. She uses her skills to get us through the tough spots. She knows no one can be their own patient, and most of the time she is only a mere mortal like me.

Hours ago we traded our tea for coffee. Through the window the sky is showing signs of sunrise. By the sound of the surf it is already high tide.

When I return with another pot of reality, Karen is still amused at the thought of me in Nebraska.

Relentlessly Karen continues, "You'll be pleased to know we took a conviction on the murder trial," she says triumphantly. "We couldn't get a repeat sex offender status on him because Judge Jones had dismissed the felony case." She doesn't have any anger in her words, which surprises me.

I am still struggling with the memories—not just this case, but all of the bad cases. Though none of the other bad cases compares with this last case.

"Since you were unavailable to testify, but were under oath on the transcript from Judge Jones' case, Judge Lawrence allowed your testimony into the record in the murder trial as motive for murder."

Karen deliberately makes eye contact, holds a beat, then continues, "With the coroner's report of sexual abuse prior to her death, we had murder while committing a felony."

"Murder One?" I nearly breathed the words, unable to say them out loud.

First degree murder usually is reduced. Plea bargaining is a reality of the justice system we have come to expect, if not accept. I can't believe the system actually worked full tilt.

Karen smiles with my appreciation of their accomplishment. We had won a battle, if not the war.

I look at the cup in my hand to avoid the clumsy moment of truce between us. My gaze strays to catch sight of the unopened letter on the coffee table. I look up to see Karen looking at the envelope too. We look at each other briefly.

Karen is correct, the letter is collateral to the "blood and guts" of who we are and the work we do. What we do is real. Judge Jones' robe was a façade for a man who made a mockery of the system and the ideals of justice. The envelope doesn't hold any power over us.

The sound of the surf is restlessly calling me to the beach. We have relived enough of the past for one night. I know that I can't take any more. Karen looks depleted and doesn't attempt to hide it behind her usual commanding composure. It would take too much effort to hide her emotional exhaustion—or maybe she doesn't feel it's necessary to keep up her guard any longer.

Along with the emerging resolution of the past, I sense the development of a new understanding between us. Karen is probably tired of our battle. I know I am. Maybe the problem had been me all along, but I feel our conflictive relationship is evolving into a more agreeable posture. At least, I hope so.

Dawn is showing fully in the bit of sky visible through the window. It's safe to go on the beach now without stepping on a jellyfish or a piece of debris that washed up during high tide. I am ready for a walk. I need to stretch my legs and clear my head, and get some distance from the memories.

In unspoken agreement we look toward the door and the waiting beach beyond it. This moment of common thought is a refreshing change.

It is decidedly awkward once it's apparent that we are officially no longer at odds with each. We will have to adopt new roles in the absence of our old ones. It might not be easy. It will certainly prove interesting, if nothing else, considering the personalities involved.

Giving in to the beckoning of the surf, Karen suggests a walk before she leaves. I don't need coaxing. There is a consolation that only the beach brings. It has been a long night and the sea air will be a refreshing change.

Karen pulls on the oversized sweatshirt I offer to guard against the morning's chilly mist and we're out the door.

The loud calls of the seagulls dull the further intrusion of memories from the past. Everything is washed new with the ever-changing tide. It's the constant renewal of the surf that I seek this morning.

Karen and I walk along the shore we both think of as "our" beach. We talk only a little before we slip into silence.

Karen seems different from how I remember her. When I worked for her, I didn't think of Karen as a person touched by the same things that haunted her staff. She always seemed to be in control of the intense emotions that raged out of control within us, especially in me. She seemed peaceful and calculated.

I had no idea she shared our humanity. I'm sorry that I hadn't taken the time to notice before now. Me running for five years accomplished nothing. I have wasted all that time being emotionally numb in Nebraska.

Now, I have a second chance to actually see Karen and the other people I had taken for granted. This time I will not make the same mistakes. I am beginning to understand myself a little better in the process. Yet the anger and hurt remain buried inside of me, seeking an exit.

It took the entire night for Karen to relate the saga that unfolded after I left. I have nothing to contribute, although it seems to have been enough to allow her to talk. Maybe receiving was exchange enough for now.

For me the total emotional dynamics of this work, and that case in particular, haven't been resolved. I know one day I will need to let go of all of my thoughts and emotions, even the anger, related to "that" case. I have not found the key to such a release. At least I have information that may come into place at the right time to help me heal and be whole again.

It was good Karen and I spent this time together, but I will have to find my own healing. Now would be a good time for a wave of clarity to wash over me. I like the feeling of confidence I have when things come into focus.

The clarity doesn't come. When I have tried to coax the feeling before, it would not be forced. I can control it no more than I can control the tide. I will have to be patient with it and with myself.

Karen and I walk quietly along the morning beach—our silent thoughts drifting out to sea with the waves.

~~~

~ CHAPTER 5 ~

Letter, Letter, Who Gets The Letter?

Immersed in our private thoughts, Karen and I walk for a mile and a half along the deserted beach. The bird calls and the sounds of the surf blend into a symphony in the background of my thoughts. The caffeine in my system is slowly being replaced with the awareness of hunger.

Breaking the silence I ask her, "Could I interest you in breakfast?"

Karen looks around as if I awakened her from her thoughts. "I should get home."

"I make a great omelet," I coax. "We can invite Maggie and open the letter," I add more incentive.

I'm tired, but more interested in breakfast than sleep. There is the constant threat of nightmares that makes me think twice before sleeping. It's not only this one bad case that I dream about, but it is the one responsible for most of the nightmares.

That little girl would be eleven now, if Judge Jones had left her removed from her abuser and in a safe home. Not only did he dismiss the criminal case, he dismissed the Child Protection case. I keep thinking there must have been something I missed that would have prevented the system from failing her.

Karen changes her mind. "Okay, you talked me into it. I didn't bring my phone, did you?"

"No. I don't bring my phone to the beach."

"Let's walk to the pier and use the pay phone." She turns back toward the pier.

~~~

Luckily, Maggie-the-early-riser is still home. I tease her, "I will serve my 'world-famous omelet' and unveil Judge Jones' letter—if you can get here by noon." It is nowhere near noon, but I couldn't resist repeating her words from before.

She laughs and accepts the challenge. By the time Karen and I return from the beach, Maggie is leisurely waiting on my patio looking smug that she arrived first, though she couldn't have waited long.

Maggie and Karen slice mushrooms, bell peppers, dice onions to be sautéed, and grate the cheeses. I add secret ingredients to the egg mixture. The omelets cooperate and are perfect.

We eat on the patio, casually visiting in the slight morning breeze. I begin to realize why Maggie seemed comfortable to dive into the conversation my first day back.

It must have been therapeutic for her to go through the department's internal investigation, rather than run away as I did. Certainly processing small increments of this nightmare is easier, and saner, than being bombarded with everything at once, as I have been since I returned.

As I listen to Karen and Maggie visit, it's obvious Karen has not healed completely, though she hides it well. I am convinced leaving when I did, the way that I did, made things worse for her. It is almost as if Karen cannot, or will not, allow herself to put this aside until all of her staff has been "accounted for."

It was necessary that I return, not just for me, but because I am one of Karen's unaccounted-for factors in her nightmare. It seems that Judge Jones' letter is another, albeit minor, unanswered question. I suspect Karen cannot find closure until everything is finished and put away in neat stacks. It's difficult to gauge how many items remain on Karen's list of unfinished business regarding that case.

~~~

When I return to the patio with more orange juice, I bring Judge Jones' letter with me. Maggie and Karen are engaged in conversation and fail to notice the letter until I refill their glasses and set down the juice container.

There is a sudden serious curiosity in both of them. They watch intensely as I slip my unused butter knife inside the flap of the envelope, then hand the opened envelope to Karen.

She and Maggie stir to sit up straighter in their chairs. Karen clears her throat. While she unfolds the handwritten letter on the court's stationery, Maggie and I settle back in our chairs to listen. My focus turns to the waves across the street while I look past Karen, listening as she reads:

"Dear Kathryn." Karen stops, looks intensely at me.

Her abrupt halt pulls my attention back to her. There is almost a discernable moment of silent pause in the morning sounds that had surrounded us only moments ago.

Karen and Maggie look at me questioningly.

I understand the question, but shrug. I don't have an answer.

> Dear Kathryn,
> Don't judge me. Tell my daughter I am sorry.
>   m. Jones

Karen settles back in her chair to begin again.

"That's it? He didn't tell us anything!" I snap, allowing my anger to surface. I am filled with disappointment that he didn't mention regret for his hand in the little girl's horrible death. He owed all of us that much. They have been waiting all this time for what? For nothing.

"Why did he bother?" The betraying tone of my voice is filled with pain and anger that is impossible to disguise.

Karen and Maggie look directly at me. Judging by the look of disappointment in their eyes, they seem to share my sentiment about the letter. They say nothing to confirm my assumption.

After a couple of minutes, Maggie becomes alert as she shifts straighter in her chair.

"Read it again, Karen."

Maggie loves a mystery. She often focused on an obscure detail that didn't quite fit together. She pulled at it until the whole case unraveled, then sorted through the pieces looking for the truth with single-minded devotion. She was relentless, even sometimes to the annoyance of those around her.

Karen picks up the letter from the table where it had been discarded.

She reads again, "Dear Kathryn."

"Stop!" Maggie turns directly toward me and studies me.

"Why the familiarity?"

"I don't know. We were never on a first-name basis," I defend my honor.

"Symbolism then?" Karen inquires.

I reply with a shrug. Honestly, I have no idea.

We toss around several possible explanations.

"A desire for a personal relationship?" Maggie suggests.

She deserves the sour-milk face I make in response to such a comment. The whole concept of a relationship with Judge Jones is repulsive. There was something about that man that made my skin crawl.

"Certainly NOT!"

"Did he hear other judges call you 'Kathryn'?" Karen asks.

"No. Never. I kept a professional distance with the court." Just to make myself completely clear I add, "None of the judges called me Kathryn. Give me some credit. I knew better than to let that get started."

"Lack of professional respect, or was it just his emotional state at the time he wrote this?" Karen submits.

"I don't know. He was a jerk!" That is the nicest thing I can say about him. I'm unable to articulate my thoughts any better than that.

Karen looks back at the letter and reads, "Don't judge me." She looks up.

"What does he mean, 'don't judge me'?" I am annoyed with him for writing a letter that said nothing. "This is dumb. Certainly not worth the time we are spending on it." But they aren't finished.

"Could there have been a conflict of interest?" Karen asks.

Maggie looks at Karen, and asks, "Then why didn't he recuse himself?"

"Maybe he didn't have a legitimate conflict." Karen sounds suspicious. Maggie and I are alerted by her tone, but we say nothing, waiting for her to continue.

Karen's eyes look thoughtful. She looks back to the paper and reads, "Tell my daughter, I am sorry."

"Sorry for what, the suicide?" Clearly, I am not getting whatever secret message he tried to convey. I have forgotten the secret handshake, and I seem to have left my decoder ring in my other jacket. If he was going to be cryptic, he should have sent the letter to someone who would understand it.

"Kathryn, do you know his daughter?"

"No, Karen, I don't think so." I slowly shake my head, searching my mind for a clue. Nothing rings a bell. Sending the letter to me makes absolutely no sense."I have no idea who she could be," I repeat.

"Then why ask you to tell his daughter?" Maggie is looking at me as she asks, hoping to trigger some recognition of his daughter among my acquaintances. "Maybe he thought you knew her."

"Sure? If you know his daughter that was a conflict of interest," Karen questions.

"He shouldn't have heard any of my cases, if he thought that was true."

"This doesn't make sense. Something is not right with this." Karen states the obvious. She has a serious, pensive look.

"Why didn't he mail the letter to her?"

"Maybe he didn't know where she was?" Maggie says.

"Neither do I!" I regret my tone. I'm not angry with them. But, this is ridiculous.

"This is getting us nowhere," Maggie admits.

Karen is watching both of us try to decipher his message.

"I agree. After my interview on Monday, I'll stop by the courthouse and see what I can find out about Judge Jones' daughter," I offer a small penance for my anger.

Maggie asks, "Was her name is in his obituary?"

"No, I don't think so," Karen rejoins the conversation. "As I remember, I thought the obituary sounded like it was written by someone who didn't know him intimately. Besides, the daughter wouldn't be new information if we had seen it in the obituary."

Maggie glances at Karen and nods in agreement. "True, you have a good point."

"I don't understand why he didn't send it to you, Karen. You're the department head. It would make more sense to expect you to give it to me. Why would he put it in an envelope addressed in care of Keith?"

"I don't know," Karen replies. "You two worked as a team, almost exclusively. Maybe he thought Keith knew where you were."

It hadn't occurred to me to say anything to Keith about leaving. Our relationship ended when I walked out of the department for the last time. I worked with him exclusively, but he worked with other people in the department. What difference would it make to him if he didn't see me again?

"Judge Jones may not have known you were gone. No one knew you were in Nebraska."

"Nebraska?" Maggie laughs heartily and looks at me amazed. "Really, Kate, how could you?" Maggie stares straight into my eyes until I look away. Without another word about Nebraska, she resumes speculating about the letter. "Why did he send it to Keith?"

"Maybe Keith knows his daughter," Karen offers.

"Even if he does, that brings us back to why write the letter to me?" I toss the original question back into the conversation.

Karen looks thoughtful, but doesn't respond. She is usually quick in seeing through these things. "May I take this, and show it to Keith?" Karen asks, holding up the letter, waving it slightly.

"Sure, go ahead. I don't want that thing." I re-fold my napkin and scoot my chair back from the table slightly. "This whole silly game with Judge Jones annoys me." I say it as if there was the slightest chance they didn't clearly get the message already.

"I have to get some sleep." Karen stands and begins to collect the dishes. She has had enough mental gymnastics about the letter for now. Or maybe she is onto something that she isn't ready to share with us.

"Leave the dishes," I say. Maggie and I stand. "I'll let you know what I find out Monday," I add while walking to their cars.

I am tired of Judge Jones. I can't even think about that ridiculous letter right now. I don't expect much to come of it after all this time. Besides, the man is dead. We aren't likely to learn the meaning of the letter. I doubt it really matters in the long run.

My mind resumes the questions as I start the dishwasher. My thoughts ramble while I change my clothes for sleep and brush my teeth. Obviously, people don't decide to shoot themselves out of the blue. Apparently he had been a disturbed man for a long time. It only became obvious how disturbed he was when he fired the gun into his mouth.

Karen answered some questions; however, the cryptic letter raised others. I detest him intruding on my life from his grave. I crawl into bed. I am furious with him all over again.

"Ooh, I hate him," I whisper as I turn over and settle into my pillow.

The rest of the morning and most of the afternoon are lost to restless sleep. The Judge came into my dreams. I wake covered with sweat, my heart is racing, and my bed looks like I have wrestled the devil. Those damn nightmares. The recurring high-pitched blood-curdling scream from the dead little girl is the worst of all. Now Judge Jones is making his debut in my dreams. Is there no escaping them or him?

In the hours after I wake, I don't accomplish anything. The shower doesn't revive me. My mind wanders and I can't stay focused on any task. I start to empty the dishwasher, but have to come back to it three times before I actually finish putting the dishes away. Coffee doesn't taste good. I sit, get up, sit, wander to the window, and sit again. I've tried all the chairs and none are comfortable. I would read, but I can't concentrate and only flip through the pages of a magazine. I'm tired, but I wouldn't nap for anything, not even a million dollars. I have had enough nightmares for today—enough for the rest of my life.

Finally, I force myself into a semblance of routine and stand in front of the open refrigerator with the intention of preparing dinner. Nothing looks good to me. But I'm not really sure I actually looked at the food. I'd go out to eat, but I don't have the energy. If I sit long enough, dinnertime will pass and I won't have to bother with it—at least, not officially.

"I need to shake this, this mood," I whisper to no one. I need time to get on with life after the little girl's scream over and over again in my sleep.

Settling back on the sofa, I pull my feet up on the coffee table and sigh. My eyes roam to my favorite movie poster hanging on the adjacent wall. I stare at the poster, feeling myself being drawn into the scene. It isn't long before the harsh, real world drifts away and music begins to play in my mind. I squint my eyes to focus all of my soul on the music and the mood of the scene. "Play it again, Sam," I whisper.

Kathryn's Beach

The Moroccan movie in my memory is interrupted by the distinctive tap at the door. Mr. Goldstein arrives for our daily walk along the beach. It takes a second to realize what stopped the music, and another second to come to my senses and answer the door. I don't mind the interruption. It's Mr. Goldstein. I get my walking shoes and ease into the comfort of walking along the beach with him.

Maybe it's Mr. Goldstein's personality or his life experience, I don't know which, but he was the first to reveal a deeper level of himself during our walks. He talked about the death camps while I talked of wheat harvest. However, this evening I am beyond talking about the weather and crops.

If my father had been alive I might have discussed with him my frustration about the letter. In Dad's absence, Mr. Goldstein is becoming a fatherly mentor to me. I feel safe and secure with him. Because of that easiness, I enjoy an unexpected freedom in his company. I always look forward to our evening walks, especially today's.

I would never tell Mr. Goldstein, or anyone, the nightmarish details of my work, even if confidentiality wasn't an issue. No, I want his perspective on the hidden dynamics of the Judge's letter.

In the beginning I thought Mr. Goldstein simply wanted to have someone around so he could venture safely farther into the world. Now, I think it is more than that. I think he is looking for companionship, as am I.

Mr. Goldstein seems willing to take our friendship wherever it leads. We both need the exercise. We both need the inter-generational friendship. And today I need to verbalize my thoughts without fear of rejection, and yet have someone I respect stop me when I veer off course.

Whatever is developing between us, it works well because, unlike a real parent, I don't have to struggle for independence from Mr. Goldstein. I can confide in him in a way unlike anyone else I have known. And he willingly, thoughtfully, guides me. There is no tangible explanation for what is special between us, but we have connected. Right now a sense of connectedness is what I crave most.

To have this conversation, this relationship, with Mr. Goldstein, I am willing to dispense my self-preserving defenses and admit that I am clueless. I am willing to divulge my private thoughts and fears about my reaction to the letter.

Mr. Goldstein listens expertly, wisely. My thoughts are disjointed and fragmented. I talk in circles with no direction. I bare my heart to him.

He asks no questions. He allows me to talk until I have no more to say, then asks, "What do you think the letter means?"

I consider the questions we had when the letter was opened. I look out at the waves, then confess, "I don't know what it means. That's the problem. I don't know how much credence to give the letter or Judge Jones, considering he committed suicide right after writing it."

I'm used to figuring things out, but can't get enough distance from my feelings about the case or Judge Jones to see the letter objectively. My defenses are completely down, which seems to be what Mr. Goldstein was waiting for.

He remembers the Judge's suicide—it was in the news. Mr. Goldstein smiles, "Katerina, maybe he just wants you and the detective to find his daughter and give her the letter."

"Maybe so," I say, "but what do I tell her?"

"Just what he wrote. Tell her 'he is sorry.' She will know what he meant."

He speaks in a soothing voice. Mr. Goldstein looks at me like he can see into my thoughts and know whether I am still making things more complicated than they need to be. He seems pleased with himself that he understands and I do not. I think that is the beauty of age. It certainly is its privilege.

"You're right. I don't have to understand the letter." I finally understand what he is telling me. He has a refreshing way of simplifying things. Eventually, I hope to learn to do the same.

Mr. Goldstein smiles again and his eyes twinkle.

We have nearly completed our walk. By the time we return home I have decided to put more energy into finding the missing daughter than I had earlier intended.

Maybe Keith can run her driver's license and find her address—if he knows her name and she still lives in California.

~~~

The upcoming job interview moves into the center of my thoughts. The anticipation of it excites me more than I had expected. True to my investigative nature, I decide to research the agency for information in preparation for the interview. With a cup of coffee in hand, I begin. Several online searches come up empty. With more coffee I try different search parameters.

I don't find any information about St. Mark's homeless program. Even the online newspaper archives reveal nothing about it. Apparently, it is too new to have hit the press. Maybe the media hasn't considered it newsworthy. After all, the homeless don't have money to purchase newspapers or advertise in them, so why cover their news, if it doesn't generate revenue? Who else would care?

There are a few articles about St. Mark's Convent that shed light on this potential employer. It has been a long time since I have interviewed for a real job, bartending doesn't count. I am probably over-preparing, but it satisfies an indescribable need in me, so I continue.

Saint Mark's is a descendant of one of the original California mission communities. They come from a group of Franciscan nuns brought here just before California became a state. The sisters celebrated their 150th anniversary a few years ago. They're a relatively young community of nuns, considering the age of the Catholic Church and religious communities.

The article indicates the convent had been quite large at one time, but it is now down to forty-six nuns. It has been eight years since their last novice made final vows. Their community is in decline. I wonder what that means.

A decline isn't entirely surprising, since many religious communities experienced a decline after Vatican II, but it is worth keeping in mind when I meet with Sister Elizabeth. Their decline could be the result of something unrelated to the changes from Rome. It could be the result of internal problems. I don't want to work somewhere dysfunctional. The information in the article is facts and figures, nothing I can grasp for security.

I'd rather not walk blindly into this situation. On the other hand, how dangerous can forty-six nuns be anyway? After all, it is not like I have to take the job if it doesn't seem right. At the very least it will be interviewing practice.

I try to keep everything in perspective, but I remind myself that I want more out of life than I had expected from it before. I want to be myself without being consumed by those around me.

~~~

Monday arrives. I am awake and stirring uncharacteristically early. The interview is scheduled after the morning rush hour, so I have time to savor my coffee before I make my way downtown.

As I drive into the heart of the city, my mind is a whirl with last-minute questions and prepping. Before long I am standing in front of the convent. It is a large, old building with a Spanish influence in its architecture.

One nice thing is that it's located only four blocks from the office where Maggie and I had worked. That will be convenient for having quick lunches with her. I give the nuns extra points for their location.

I pause for a moment or two at the large double front door of the convent. It doesn't seem right to walk into a convent as though it were a place of business, but there is no doorbell. I use the heavy black metal ring-shaped knocker on the weathered wooden door. I take a breath and straighten myself as the knocker hits the strike plate.

A sister in a traditional brown habit appears at the door. She looks to be in her mid-forties, slim, cheerful, and holy. Very holy.

She says politely, "Good morning, I am Sister Theresa."

I tell her who I am and why I have come.

She nods awareness of my appointment and says softly, "Follow me, Kathryn."

After she closes the door, her hands briefly go to her side and disappear as the long sleeves fall over them. I notice with interest as she clasps her hands together in front of her stomach, where her hands remain completely covered in the sleeves of the rough brown fabric. Her slim face is the only part of her humanity in the open.

She says nothing more. Abruptly, she turns her back to me and walks swiftly through the quiet halls. It strikes me as funny, but I contain my humor from erupting into a nervous laugh.

I begin to question my choice of attire as I follow her. I didn't know they still wore the habit or I might not have worn slacks. The newspaper articles didn't mention the habit and there were no photos included with it. It's too late to worry about that now. I hurry to catch up with Sister Theresa.

I steal glimpses of the convent decor as we pass through the halls. It is stark. I feel out of place here. Several large statues, set in alcoves in the walls, loom over us. The delicate statues are beautifully hand-painted. Their faces are serene. As I look into their eyes, I feel their calming influence on my nervousness. I take a deep breath.

Sister Theresa continues to walk silently and swiftly through the hallways. Suddenly she stops before an open door, turns toward the opening, steps past the threshold, genuflects, backs out, then hurriedly continues down the hall.

When I arrive at the doorway, I see a dimly lit chapel. No one is inside, but there is a red candle burning near the altar and the faint smell of lingering incense. It seems strange that incense was used at a weekday Mass. I do what she did and hurry to catch up without letting my shoes make too much noise on the tile floor. It is difficult to walk fast and maintain the look of confidence I want to portray.

Sister Theresa shows me into a waiting room and smiles slightly before quietly disappearing. I sit up straight on the old no-frills leather sofa, waiting uncomfortably.

In about ten minutes, right on time for the appointment, another sister dressed in a brown habit enters. She moves with the same commanding confidence and grace as Sister Theresa, maybe even more. I automatically stand because of the respect she commands.

"Hello, Kathryn. I'm Sister Elizabeth," says the mid-fifty-ish woman. I am just guessing her age, because all I can see is her face peeking out of the headpiece. A white hand appears from her sleeve as she offers a businesslike handshake.

Protocol. I will have to learn the convent protocol. "Sister, it's nice to meet you."

"I understand you worked for Karen Craig," she says as she leads me into the inner office. "Tell me about that, if you would."

She sits behind her large desk, motioning me to sit in the chair across from it.

There isn't time to acclimate to the environment. I begin the textbook description.

"Our department was responsible for investigating suspected child abuse. We worked with the police department on sexual abuse cases, then the district attorney's office—if a case went to court."

I relax speaking about a subject I know well. "I worked exclusively on sexual abuse cases." I make the transition from talking about the department to speaking of my role there. I have never told anyone the exact work I did as a social worker. Talking about it feels awkward and yet comfortable with her.

With the habit disguising everything about here, I can't get a sense of her personality. Even her eyes, don't yield information about her as an individual. Consequently, I have to answer her questions blind of external clues about the best way to present myself or how well I am doing in the interview. Since she doesn't give me verbal feedback, I am left to follow my instincts.

"And your co-workers?"

A smile fills my face and I feel my eyes dance. "We were a good team, Sister. We worked extremely well together," which I believe with all of my heart, and say it with passion.

"What was your relationship to your supervisor?" She looks straight at me with each question, with the knowing look only a nun has.

This is not the time to confess how often we butted heads. "Dr. Craig gave us direction when we needed it, and room to work when we didn't." I am surprised by my answer. "She has confidence in her staff. We—we were an incredible team."

Overall I am proud of my answers. However, I am beginning to wonder if I will regret not taking my old job back while I can.

"Then, why aren't you working there?"

"I am ready for a change from CPS. Dr. Craig suggested I apply here." I hope she is satisfied with my answer. Now I am unsure why I'm not back at my old job. As a matter of fact, my old job paid more than twice what this job offers—plus benefits. Worse work, though.

Sometimes money isn't the deciding factor in the choices we make. This is one of those times. I want more than money from my next job. I want a life.

In an open file folder on her desk, she has the résumé and copy of my diploma I had emailed to her. There are a couple of other papers. Perhaps they are letters of reference, but I don't know for sure, and I can't imagine how she has them in two days. One thing for certain, I didn't give them to her.

Without obviously staring, all I can do is glance intermittently at the papers, hoping to figure out what they are. There are clippings from the newspaper sticking out from under the other papers, but I can't see enough to determine which they are.

"I see there is a five-year gap in your résumé," she says.

I'm busted. I hope she doesn't back me into a corner, forcing me to mention the bar. I'm not ashamed of being a bartender, I just don't want to talk about Nebraska and the events of my self-imposed exile, or recent return to L.A.

"Yes, Sister, I was out of state during that time, so I omitted it," I say smoothly. I will probably never mention the bar to anyone—except Karen and Maggie.

To my amazement, Sister Elizabeth lets it slip by without asking additional questions. A slight relaxing smile comes over me as I think about my hidden "wild" past.

Sister Elizabeth looks at my résumé for another pausing moment, then looks over her reading glasses at me.

I would feel better if she would smile or something to give me a clue about how this interview is proceeding. In the absence of indicators, disappointment creeps over me. I brace for the inevitable.

Unexpectedly, she continues, "Do you know anything about homelessness, being hungry, or alone with no one to help?"

I understand the sense of the hopelessness she is describing, but the perfect words don't come to explain the concept in terms of human reality. I'm doomed. I simply answer, "Yes."

She begins to provide a quick overview of her program. She must have decided to hire me. Otherwise, she could have ended the interview. Why else would she tell me about the program? I must have the job. I listen carefully to her review—just in case I am correct in assessing her behavior.

Sister Elizabeth's face lights up and her eyes dance. "This is a pilot project. It is designed for families who have been homeless less than two years." She pauses for a minute before revealing her hope for the future when she adds, "Then we will expand the program to people with less chance for success."

There are several innovative social work aspects in their program. And she wants staff who are creative, diligent, and committed to get the program off to a good start.

No, not committable, committed. I nervously joke to myself in this foreign environment that is making me feel like I am trespassing.

"Kathryn, can you start tomorrow morning at 9:00?" Sister Elizabeth asks as she stands up from behind her huge old desk, obviously concluding the interview.?

"Yes, ma'am." I stutter, "I, ah, yes, Sister." I feel my cheeks blush. I wish they hadn't betrayed me, but I will survive.

"Dress casually, and we will review the program and your duties."

That will be a nice change of pace—something between business suits for court and blinking bow ties at Ruthie's Bar.

Unaware of my inattentive thoughts, she smiles warmly before directing me back to the main hallway. She stops and looks at me squarely. "And, Kathryn, you don't have to genuflect at the chapel, if you are not Catholic. It's acceptable to walk past the doors."

Did nothing escape her? I wonder how she knew I had genuflected at the chapel—maybe it was just a lucky guess.

Walking beside Sister Elizabeth through the halls to the front of the building, I am aware that she behaves in a motherly manner reminiscent of Karen's new manner.

Sister Elizabeth genuflects expertly despite the yards of brown fabric that balloon on the floor as she kneels. She smiles at me, then turns back in the direction of her office, leaving me on my own to find the way out.

I do genuflect at the chapel doors. I am glad to have a job, and it won't hurt to show that I'm thankful.

Sister Theresa joins me near the front door and conducts me out into the waiting California sunshine.

~~~

Inside the main entrance of the courthouse, I wait for the arrival of an emotional avalanche from returning to the setting of my nightmares. Nothing happens. Nothing? Certainly, not the response I expected. Either I am in denial or stronger than I think. Could it be I really don't feel anything in this place? For five years I have felt broken. Was it all a lie?

The routine security check hardly interrupts my thoughts. I pause in the middle of the foyer, still waiting for the emotions that should have come. To buy time to adjust, I choose the stairs over the elevator.

It concerns me that I feel nothing, although it is convenient not to deal with rampant emotions right now. I have no plan to return to the courtroom we were in that day—that's too risky.

The place to start my query is the Clerk of the Court's office on the third floor. If anyone knows anything, Agnes will. She has been the Clerk since the courthouse opened a hundred or more years ago. Well, maybe not quite that long, but almost. All I have to do is get her talking, then move her on topic.

After several unrelated stories, Agnes finally comes up with a gem—Judge Jones' law clerk, Sam Jackson, now works for Judge Lawrence.

One of the criminal lawyers, who is filing documents in the Clerk's Office, overhears the conversation and says, "I saw Sam in the law library about fifteen minutes ago. He looked like he planned to be there for a while."

"Thanks." Well, that was easy enough.

Since I have no idea what the guy looks like, I hope Mr. Jackson has stayed put. As it turns out, it was a useless concern. There is only one person in the library.

He and his laptop are surrounded with stacks of law books and a legal pad on the table. He is typing at a fast clip, and he doesn't look up from his work when I enter. Finally he stops typing and flips through a fat file of papers.

"Mr. Jackson?" I ask, approaching his table, ready to extend a handshake if he responds affirmatively.

"Yes?" He looks up and smiles. He is a handsome Black man, appearing to be about my age—maybe a little older. He wears thick-lens glasses and an engaging smile. There is a sense of approachability about him, though he is dressed in a tailored suit that looks strictly business.

"Hello, I'm Kathryn. I am looking for Judge Jones' daughter."

"I don't know anything about Judge Jones' family. I only clerked for him a few months before he killed himself." He is soft-spoken with a deep, rich voice.

"I see. Well, thanks for your time." I smile and turn to leave.

"Wait. I do remember something. I think Judge Jones' wife died years ago, but now that I think about it, he did have a picture of a young woman on his credenza."

It isn't much to go on. Oh well, it was a long shot anyway.

"It is probably still around here somewhere. No one claimed his personal belongings after he died, that is, those not taken by Homicide."

His comment reminds me that suicide is just another form of murder. That old case is a collection of one damaged life after another. I feel terribly sad about the whole ordeal. Even more odd is that no one collected his personal property.

"I'll make some inquiries. Give me a number where I can reach you, Kathryn. I'll call, if I find the picture."

"Thank you. That would be great."

I wish he knew more. This will have to do for now.

Agnes left for lunch. I know several other people who worked in the courthouse. I spend a little time visiting the offices in search of someone who might be helpful.

Unfortunately, after an hour, I don't find anyone I know well enough to ask directly about the Judge's daughter. I'm sure there were rumors about Karen's investigation, and I don't want to raise suspicions. No one mentions Judge Jones or his death, so I'm unable to maneuver the conversation to get what I want. It was probably a dumb idea anyway.

~~~

As planned, I meet Maggie for lunch and tell her about my new job. Maggie, like any good friend, is pleased I am still employable in my field.

"Will you adjust to a job without tips?"

There is no resisting a laugh at her wit, even if it is at my expense. Tips aren't the issue. We both understand that the bar brought no nightmares. She must appreciate why I needed a job like that. In this moment of pause, I feel deep appreciation for Maggie's friendship and for Karen's lead on the new job.

"Before I head back to Orange County, I'm going to thank Karen for the job information."

"Have a nice trip. She's in Sacramento all week for a conference." Maggie laughs.

~~~

Even though I haven't learned anything about the Judge's daughter, I have accomplished quite a bit for one day. Time to go home and start reconnecting the rest of the pieces of my life. Until I had the basics—a car, job, and an apartment—I didn't feel ready to reconnect with my extended family.

There are twenty-seven first cousins in my family, so it is not terribly unusual to lose track of one of us from time to time. I am certainly not the first or likely to be the last to disappear for a while, then return. I tend to be one of the less colorful members of this family. I guess running away for five years is my turn to fly in the face of convention. My world is steadily expanding now that I'm home again. Once I reconnect with my family, my world will expand exponentially.

I begin with a call to my cousin Ilene. We decide to meet at Laguna Beach on Saturday morning. Her schedule only allows a little over an hour, but it will be enough time to touch base. Baby steps.

~~~

Mr. Goldstein comes after dinner and we go for our walk. I've lost focus on the physical exercise and look forward to our talks. Hollow conversation is a thing of the past. Instead we speak of feelings, dreams, and hopes.

He is genuinely happy I managed to get the job. I am pleased too. It was easy, wasn't it? Things are moving along effortlessly, taking on a life of their own—or rather, giving me a new life. The balm of a new life is something that I desperately need now.

Mr. Goldstein asks numerous questions about the homeless program. He is very knowledgeable about the homeless issues. It's his passionate cause. I promise to tell him more tomorrow.

The day's activities have energized me. I make a new pot of coffee and settle in with my computer. The online newspaper archives produce the Judge's obituary.

Karen is correct. There isn't much to it. There is no mention of a daughter. It does mention his wife preceded him in death, but doesn't list her name. I have no idea how long she has been dead. I know it is absurd, but I put the name "Jones" into the obituary search and hope that the daughter would be mentioned in Mrs. Jones' obituary. As expected, the archives pull up an unmanageable amount of obituaries for people named "Jones."

I begin to mark off names that are obviously male names. I wish I had asked for her first name while I was at the courthouse, but it hadn't occurred to me then. It doesn't seem anyone would have known her name anyway.

Starting at the top, I skim each obituary listed looking for one mentioning a spouse named William Jones. I had hoped to have a lucky break and find Mrs. Jones' obituary quickly. It doesn't work that way. I get through the list as far as the letter "H." That's enough for tonight.

~~~

Standing before the closet, I prepare for my first day at my new job. I select a blue blouse, black slacks that I think look casual enough, and a pair of flats. I set two alarm clocks out of reach of my bed, so I won't shut them off. I feel excitedly ready for tomorrow morning.

Lying in bed, working through the morning routine in my mind, I decide to take the mass transit to avoid any unexpected delays on the freeway. It has been five years since I drove that route during morning rush hour. I won't be late the first day at my new job.

I'm not leaving anything to chance, so I get up and check the transit schedule on the internet. Finally, I crawl back into bed. The activity of the day settles on me. At last, I am tired enough to fall asleep.

~~~

~ CHAPTER 6 ~

Nun Other Than...

The morning transit takes less time than I expected. I decide to wait at the bus stop a block from St. Mark's, so I won't be too early for my first day at work. There is nothing worse than appearing too eager.

Finally, as nine o' clock approaches, I walk down the street to the convent. Like last time, Sister Theresa greets me at the door. She is not hurried today. Instead, she directs a tour of the old school and convent, at least, the public areas of the convent.

The Catholic grade school is still in operation, but three years ago the high school merged with a larger school in a better neighborhood. The nuns converted the old high school building into living quarters: one classroom for each anticipated homeless family. Sister Theresa identifies the other rooms by their new use rather than the former function, even though she acknowledges that some remodeling still needs to be completed.

The cafeteria is now the common dining room. The families will eat in a communal fashion, much like the sisters do in the adjacent convent. There is a playroom for the children and a community room for relaxing.

"One of our sisters and a local artist painted a mural around the walls of the playroom," she beams.

I stop in awe just inside the playroom door. Amazingly, it isn't overwhelming to have the mural from floor to ceiling on all four walls. It's detailed, but not too busy. All in all, it's calming. I feel its effect just standing here, though my eyes are eagerly moving from one surprisingly delightful detail to the next.

To the left of the door and around the nearby corner is a country scene with a cottage and a variety of domesticated animals and squirrels that ventured near the dwelling. Midway along the wall the terrain rises slightly to gentle rolling hills covered with wild flowers. A paved road emerges from the far side of the hills and turns the corner onto the next wall.

The road quickly grows into a freeway system with bridges over a barge-filled river in the forefront of a city, which includes a collection of tall smokestacks belonging to a factory. Towering apartment buildings glow with the setting sun. The buildings blend into silhouettes with light-filled windows as the painted sky fades to darkness, except for the moon and stars in the heavens. The cityscape takes nearly the entire wall opposite the door.

Beyond the city, nearing the third corner of the room, the ground rises to a high meadow at the edge of a forest which begins on the third wall. The forest grows dense with hardwood trees that reach to the ceiling, blocking most of the painted light to the forest floor and a small overgrown footpath. Tiny shimmering rays of sunlight filter through the forest canopy to illuminate deer, bears, and other indigenous adult animals in the distance, keeping watch over their youngsters in the forefront —within reach if a child wishes to touch them.

Moving along the wall, the forest thins and a stream gives way at a steep drop. The rising sun glistens through the mist of a waterfall cascading down the corner of the room and splashing into a freshwater pool with brightly colored trout, frogs, and dragonflies. At the far edge of the lake, the water rushes to the sea and the waves splash with a pair of dolphins. Farther back, a California gray whale spews a waterspout while another breaches into the water. Beneath the surface, a whale calf is visible swimming at an adult's side.

On the fourth wall the waves rush onto the shore where there is a wonderfully intricate sandcastle. Beyond the grassy sand-dune beach, a desert materializes. It is full of cacti, Joshua trees, horny toads, a burro, and a scorpion with its tail turned up. The sand grows green and golden with California poppies that end at the door. The entire picture connects together, and I love it!

Sister Theresa says they will have a story hour as she points to the overstuffed pillows and beanbag chairs.

My eyes go around the room a second time looking at the details. There are butterflies, seagulls, hummingbirds, soaring eagles, and a cactus wren—all in the appropriate habitat.

I assume there are no people in the mural because the children are encouraged to place themselves into the settings, stimulating their imagination. No explanation about the missing people is offered, and I don't venture to ask. The idea and the art are brilliant.

Inconsistent, inadequate education, and housing erodes the homeless children's confidence, social skills, and emotional security. Sister Theresa says they have a place for craft projects to facilitate communication among the children and the supervising adults. They have group activities planned and are always looking for others. They have a whole forest's worth of stuffed animals for the children to cuddle.

Sister Elizabeth and her staff thought through the entire program. The children will attend the parish school, tuition free, and there will be after-school tutoring to catch them up academically while helping them with their current homework.

Sister Theresa moves the tour along. Two sisters are near storage closets in the school's auditorium, organizing musical instruments.

Sister Theresa introduces Sister Mary Veronica, the grade school music teacher, and Sister Marie. Sister Mary Veronica slightly nods her head in my direction in response to the introduction. She looks older, well past retirement age, but full of energy. I can only imagine the kind of music she teaches.

We had an old teacher like her when I was in grade school. We sang "Salve Regina" and "Ave Maria" until our Latin was perfect. Unfortunately, she was so particular about diction that those were the only two songs we sang the entire year, but we sang them beautifully.

Not to be left out of the action, Sister Mary Veronica explains her plan to make musical instruments available to the families. "Maybe we can have jam sessions!" She admits to secretly hoping, "Maybe I will be asked to give music lessons."

Jam sessions? I think to myself how things are rarely as they appear. Sister Mary Veronica smiles at me as if she can read my thoughts. I am sure that she can't really read minds—can she?

Sister Theresa turns to me to explain, "The new residents will need a form of expressing what they have been through, and words don't always come easily. Music may become their voice for a while, maybe for the rest of their lives."

Sister Mary Veronica adds excitedly, "We can start a choir!"

These two nuns act like children scheming a wild adventure. Their enthusiasm is contagious. A smile rises to my lips and I realize I am happy to be here in this place, and to be a part of this wonderful scheme to help people. I love it. I simply love it.

Gesturing her hand toward the other nun, Sister Theresa continues, "Sister Marie teaches mathematics—she also studied dance all her life and wants to teach dance to the children."

Sister Marie smiles sweetly and nods agreement with Sister Theresa. "I would love to teach ballet, but they will like jazz or tap better."

Tap? Tap is noisy. The image of this woman in a habit teaching dance flashes into my mind. How is she going to teach isolation exercises for jazz to the children? They won't be able to see the incremental movements under her habit.

"Dance is a physical activity, but more importantly it will free their little spirits. They can benefit from something setting them free of the weight of life's reality, while giving them the success of mastering the steps." Sister Marie lectures her opinion in a math teacher matter-of-fact way. "Performing arts are esteem builders. Besides, everyone should learn to dance."

Looking at Sister Marie's young face and bright eyes, she must be the one in the newspaper article who made final vows eight years ago. I think the kids will like her. For a nun she seems pretty cool, but I still can't imagine her in a leotard leading a rag-tag dance troop across the gymnasium floor.

We progress in the direction of Sister Elizabeth's office. Sister Theresa deposits me at the door, as she had yesterday, and points me to a leather sofa. Then she announces our arrival to "Mother Elizabeth."

What? Mother? She caught me off guard. I don't know what I expected. They do wear habits, so it makes sense they still use the formal title Mother for their leader. With increased interest I think how now I can see what a real Mother Superior is like and see if Karen's nickname fits her.

The unexpectedness of this new job is definitely a refreshing change from child abuse investigations. Working in this place promises to be mentally stimulating, plus the program has creative social work elements that satisfy me.

An abrupt noise interrupts my thoughts when Mother Elizabeth shuts the drawer of her desk. She stands up and moves a wooden chair she was using as a credenza back to its place in front of her desk.

I don't mean to watch her, but the sound caught my attention. I am embarrassed when our eyes meet in an awkward moment. I look away.

To the left of where I am seated on the leather sofa, I see into a conference room that I hadn't noticed yesterday. People are beginning to congregate in the meeting room via a door from the hallway. Mother Elizabeth comes from her office and motions for me to follow her through the door to join the group.

Apparently, I am the last person hired. Everyone else seems to know where to go and appears comfortable with their surroundings. Inside the conference room on the table near the door there are stacks of folders along with other materials arranged in neat piles, ready to be disseminated.

After we have filed through the line to pick up our folders, we sit on one side of the dining-room-style tables surrounded by straight-back wooden chairs, so we are all facing Mother Elizabeth. I glance at my new co-workers at the table I join, and smile at any who makes eye contact with me. I look around to see if I know anyone. I know this, I'm in a good place.

Mother Elizabeth begins immediately after the last person takes his seat. There is so much new information to absorb that previewing the entire staff will have to wait until later. For now I stick to scribbling notes as Mother gives a précis of the handouts. I can work with anyone for the good of my clients, so the staff are secondary to my mission.

It has been a long time since I have had a new area of study. Bartending doesn't count. I take copious notes. My attentiveness is based on my desire to understand so completely that the knowledge will be second nature to me by the time the clients arrive. It is stimulating to hear new information in my field. I feel alive.

Mother Elizabeth reviews the program with us, her secular staff, explaining that whatever it takes to help these yet-to-arrive clients get back on their feet, is what will be done. At the end of an hour, Mother Elizabeth announces, "You have the rest of the week to learn the information in the packets. You will be paid for forty hours of work this week. Take the material home—study it. Come on Monday ready to work." She dismisses us, and that is that.

There are no questions from her new workers. What she expects of us is clear. Apparently she has determined we are capable of the task. Just like in Catholic school, we line up in an orderly fashion and file out the door past Mother Elizabeth.

~~~

The week passes quickly. Reviewing the material from work is an all-consuming task. The days are spent devouring the material and internalizing it. I do nothing else during these days except walk on the beach and study. The hours blend with each other. I lose track of time. I eat when I am hungry. I sleep when I am tired. The rules of night and day become meaningless.

I enjoy the freedom from the constraints of time and external schedules. It is an interesting experience, one that I want to explore further when I have more time. For now, I focus on the assigned task.

Reading about the reality of the situation of these yet-unknown-to-us homeless families makes me cry. It overwhelms me to think about the kindness of these nuns who are opening their home and resources to strangers.

Mother Elizabeth's material reminds me why I switched majors to social work during the first year of college. The sisters' project seems to have real potential to make a difference for the people they will serve. The prospect of making a difference sparks a renewed enthusiasm for my chosen life's work. Finally, slowly, I am regaining my focus of who I am as a social worker. I had wanted to make a difference. Perhaps it's possible to do that at St. Mark's in a larger way than I could by doing child abuse investigations.

Mother Elizabeth maintains absolute control of the program. No one can vandalize this program like Judge Jones did to our cases ensnared in the judicial system. I don't think anyone with any common sense will try to sabotage her plans. This woman runs a household full of nuns; she is not someone to mess with.

We are as safe from the craziness of the system as anyone in this business can be, something I desperately crave.

At last I reach the final information packet. It contains the referral criteria. The grant the nuns wrote specified traditional families—father, mother, and children. That, and limiting the length of time of home- lessness to two years or less, is clearly designed to help the program succeed. Mother Elizabeth impresses me with her insight to anticipate unexpected problems before admitting people at greater risk of failure; people who will need more support and resources that will need to be developed to meet their critical needs. Hopefully, that will improve the families' chances for a sustainable success, as well as renew funding for another three years of the program.

In addition to everything else, I like the name she gave the program, "Spirit of Hope." As I learn the material, I find myself caught up in the spirit of hope that the program emanates.

~~~

Mr. Goldstein continues to come for his evening walk during my study week. Now that he is physically stronger he has started attending the Senior Center on a regular basis. Sometimes while we are out for our walk he tells stories about the goings on at the Center, especially about the older women. (As if he is so young.) In truth, he is enjoying the company of the women his age. He does seem younger than before he started getting regular exercise. The companionship and fresh air probably helps too.

We talk endlessly during our walks. Our hands are animated, and we nod in agreement or disagreement. This week he is especially interested in the material I am studying. It helps me internalize the information more easily to discuss it with him.

Mr. Goldstein makes a curious sound when he hears the program's name, thinks it over, then indicates his approval. Of course he likes the name. Who wouldn't like "Spirit of Hope"? His unpretentious response amuses me so much that I have to fight back a laugh and the urge to hug him. I don't think he would mind either, but it doesn't seem to fit the mood of our conversation.

I return to California late enough in the winter to miss the worst beach storms that come in November. As the days pass, the winter skies are beginning to show signs of the approaching spring. The beach doesn't seem as cold and desolate as when I first came home, yet the tourists are still months away. It is a peaceful winter-beach. With Mr. Goldstein's help, it is a place of refuge.

About mid-week Maggie stops by to check on my progress with Mother Elizabeth's homework assignment. For "graduation" she offers dinner at her place—Friday night. "Besides," she tells me, "Dave" (her long-time live-in partner) "thinks you are a figment of my imagination." She laughs as she tosses her head back in her usual mischievous manner.

"Dave," I whisper. "It will be good to see him again." I smile and I accept her invitation for a good meal and conversation among old friends.

The days continue to blur together. Wisely, Maggie calls Friday afternoon to remind me of the graduation dinner in a few hours. In the course of our conversation she mentions that Dave invited a friend from the law office where he works. I am beginning to get suspicious, but since I am already committed to the evening, I still plan to attend. After all, I can claim fatigue and leave early if the evening turns disastrous.

Dave greets me at the door with a kiss on the cheek and a hug. He is a full partner in a large law firm downtown. He and Maggie became an item during Dave's last year in law school, when she was a freshman. They have been together ever since. Surely they must have discussed marriage at some point, but never married. Whatever their arrangement is, it works nicely for them.

Joseph McLean, Dave's friend, arrives shortly after me. Joseph is heart-stopping handsome. He has beautiful dark eyes with the blackest lashes to match his wavy black hair. There are laugh lines around his mouth and eyes. He is quick to laugh, flashing his bright white teeth. Joseph is charming, and he knows it.

I catch myself staring at him several times in the first few minutes after he arrives. This is embarrassing, but I don't stop admiring him. He has an Irish accent. I love to hear him talk and see him flash his big, easy smile.

Maggie makes an excuse for me to help her in the kitchen where she gives me Joseph's condensed biography.

"Joseph is spelled I-O-S-E-P-H, but pronounced 'Joseph.' He is thirty-seven, a successful criminal lawyer, AND never married. At least not yet," Maggie says with a disturbing amount of delight as she grins at me. Eros has nothing on her. No doubt she is hiding Cupid's arrows behind her back as we speak. Yikes!

Dinner is relaxing. The men don't occupy the conversation with discussions of their conquests in the courtroom. Dave allows Maggie to shift the conversation to discussing my new job. As I explain the new program at St. Mark's, they seem genuinely interested in the homeless.

Dave and Joseph ask many insightful questions about the legal needs of our clients. I agree legal services probably are needed by some, but unfortunately it is unlikely there is money in the budget for it, and I'm not sure even the filing fees would be manageable. There probably isn't much hope for these two to add to their client base at Spirit of Hope.

Dave offers pro bono work. Joseph says he can swing a case or two to clear some old offenses, then flashes a toothy grin. The guys talk about asking the bankruptcy attorneys to send a paralegal or two to Mother Elizabeth to see if any of the clients need a bankruptcy to get a fresh start.

Their generosity catches me by surprise. It suits the altruistic social worker in me. They both draw business cards out of their pocket business card holders as if it is a contest to be first-draw in a poorly scripted Western showdown.

For Joseph's benefit Maggie tries unsuccessfully to divert the conversation back to me. I resist her efforts to take it to a personal level, and she gives me a disapproving look. I don't care, she can disapprove all she likes. On the other hand, I want more information about him.

Much to Maggie's distress, I am spared the problem of things getting personal. We continue discussing the program and the likely needs of the clientele.

Eventually other safe topics of interest make their way into our conversation. Regardless of the topic, I like listening to Joseph's thick accent. Verging on being obsessive, I ask him as many questions as I can to keep him talking. I try not to seem too mesmerized by him, but I doubt anyone is fooled. Needless to say, there is no need to attempt an early escape.

~~~

Driving home, I wonder what Joseph thinks of me and if I will see him again. Maybe Maggie and Dave can be persuaded to arrange another dinner party in the near future. I can only hope.

My thoughts are still occupied with Joseph when I reach my apartment. I need to refocus. Though it is not entirely the wisest thing to do alone at this hour, I walk to the empty beach and listen to the waves come to shore.

I think about how pleasant it was to see Maggie. When I left California I didn't say goodbye to her, which makes no sense. Strangely, she still has not asked me why I did not contact her during my five year exile. She hasn't pushed discussing work since the reading of the judge's letter with Karen.

I am glad not to continue either conversation. Perhaps now that we are working at different agencies our friendship will continue in new and different ways.

The longer I sit on the beach, the more sentimentality washes over me. I think about Maggie and Dave and what a treasure their friendship is to me. I think about Joseph. The mysteriousness of him intrigues me. And Mr. Goldstein, an unexpected welcomed friendship bundles all into coming home.

I have missed California and all the nuances of life it holds for me. Contentedly, I sit soaking in the experience of the beach, smelling the sandy saltwater scents, and listening to the sound of the crashing waves as the tide comes in. My mind settles softly into the rhythm the waves play in my thoughts.

As the tide rises, the mist of the breaking waves reaches out to touch me from the darkness. Behind me on the lifeguard station, the handless clock confirms time is truly standing still. I look up at the moon in the black night sky and think, if this was a movie, they would be playing the good music right about now.

~~~

In the morning, my cousin Ilene and I meet at Laguna Beach. She is standing on the beach looking out at the ocean as I approach her. She looks just as I remember her the last time we were together. The greeting is always the same whether we saw each other last week or five years ago. She greets me with a hug as if I am her little sister. This warm and genuine affection is the hallmark of our family. I reciprocate. In this family any other behavior would be alien to our nature.

We have only an hour to visit before her tennis date. Ilene tells me she is a grandmother now. I tell her about my job. We make plans to get together for lunch at her new house when we can really catch up with each other. We move the boxes I had shipped from Nebraska out of her car and into mine. She asks if I want to talk about going away. I know there isn't time to get into that conversation, so I decline.

~~~

Monday morning Mother Elizabeth appears with shopping lists. She divides us into two groups. One group is assigned to descend upon the local merchants in a never-before-seen swarm. She dispatches the first group of staff out into the world of commerce, two-by-two, to purchase shampoo, bath towels, hairbrushes, laundry detergent, and everything from aftershave to nail polish. She gives specific instructions to her shoppers: "Get the good stuff, the bright cheery colors, the fluffy towels."

She turns her attention to the remaining group. Mother Elizabeth assigns the non-shopper group to sort through the sizable stacks of applications under the watchful supervision of Sister Theresa. I am assigned to this group. We are to stack the applications in piles based only on the initial screening criteria, families and length of time of homelessness, nothing else.

I know several of the social workers among the staff. We've met at professional conferences. We never worked together, but all of the staff have excellent reputations in the social work community. It is rumored the others with essential specialties are equally as good as the social workers. We are the quintessential staff. We can do more than basic paper-sorting tasks.

Mother Elizabeth is counting on us to make this program work despite the odds. I wish she would trust her judgment in hiring us and let us jump in and use our talents and training. However, she is specific with her instructions. Perhaps eventually she will trust us with more responsibility once we have proven ourselves to her. For now she alone has taken on the task of deciding who is admitted to Spirit of Hope and who is refused. Maybe she is being cautious. I hope she isn't one who tends to micro-manage projects.

At our coffee break two staff members report they heard that Mother Elizabeth requested the referring agencies not to tell the families they refer. In that small way, if they are not selected, she can protect them from one more disappointment. She can't take them all in, not yet, anyway. But I bet she finds a way to increase the number of people she can get off the streets.

As I triage the applications, I am beginning to respect Mother Elizabeth for not asking anyone else to make the hard decision of who will be turned away. I had only thought of the screening as who would be accepted, not those rejected. That must weigh heavily on a person—even a nun who has God's benediction.

We silently continue our screening duties. Whatever their opinion is, none of the staff mention their thoughts. After failing to be acutely aware of the struggles of my co-workers at CPS, I intentionally make the effort to be astute regarding what is going on around me at this job. It is a fresh start with a new program, and I plan to pay attention.

As I reach for another referral from the stack I see Mother Elizabeth rubbing the back of her neck. When she looks up and sees me watching her, a strange look comes over her face.

Quickly, I look at the papers in front of me, but I am not really reading them. I am still thinking about Mother Elizabeth's fatigue. Perhaps she is a little embarrassed with being caught as a mere mortal that gets stiff muscles like the rest of us. Though I shouldn't, I look back at her—squarely at her.

Mother Elizabeth removes her reading glasses, but leaves her hand suspended at half-mast. Her eyebrows move slightly, and it is hard to tell how much they would have moved if the forehead piece to her veil hadn't restrained the movement. It seems like a long pause. Finally, she lays her glasses on the table and addresses me from where she sits.

"Kathryn, you are an expert on children, aren't you?"

"Mother, I don't have children," I answer, noting the nearby co-workers are listening to the conversation without looking up.

"No, but you know about children, don't you?" She tips her hand to the answer she expects.

"Yes, Mother Elizabeth, I do." I understand her directive.

"Then, come with me," Mother Elizabeth says as she stands to leave.

As I rise, I look to my co-workers for a clue, a hint, about what Mother has in mind. A few of them are now looking up from their work. Their expressions make it obvious that none of them know what she is up to, either.

I follow her out of the room and down the hall. Unlike Sister Theresa, Mother Elizabeth waits for me to catch up and walk beside her. She doesn't talk en route. She genuflects at the chapel doorway. I do the same. As we walk to her office, this reminds me of Karen summoning me. She takes a checkbook and a small wallet from her desk drawer. She removes a set of keys from one of the hooks on the inside of the coat closet door. I follow her out the back door to the garages, slide in the front passenger seat of the vehicle, and secure the seat belt.

Mother Elizabeth drives carefully through the narrow alley and pulls into the traffic. Silently looking directly forward, I sit motionless in the front seat, insuring I don't distract her from her attention to driving.

This ride reminds me of the other time I rode in a vehicle with a nun at the wheel. In first grade one of the sisters drove me to the hospital to be with my mother after my parents had been in an auto accident.

I remember Sister instructing harshly, "Sit quiet," while she concentrated on driving. She seemed uneasy and nervously hesitant with the traffic. Thinking about it now I wonder whether she even had a driver's license. Some didn't back then.

During that entire trip I clutched the strap of my book bag until my knuckles were tight, while staring at my oxfords dangling above the floorboard. My father died later that afternoon. I haven't been in a car with a nun since then.

Mother Elizabeth begins to speak casually. It takes a moment for me to leave that memory of long ago and mean old Sister Dominic. The sound of her voice comes through the memory, relaxing me into the conversation.

Mother Elizabeth has never given me a reason to distrust her. It was the unknown element in her request that made me uneasy. Eventually I will to adapt to her expectation of blind obedience without responding with uneasiness. After all, how threatening can a nun be?

Mother Elizabeth expertly turns the car across three lanes of oncoming traffic and into the parking lot of the shopping center. Curiosity crowds the other thoughts from my mind. I forget my concerns about riding with a nun or being summoned to blind obedience. Why are we going to the mall? What is her mission?

Inside the store, our task turns out to be shopping for children's sheets and blankets. Well, this is easy enough.

In my previous job I learned the children's modern heroes. It was one of the tools of my trade. Children are not going to tell their deepest secrets to someone who doesn't know the name of the character pictured on their shirt or the doll tucked under their arm.

It is purely a matter of credibility to know their heroes. There is no such thing as winging it with kids. Either you know what you're talking about or you don't. Instinctively they know too much to ever be fooled by phony credentials. Some social workers try it, but it never works—not in a million years. Working in children's services requires advanced studies in the children's section of the bookstore, hours of children's television, and browsing toy store aisles to know the neighborhood where kids live and play.

Mother Elizabeth and I cruise the linen aisle looking at the displays. All of the characters on the packages are familiar to me. I differentiate for Mother which characters are the good guys and keep her from purchasing those with a questionable reputation, even if they look cute. Mother Elizabeth appears to enjoy purchasing children's bedding for a change of pace. It was thoughtful of her to even think of children's sheets, considering she has never had children.

After shopping, Mother stops at the soda fountain at the food court. She whispers, "They make the best vanilla colas here."

It intrigues me to have an unexpected moment off the clock with her. After Karen's honesty about the emotional and physical strain of being in charge, I had been concerned when I noticed Mother Elizabeth assumed all of the weight of the program for herself.

It is a relief to realize that she monitors her own barometer. She paces herself, obviously something I need to learn after my experience five years ago. "All or nothing" is too stressful of a way to conduct work or life.

As we enjoy our drink, we visit about the Dodgers upcoming season—she is quite the fan. A fashionably dressed woman walks past us, moving our conversation to fashion—somewhat surprising me, considering what Mother Elizabeth wears. I remind myself she hasn't always been a nun, but it's hard to imagine. She is very much a nun, even with a cherry-vanilla cola in her hand, and fashion or baseball in her words.

Mother Elizabeth turns her attention to the people carefully selecting plants from a potted plant display. She remarks she loves to garden without removing her gaze from the plants. She moves to the display and carefully examines the specimens, but purchases none of them. That is not the purpose of this trip. She is very disciplined.

Watching her, I recall seeing the usual convent vegetable garden while on tour with Sister Theresa. Of course, there are flower gardens around the outdoors grottos. She speaks fondly, though briefly, about her own private garden.

In my mind's eye I can imagine Mother Elizabeth outside, alone in her own garden, recalibrating her self-monitoring systems. The idea seems to fit with the character of this woman I am becoming acquainted with today. I wonder who she turns to when gardening isn't enough? God? Yes, probably.

When we return to the convent we put away our new treasures until they are needed. She wants them left in the packages so the children know they have new sheets, and to select their own. There will be hand-me-downs later, but she wants as many new items as the program can afford in the beginning.

While we work side by side, her thoughtfulness for the children continues to amaze me. Most people, especially virgin nuns, would not have thought of special linen for the children. I have come to believe she has a detailed plan for everything. I admire her tenderness and her gentle ways.

~~~

Throughout the week Mother Elizabeth takes other staff on errands. No doubt she is getting to know each of us away from the convent environment. It is rumored that each of the staff was recommended to Mother Elizabeth by people she knows. Equal opportunity employment doesn't seem as important to her as a hand-picked team to help the people who will soon come through the front door of St. Mark's convent, school, and now, home for the homeless.

Mother Elizabeth applied for grants from private foundations. Thanks to her savvy ideas, there is no danger this program will be one of those giving the appearance of helping, but in reality just creating employment for otherwise unemployable staff. Spirit of Hope is real, and I desperately need to be part of something real.

These nuns touch something in the core of my being. Most real social workers, as Maggie and I call our breed, chant the prayer, "God save us from the do-gooders." It looks as though Mother Elizabeth knows the same prayer. Or maybe God has heard our prayers.

~~~

The next Monday morning when the staff arrive, we encounter a group of men, women, and squirming, clutching children in the foyer of St. Mark's Convent. Small groups of homeless families continue to arrive in bunches every few minutes. There is a sense of uncertainty and excitement that grows with the increasing population.

Sister Theresa is at her usual post by the door warmly greeting each arriving person and directing them down the hall to the left toward the school.

Stationed strategically along the way, sisters are posted at the intersections in the hallway like brown-robed traffic cops keeping everyone from getting lost in the catacomb corridors connecting the buildings.

The disbelieving newcomers walk hesitantly through the hallway, suspiciously examining their surroundings. It is as if they are taking in every inch of the place in wonderment. After all, the convent is spotless, as one would expect. There are no rodents, nor drunks in the doorways to step over. The homeless families are understandably unsure of the validity of their surroundings and the program they have heard so little about—only enough to get them here. Too good to be true? I think not.

It doesn't take clients long to learn that the worst thing to do is believe too eagerly that the do-gooders will actually do good. I don't blame anyone for being skeptical. There are far too few real professionals to offset the havoc the ne'er-do-wells cause before they skip off merrily to yet another worthy cause. Those do-gooders only help the deserving poor.

I'm not sure who that is—I haven't seen anyone who deserves a life of profound poverty.

Now it is Mother Elizabeth's task to convince them, within a short period of time, to commit to Spirit of Hope project for a minimum of one year, and that she and her band of sisters are worthy of their trust. The request to trust strangers to help them, one more time, is a big request. She'll have to be patient.

The families move slowly toward the school auditorium under the protective guidance of the nuns. Meanwhile, Sister Theresa instructs the staff to go to the convent dining room and wait at the ready to assist with registration as soon as Mother Elizabeth finishes her presentation.

It is no surprise we find the application forms in neat stacks on each table. We spread through the room to allow comfortable space for everyone to register. Privacy is a luxury the poor can't afford. Space is the best we can offer them.

During our orientation, Mother Elizabeth made it perfectly clear she didn't intend to spend time holding our hands through each detail that was to follow, though I worried about micro-managing. She has been true to her word. Quickly, I review the registration form and prepare for the families' arrival. Other staff members are doing the same. There is no doubt in anyone's mind that Mother Elizabeth expects us to think on our feet once the families arrive. That day is at hand.

The form is straightforward enough—not too prying. I anticipate no real problems with registration. We wait quietly at our posts, patiently watching for signs of approaching families. We know this is it—the moment when life surges into Spirit of Hope and it becomes real.

~~~

It is an hour before the meeting concludes and families begin to congregate at the tables in the dining room. They stay huddled in family groups, some children are straining at the hand holding on to them, others are clinging tightly to a parent's clothing. Sister Theresa directs each family toward a table, while we motion them in our direction if they hesitate along the way. The room fills with people sounds and chairs scooting toward table sounds.

A few minutes after the families' arrival, Sister Bridget appears in the doorway, announcing she has paper and colors in the adjacent room for children who want to draw while their parents fill out the forms. Sister Bridget is the robust art teacher on loan from St. Mark's grade school next door. She is large, and I imagine, from a child's perspective, scary.

The children hesitate, crouching in their seats near their parents, while some are peeking over the chair back to keep an eye on Sister Bridget. Some of the older children look like they are sizing her up in a streetwise manner, not sure if she should be trusted. A few younger children look as if they want to go, yet aren't sure if they should leave their parent's side. Their eyes say, "Maybe this is a trick."

A little wisp of a thing, with unruly, curly blonde hair and big, dark eyes is kneeling in her chair with her hands on the top of the backrest, studying the nun. She whispers something to her mother. She makes the first move to join Sister Bridget once she decides Sister is worthy of the risk. The little girl walks up to the towering, round nun, and takes hold of her hand. Almost immediately there are whispers to parents and the scraping sound of chairs as most of the other children move to follow the mismatched pair out of the room.

Within minutes Mother Elizabeth walks in and heads for the table where I am sitting with my family. "Kathryn, please help Sister Bridget with the children," she says as she sits down next to me, taking my place with the parents.

Mother Elizabeth is confident and commanding, without being intimidating. Obediently, I follow the children out of the room. After all, I am the resident expert on children, am I not?

Twenty families accept Mother Elizabeth's invitation to commit to Spirit of Hope for a year. I easily calculate forty adults. However, the number of children is significantly greater. Each family must have three or four children, occasionally more. Most of the children are under the age of ten.

It doesn't take long to figure out that Mother Elizabeth selected families with the most kids in order to get the largest number of children off the street and into school as soon as she possibly can.

Sister Bridget and I are outnumbered, even if one of us in the room is a nun. Seemingly unaware of this mathematical fact, Sister Bridget already has all of the children seated with colors in hand. For the most part, they are quietly coloring. She's amazing.

We move around the room visiting with the children, helping where needed. The little artists are strained, reserved, and withdrawn. There is not the usual chatter and giggling that accompanies a room FULL of children. The kids steal sideways glances to watch the jolly, round nun, the other children, and me. They are careful not to let their eyes meet Sister's or mine as they sneak peeks of us. I am careful not to let them know I'm watching too.

As soon as registration finishes, the cafeteria ladies appear, announcing they have milk and homemade cookies, fresh from the oven, in the grade school cafeteria. The children pause—it has been a long time since they had cookies, never mind fresh cookies.

They exchange stealthy glances with each other to confirm what they heard is true. Their bond with each other is beginning with a mutual admiration of sweets.

Sister Bridget and I exchange glances, as well. All of us pause for a minute as the information sinks in and the children look like they are beginning to believe—at least in the cookies.

After the parents collect their children in anticipation of the welcomed snack, Sister Bridget and I are left alone to collect the art supplies. Sister is an outgoing, cheerful person, full of excitement about Spirit of Hope. She confides that the sisters have been developing the Spirit of Hope project for four years.

"The planning was difficult. We were impatient and wanted to begin helping people immediately, but Mother Elizabeth kept reminding us that we must be truly prepared." Her expression dulls slightly as she looks at the door. "The little darlings weren't sure about the cookies, were they? They're in for a treat."

As she speaks, Sister Bridget's hands move about in an animated fashion that I haven't seen in the nuns until now. Her face bursts into a hearty smile as she loses her sisterly composure and giggles with open delight.

"I can't believe our families are finally here!" Sister Bridget squeals with excitement. For a brief moment I think she is going to grab me by the shoulders and shake me, but she doesn't.

When she notices her behavior, she immediately regains her sisterly composure, retracting her hands into her sleeves. To ease the awkwardness of the moment for her, I capitalize on her enthusiasm for the final reality of Spirit of Hope, the admission of the homeless families. It is obvious she loves children and is a natural at working with them.

"Sister, the children will love the playroom." I smile at her, and we resume picking up the art supplies. I take the risk of being wrong and guess she is the one responsible for the mural. "The mural you painted is beautiful. I love it!"

She stops working and smiles back. "Thank you. I had help." She smiles to herself as she busies herself with full focus on the task.

That ends the unrestrained interaction. We never again mention the sadness surrounding the children's uncertainty of the cookies or her response to the long-awaited arrival of the families. I do understand her excitement. It feels good to be a part of something that is really going to make a difference in their lives.

We finish putting away the art supplies in the grade school cabinet, then join the others in the cafeteria. I'm having coffee. Sister Bridget heads directly to the cookie trays. Our arrival coincides with preparations to show the families to their homes.

We take a minute to have a cookie, then she returns to class and I catch up to the rear of the tour. There is no indication how they decided which family gets which room. Most likely it is random, but no one says. I relax, realizing none of the decisions are on my shoulders.

At the end of the tour, Mother Elizabeth asks the men to return to the gymnasium—she needs their help to assemble the cribs that arrived yesterday afternoon.

There is a slight laugh from the men as she admits the sisters don't have any experience in such things.

It is obvious the sisters can easily master assembling the cribs, blindfolded. I don't believe anyone here really thinks the nuns need help. These are not helpless women by any stretch of the imagination. Mother Elizabeth is thoughtful to give the men an immediate physical task, one with rapid, measurable success.

Each family is assigned a staff person for the week, beginning with the family we registered. The nuns and staff help our families move their belongings in and get settled. We make beds, do laundry, and bathe children while the parents unpack their meager possessions. I have no idea where all of the hot water comes from, but, surprisingly, there is an ample supply.

Mother Elizabeth had previously arranged with Sister Barbara, the elementary school principal, for the school children to have a picnic lunch in order to make the school cafeteria available for our families, the staff, and the good sisters on the occasion of this our first meal together. After today, the nuns will resume eating in the convent dining room, and the staff—well, I'm not sure where we will eat.

Each family huddles together at a table, though there is ample room to spread out. As it should be, the staff and sisters are last in the food line. It seems a little awkward. I don't want to intrude. It is more my nature to not push my clients into a forced affiliation. I like to ease into the client-social worker relationship.

Sister Bridget returns and sits at the table with her little curly-haired friend and family. The woman I was to register makes eye contact. That is good enough for me, and I ask if I may join her family. Everyone scoots down a bit and I take the movement as an invitation.

Lunch is quiet, barely more than introductions. The woman's name is Monica. The children talk to each other in Spanish. I don't let on that I understand that the youngest boy thinks I am pretty. The children giggle. Monica is uncomfortable that her children are speaking about me in Spanish. She shoots them a quieting parental look. I act like I don't notice and continue eating. The dad teases the youngster about our romance in English until he squirms, then grins with a first grader missing-tooth smile, and looks at me.

The families are hungry for home-cooked food. The cafeteria ladies are standing at their post, announcing how inconvenient leftovers are. A big man named Race gets up and goes through the line again.

The cafeteria ladies beam. He smiles back and takes an additional helping of food. His wife and others follow Race's example. The children aren't shy about the cookies. There is not one crumb of food left when the meal is finished. It is spiritual to watch hungry people eat until they are satisfied. The cafeteria ladies are visibly pleased to have their meal appreciated.

After lunch one of the staff, Rhoda, walks around with a large box of individually wrapped toothbrushes. Pete, previously an elementary teacher, hands out donated boxes of toothpaste. Rhoda has a permanent marker in her hand, in case siblings want the same color toothbrush. Otherwise we refrain from marking their belongings. Marking them is too institutionalized. Like everyday life, the families will have to keep track of their things the old fashioned way—just like the rest of us.

The day passes quickly. Our families are getting settled. They seem tired from the burden of life, though they are free with their expressions of appreciation for the smallest thing done for them, and sometimes for nothing in particular.

Generally speaking, this is a day job. The sisters will be available, if needed, when the staff is gone. The parents will retain their positions as heads of their household, and the nuns will only be on call.

When five o'clock arrives, the staff gather at Sister Theresa's desk to sign out, and the sisters begin moving in the direction of the chapel.

It was a good day.

As I reach for the door to leave, I hear the sound of female voices chanting, signaling the beginning of Evening Prayers.

Pausing to listen for a moment, I feel a sense of satisfaction with our first day at Spirit of Hope. I feel a sense of hopefulness again, like when I was a wide-eyed, young social worker.

~~~

~ CHAPTER 7 ~

Go Forth and—and What?

By the time I arrive home, fatigue outweighs my hunger. I am content with my new job. One thing for sure, I will wear more comfortable shoes tomorrow—ones equal to the adobe tile floor. The sisters wear black shoes with thick rubber soles. While leather soles may look better, the more practical shoes are a wiser choice.

Relaxing with a cup of coffee and my feet resting on the coffee table, I think about Spirit of Hope and everyone involved in the project. If I am tired, I can only imagine how the parents feel. They had a big day, the beginning of a new life. Hmm, a new life. I drift off to sleep sitting on the sofa.

It's dark when the phone awakens me. It takes a disoriented minute to realize it is Karen's voice on the phone. I have been so distracted with Spirit of Hope, that I forgot to call to thank her for the reference she gave Mother Elizabeth on my behalf.

I give her a brief review of the last three weeks. Karen is pleased to hear I am happy with the change in direction of my career. I remember to tell her I met Sam Jackson, but he didn't know anything helpful about the Judge's daughter. With my new work, I forgot to finish looking through the obituaries, but I told her what I had accomplished thus far.

Eventually, I notice the correlation between her telephone call and the first day of clients at work. Ah, it was probably just a coincidence. I pause long enough for her to understand it is her turn to speak.

"You will never believe this. I just returned to the office and found a note from Keith. He learned Judge Jones' wife's name was Kathryn!" she says with an excited voice.

I sit up straight and put my feet on the floor. "How does she spell it?" I ask suspiciously.

"K-A-T-H-R-Y-N," Karen adds a dramatic flair to her voice.

"That is too weird," I whisper. "What did Maggie say?"

"I don't know if Keith told her or not. She was gone by the time I came back to the office."

"So do you think the letter was really to me or, or to her? To his Kathryn?" I ask barely audibly, as a spooky feeling shoots up the center of my back, giving me a shiver.

Karen offers no insight into my question. She is intrigued with the name issue too. We talk for at least a half hour about the new development in our mystery.

Now I am fully awake. I pop something quick for dinner in the microwave and make a pot of coffee. While my dinner is cooking, I hunt for the obituary list I printed earlier.

Driven, I scan the list while I eat. I hadn't looked ahead while I was searching the obituaries. I wonder if I had previously seen the various spellings of "Kathryn Jones" if I would have thought to try them all to find Mrs. Judge Jones and skipped the name-by-name search.

In minutes I am online in the newspaper archives. There she is. There is "Kathryn Jones, wife of Judge William Jones." Kathryn's obituary lists a couple of siblings that may be helpful—if they can be found—AND a daughter, LINDA.

"Ah, Linda, we have been looking for you," I whisper while the printer produces a copy of the obituary. I email the link to Maggie at work, knowing she will forward it to Karen and Keith, since I don't remember their email addresses from before and haven't thought to ask for them.

Despite my satisfaction with Linda's discovery, I am furious all over again that the Judge invaded our lives with his absurd letter. He should have sent it to his daughter. If he was going to kill himself, why didn't he make a clean break with the living? Why couldn't he just go away and leave us alone? Hasn't he stolen enough life-spirit from us with his inept rulings?

In my heart, I have no doubt Judge Jones killed that little girl as surely as if it had been his hand on the knife stabbing her ninety-six times. She had died long before the stabbing to her still, lifeless body stopped—that shows how demented the guy was.

Her father must have been out of his mind when he killed her. Maybe she threatened to tell on him again. Only he knows what happened. It wasn't the fault of drugs, as his tox screen was negative. It was him, all him.

I shudder violently with the thought of her needless demon-ridden death, while my mind remembers the vivid crime scene photos of the beaten, stabbed bloody body of the defenseless little girl with blood matted in her curls.

We all knew he was sicker than most. That's why the Judge's ruling was so unbelievable. Eventually, in one way or another, death reached out and touched each of us, literally or spiritually.

Kathryn Jones' obituary is on the coffee table. I decide not to pick it up. I plan to be careful with my new life, to not spend time on anything that could become consuming, then consume me.

I sit for a long time sipping my coffee on the patio while listening to the sound of the waves from across the street. It is good to be home where I am not an outsider.

With a change of location, back to the sofa, Joseph comes into my thoughts. Every thought of him is pure speculation, fantasy, daydreams. Every ounce of my being tells me I should not entertain this fantasy. It was only a chance meeting. It has been two weeks, and nothing seems to have come of it. I cannot dare to indulge in such thoughts. I need reality, a sane reality.

My thoughts turn from fantasy lovers back to my present life. I seek to remember how Maggie's friendship had grown out of a simple working relationship. There is this new Karen that I do not understand. And, of course, there is Mr. Goldstein—my dear, dear Mr. Goldstein.

Mr. Goldstein is the only male in my life with whom I spend significant amounts of time. From him I learn about overcoming the difficult, impossible moments in life. As he continues to tell me dreadful details of his confinement in the death camp, I am more and more amazed with humanity's resilience.

As I look up, lost in thought while pressing my tired body into the back of the sofa, my gaze catches the clock on the wall. Suddenly I am aware of the time—in a few hours I have to get ready for work. Almost with a jerk, I am on my feet and shutting off the lights. In no time, I am in bed and asleep.

~~~

Morning seems to arrive only minutes after I close my eyes. Pushing myself to get ready for the day, moving reluctantly into my routine. I feel a little wobbly this morning after last night's encounter with the haunting memories of the crime scene. There is no time for indulging my wounds from the past now. I have other duties—other people need my undivided attention.

I manage to miss the bus. To get to work on time I have to drive aggressively. The families are up and around by the time the staff arrive. They look more rested today than yesterday, but their eyes are still dull. Their expressions reveal their continued disbelief in the longevity of their good fortune. I suspect the dullness is due, in part, to poor nutrition, but largely to living in unending hopelessness on the streets and in their cars. Even the children, though scrubbed and combed, look dull.

Understandably, their recovery will be slow in the beginning. First, they have to learn to trust in us to truly help them. Then the adults will have to give their children a sense of security again.

Resilience. Hope. Security. All of these come from the human spirit, and they are not things easily taught, nor replenished. We have to be more than a dry-dock along their journey. In the beginning, I suppose that is what we are, but we will have to transform into a harbor pilot and guide them on their way again.

Trust is a slow process. Self-sustaining trust is fragile and elusive. More than usual, today I fully appreciate the reality of wobbly feelings that come and go with a will of their own.

Strength of character demands facing those weak moments squarely. Oddly, we seem to manage to have the strength we need when it is needed the most.

Our homeless people will find their strength to begin again, as it is human nature. Thank God, it is even possible.

Perhaps, I am feeling philosophical because of the vivid memories of the bloody photos. Regardless of my life's complexities, work has its own demands. We are to assess clothing needs and to get everyone a new outfit to start rebuilding their lives.

The nuns are sharp negotiators and have made deals with their usual vendors, and others who are seeking to gain the convent and school's business through this back door. Some of the benefactors are "good Catholics" who attended St. Mark's school. To capitalize on this the nuns use one motivation—Guilt! It works miracles.

At any rate, each staff person is given a list of merchants who have agreed to provide for our needs at cost or below, and the store representatives to contact to smoothly facilitate the transactions.

Without expression, my family goes through the motion of assessing their clothing needs. It is glaringly obvious they don't have much. What they do have is too small or too ragged to count as clothing.

Lunch is slightly early, so we can get a running start with our shopping trip. We are given an envelope of cash and Sister Theresa tells us to "go forth" with our families. She hands a set of convent keys to each of the staff who do not have an adequate size vehicle, including me.

My family is polite but reserved as they climb into the cream-colored van with a St. Christopher medallion hanging from the rearview mirror. Keeping in mind the shopping trip with Mother Elizabeth, I take a detour to a shop in the neighborhood and treat us to ice cream with my own money. I am careful to protect the identity of the source of the finances for the ice cream, so it doesn't seem like charity.

It takes coaxing to get the parents to have more than a single scoop of vanilla ice cream. "At least sprinkles?"

These people strike me as too unassuming and polite to reach out and grab life. It's not a criticism—I do understand. We will have to start small and work toward believing they deserve more than vanilla when they really want something more exotic.

The young daughter slips free of the constraint and asks her mother if she might have strawberry sauce on her ice cream. Her mother looks at her, then at me. I smile and tilt my head in a "Why not?" way. After a considering pause, she approves.

The little girl squeals with delight. It wouldn't ordinarily have been my choice, but I order strawberry sauce on my ice cream too. It is as if a dam broke and we all indulge in various toppings on our vanilla ice cream. The laughter that might ordinarily accompany a moment like this—is silent. I watch Monica with her family and love her immediately. She is a good mom.

With ice cream treats in hand, we walk to the shaded picnic area. There we examine our shopping list while we eat. Choosing the stores from the merchant list, we plan our attack on the world of commerce. I ask what style of clothes they like in an effort to plant the idea that they have choices, something that has been lost to them in their homeless state along with everything they owned.

The parents go through the motion of complying with my requests without being an inconvenience to anyone. Not to be stopped so early in my mission, I turn my focus on my previous ally, the little girl, and her three brothers who willingly engage in the conversation. After the experience with the ice cream, the children are quite adamant about what they want to purchase. They are not visibly excited, but decisive nonetheless.

Returning the question to the more reserved parents, they comment that "anything would be fine" with them. Conversely, I reply they might as well have something they like. Hesitantly, the man suggests that he needs clothes for job interviews. We talk about what type of job he wants, so we can decide what will be the best attire for his interviews. Gradually they relax—slightly. I only wish I could have figured out a way to facilitate an even more relaxed atmosphere for them.

At the store the parents are stoic until the children and I begin voting on the parents' clothes with thumbs up or down, and make faces when necessary to further cast our vote on the items they select. I admit it, I am the instigator of this spectacle, but it worked to make shopping less awkward for the parents. They stand a little taller when they see themselves in the mirror wearing our final, best pick of outfits in our budget.

Before long the parents are enjoying our outing almost as much as the children. They seem to get a flicker of hope for the moment, but I know it is not self-sustaining, not yet anyway. It is a good start— something for them to build on as they work their way through the Spirit of Hope program.

While we are in the check-out line at the service desk, I slip the money to the father to pay for the items himself. His eyes meet mine, but overall he is agreeable with the covert money exchange. I will have him give Sister Theresa the change and sales receipt. The rationale is that it takes me out of the middle of this transaction and keeps him in the position of head of his household.

~~~

Back at the van, he seems surprised when I refuse the change and receipt. Gently I push his hand back. "You give it to Sister Theresa when we get home." I figure exchanging trust has to start with one of us. His eyes understand, but he says nothing as he pockets the money.

We arrive back at the convent with plenty of time to admire the purchases they made before carefully putting dad's interview clothes on hangers until needed. The children want to wear something new, now— right now.

The husband sits back, lovingly watching his wife and children with their first new clothes in a very long time. It is almost a spiritual experience. I watch them too.

Our eyes meet. We don't speak. He must sense that I understand his pleasure. He makes no indication with his unchanged facial expression. When he looks back at his family, I quietly slip out of the room to leave them alone.

In the hallway, little Shasta, Sister Bridget's newest best friend, can be heard insisting on wearing her new white sandals with the pink "diamonds" with her pink shorts outfit. Her mother adds pink barrettes to keep her curly strands of hair out of her face. Shasta dances around their room trying to go up on her toes like a ballerina in her sandals with the pink diamonds.

Watching Shasta dance is a "Spirit of Hope" moment that will be repeated many times in the days ahead.

Mother Elizabeth must have been notified that her first dispatches had returned home, probably by the watchful Sister Theresa at the front desk. Mother locates me in the hallway and invites me to her office.

As we walk together I wonder why it is that I often find myself being summoned to the boss' office. This is reminiscent of working for Karen, only more pleasant.

~~~

One family left their three youngest children with relatives while they migrated to California to find work. Work didn't come.

They haven't seen their children for over a year. With that one piece of information, I know exactly why she accepted that family into the program.

"We contacted each airline in person until we found one willing to fly the children to be united with their parents—at no expense."

I am only slightly surprised. Who among us can refuse a nun in full traditional habit when she needs help to reunite children with their parents? Surely, I don't know anyone that brave.

Mother Elizabeth asks me to take Sister Theresa to LAX on my way home. On my way home? It is obvious Mother Elizabeth needs only twenty-four hours to request and receive miracles.

Of course, I agree to take Sister to LAX, since Mother Elizabeth already seems to assume I have. Besides, it's an opportunity to get to know Sister Theresa a little better, on my turf, or at least off hers.

Sister Theresa is near the front door ready to depart for Detroit to escort the children back to their parents. The children have never flown before, and even if they had, Mother Elizabeth would never consider allowing them to travel alone. Sister Theresa will leave today and return with the children tomorrow. She'll spend the night with the local nuns who meet her at the airport. Someone will pick them up in a convent van when they return.

During our road trip, Sister Theresa is pleasant when I speak to her. She briefly answers my questions, but she doesn't initiate any conversation of her own. Maybe she has the trip on her mind. Nonetheless, I am disappointed with her silence. I amuse myself with the thought that she is probably desperately conversing with Saint Christopher, the patron saint of travelers about traveling with three children.

As I drive through the heavy traffic on the way to LAX, I glance at her from time to time. She is tall and thin. She has laugh lines around her mouth and bright dark brown eyes that hint at the person behind the holy exterior.

When I drop her off at the airport I say, "Have a good trip."

She bends down to look in the open car window and smiles broadly. "Thank you, I will—I love to fly!"

With that, she turns and quickly disappears into the terminal with a small black travel bag in her hand and her full-length veil blowing behind her. I hadn't expected her response and laugh at the thought that she is happier to fly than to ride in a car. She is probably skipping down the concourse, for all I know.

~~~

After taking Sister to the airport, I take advantage of the early release from work. First, I'll catch up with my cousin, Ilene, via email, then go for a walk on the beach before the sun sets and it gets chilly.

Just as I am about to log off the internet, an email from Maggie arrives. She is coming over tonight after dinner to work on our "missing Linda" project. I am glad to see Maggie, but a little annoyed with the intrusion of the past when the present is much more pleasant.

Now that we have a lead on the Judge's daughter, I feel the urgency is gone. My new job is more interesting than dedicating time to the past, a past that is not at all enticing to me. I hope Maggie doesn't want to go at this with too much enthusiasm tonight. I don't need a second full-time job. I am enjoying discovering who I am now, or maybe who I have always been. The interruption from the past interferes with the present.

The work at the convent is refreshing, but I intend to enjoy being in California again. For one thing, I want to spend time going on walks on the beach with Mr. Goldstein. Luckily, there is time for a walk before Maggie is scheduled to arrive.

~~~

For a week now Mr. Goldstein, who is developing friendships with several females at the Senior Center, has been giddy. I am curious to learn more about this new adventure in his life.

Mr. Goldstein comes for our walk right on cue. He doesn't say much about specific friends at the Senior Center. They had taken a short trip to the Huntington Library today. It is hard to tell what he liked best, the art or the one-of-a-kind rare books. He really loved the gardens, especially the desert garden.

He had never seen so many different varieties of desert plants before, and was pleased some of the cacti were in bloom. It is delightful to see the world through his eyes. It' is amazing how quickly our walk is done and he is heading up the stairs to his home.

There is barely enough time for a cup of coffee before Maggie arrives. I enjoy reconnecting with Maggie. However, I have waited five years to deal with the past, so I am in no hurry for it to become an all-consuming activity. I would rather spend time visiting—casually visiting.

Unfortunately, as it turns out, Maggie wants to do more. She indicates Keith said that with a name like "Jones," he needs a middle name before he runs Linda through the system to get her current address on her driver's license.

At Maggie's insistence, we search the online newspaper archives for articles about school activities, awards, anything that might indicate which school Linda attended. Almost two hours pass before we discover Linda had received several awards in debate and always did well in tennis. One article lists her high school in the valley. The school does not have past yearbooks posted online. Finally, Maggie is content to sit and relax. For this I am more grateful than she will ever know.

We have eased back to the level where we had left our friendship and perhaps beyond where it was five years ago. I am beginning to feel less guilty about not keeping in contact while I was away, now that I realize our friendship transcends time and location.

Better than I, Maggie seems to understand why I left. I admit I had been too self-centered in thinking, "It was about me," especially the failings at work. We leave it at that, sparing me from divulging the details of my emotions then and now.

We are both older and wiser. Soon I will be thirty and she is thirty-four. We are enlightened—and proud of it.

Somehow, Maggie has learned to find a little distance from the emotions of her cases. It's probably her "advanced age," I laugh to myself, since she is only a couple of years older than I.

While we talk, I have become lulled into a sense of contentment with our friendship. I tell Maggie about the trip to the airport with Sister Theresa. I relate how difficult—no, impossible it was to draw Sister Theresa out and meet the person hiding inside her shielding habit.

Maggie begins in a serious tone of voice, "Kate, you have an impenetrable 'shield' around you too."

I tilt my head in surprise. I study her eyes, trying hard to read her thoughts, while fearing where she is taking this conversation. I shouldn't have bothered guessing where her comment was leading. She is about to tell me what is on her mind, whether I want her to or not.

She looks at me long and hard. "The problem is your protective shield is much larger than usual, larger than everyone else's." She does not smile. "Your defense mechanisms set off too many alarms when anyone gets close to you."

"Maybe in the past that was true," I begin my defense, "but no more than—"

"With you, Kate, it's a one-way street." She barely takes a breath, leaving no time to interrupt again. "You are there for others, but won't allow others to reciprocate." Her voice is confident.

"My personal problems are mine to—" I start to agree in a revealing, but justifying tone.

Maggie interrupts, "Don't misunderstand. You're a wonderful friend and exceptional social worker. When people are around you, they open up the deep recesses of their life to you." Maggie softens her tone and continues, "Instinctively they feel your strength."

I look at her, then look away. What can I say to that? Of course I'm strong. My strength is one of the things that makes me good at my job. I deliberately set out to be strong. I consciously work at it. How can that possibly be bad?

Maggie leans forward, reaches across the table, and touches my wrist.

I fight the urge to pull back my hand. I decide not to confirm her comments with such an action. She can think what she wants, she does anyway. There is no point in proving her point.

"You are too self-sufficient, Kate." She lets go of me, but continues to speak—even more softly this time. "You only allow glimpses of who you are and your struggles," she says, then she leans back in her chair again. "When things get to be too much, you pull away from everyone."

At last, Maggie finally smiles compassionately. She adds with a slight laugh, "I understand running to the beach on occasion —but Nebraska?"

I may deserve the Nebraska wisecrack, but I take advantage of her pause, "Maggie, what can anyone really do?"

She draws a slow, deep breath before she speaks. "Listen, care. The same things you do for us."

"I need to process things for myself. I have to understand—" I counter her comment.

"Maybe, but not alone." Maggie continues to look at me more intensely than I like. "This isn't about me being hurt because you keep part of you out of our friendship, this is about you hurting —alone."

"But—" I protest, then comply with her silencing glance.

It is obvious that we have opposing opinions on the subject, but I expect more understanding from her than that. She knows the horrible things we saw and heard in the worst of the child abuse cases. She knows the details don't always come out in court because we aren't asked the right questions on the witness stand. Some things are too bad to tell anyone. She knows. We have to keep it to ourselves.

In the end, the most we can do is write about them in our case notes and try to leave them there. Sometimes the cases haunt our dreams for years. She knows that too. I feel trapped, and it must show on my face.

Maggie gives me the don't-argue-with-me look as she pushes on. "You aren't the only one who has nightmares over this job," Maggie confesses for the first time, leaning forward again. "I just want you to know that Karen, Keith, and I understand." She tries to be consoling. "Sexual abuse cases are the worst. You don't have to do this alone. You never did."

This time I can't help moving my arm out of her reach as a precaution in the event she attempts to go for my wrist again. I appreciate her friendship and her words, but I can't do this right now.

She knows my parents are dead, but I am not alone. I have a close-knit extended family. Even though I don't have siblings, I have a lot of cousins. They fill any gaps that might exist.

"Kate, please don't leave us out again, if things get to be too much for you." With that, Maggie concludes her lecture.

So much for my relaxing evening. This bonding thing Maggie is doing isn't what I am in the mood for tonight. I go to make more coffee in an effort to permanently disrupt the conversation.

Maggie follows me to the kitchen, telling me how Karen holds the entire system to a higher level of responsibility than before, and everything is not on the department now. I guess this is in some sort of response to what happened to me. I don't know.

When I reach for a new coffee filter, I nearly trip over her. I express appreciation that things have changed for the better. Yet, I am thankful to be out of Child Protection and into the Spirit of Hope project.

She waves off the offer of a refill of coffee. Shamelessly, I am glad that it's getting late and Maggie is talking about going home. This conversation has become exhausting.

Just as she is leaving, Maggie turns back and says, "Oh, by the way, Joseph asked me for your phone number." Her eyes have a dangerous twinkle.

Maggie always knew how to get my attention. The evening might have played out differently if she had mentioned it when she arrived. It pleases me that Joseph wants to call me.

I smile and whisper, "Give it to him."

~~~

Long after Maggie drove away, I stood on the patio looking toward the ocean. I need the beach after the intensity of the evening's conversation. The rhythm of the waves always seems to calibrate my soul in a way nothing else can. It is too late and too chilly to go to the beach tonight.

I turn and go inside. Mostly I just want to go to bed, sleep, and get up to my new job in the morning. There is no point in living in the past or a daydream future involving Joseph.

~~~

~ CHAPTER 8 ~

Romance? Are You Kidding?

More than I want to admit, I think about Joseph. I remember the sound of his laugh that came so effortlessly during dinner. The essence of his smile and dark eyes still lingers. What is taking him so long to call me? Has he changed his mind about wanting my phone number?

When I don't hear from Joseph by the end of the week. I get his number from Maggie with the intent to leave a message on his voicemail Uncharacteristically, I decide to take the initiative. After considering several messages, I decide to leave only my name and phone number. He's a lawyer—he should be able to figure out the rest for himself.

At first I don't wander far from my phone, except for work and walks with Mr. Goldstein. Finally, as the days pass, I decide staying by the phone is silly, especially since the answering machine is always on.

I am glad no one knows I have behaved so pathetically. Apparently Joseph isn't worth pursuing. I refuse to call him a second time. I am not desperate. There will be others who come along in time. No rush.

~~~

The week passes. I venture out to sit on the moonlit beach most evenings. I sit in silence for hours after the sun blazes into the ocean, until the damp cold or the beach patrol drive me inside.

When I am on the beach, time drifts away. I sit and think of nothing more than the sound of the waves coming to shore.

Several weeks after Maggie's visit, I'm on the beach, remembering the bitter Nebraska winters in contrast to the agreeable California weather. It makes me thankful I will have no more cold winters in my life. Those days are gone for good.

"Never again!" I say, as thoughts of the below zero temperatures make me shiver. The sound of the waves and the hum of my thoughts block out everything else.

"What did you say?" asks a male voice from behind me.

I jump at the unexpected human response. He repeats the question as he moves to where I can see him. It's Joseph!

"So this is Kathryn's Beach?" He smiles.

It has been nearly a month since Maggie asked permission to give my number to him. My surprise quickly fades into curiosity at how he found me. He says it was the message on my answering machine saying I was either ignoring the phone or on the beach.

Joseph had telephoned Maggie to find out the location of the alleged beach. And now he is here beside me. Instantly I forget, or forgive, that he has taken his sweet time in calling. A visit is less awkward than a phone call would have been anyway.

I take a deep breath to calm my giddy heart. I'm more excited to see him than I'm ready to admit. I'm acutely aware of his presence. I can smell his aftershave and hear his breathing.

Sitting near me on my blanket in the sand, Joseph takes a deep breath. Clumsily, we silently watch the moon reflecting on the waves for a while. Then we speak at the same time about the scene we are watching. After a nervous laugh, we start again and ease into talking about general things at first, things that don't really matter.

Joseph says when he was fifteen, he left the fighting in Dublin to come to a boarding school in the U.S. He is excited about going home for the holidays this year. He talks fondly of his homeland, his family, and his friends. Listening to his accent makes everything he says sound romantic.

He intrigues me when he speaks Gaelic. I love the soft sound of it. His bright white teeth flash in the moonlight when he smiles, and he smiles easily. He is kind, almost gentle, in his way of talking about life. I like him. I really like him. Beyond that, well, one can always hope. Love doesn't come easily for me. But this time seems different.

The spray from the rising tide makes us get up to move toward higher ground. Once we're up, we decide to go to my apartment for freshly brewed coffee to warm away the dampness.

To my surprise, Joseph welcomes the coffee despite the hour. Maggie found it unusual that I drink coffee every night before going to bed. Joseph doesn't seem to mind. There is another thing to like about him, he likes coffee as much as I do.

The stereo provides background music, so that the pauses in conversation won't be obvious or awkward. It may be nothing, but I take it as a good omen that the first song we hear is Ella Fitzgerald and Louis Armstrong's "Summertime"—my favorite jazz song. I savor the moment listening to the brassy sounds.

Eventually it is time for Joseph to leave. I want him to stay, but I am too tired to stay up much longer to entertain my guest. Of course, staying the night is out of the question. We have barely met. No, I do not want him to stay and complicate my life in that way. Besides, I do hope this is more than a physical attraction.

After Joseph leaves, I lounge on the sofa with my feet on the edge of the coffee table finishing my cup of coffee. I am incredibly tired, but my mind is not quite ready for sleep. I stay up a little while to savor the evening. I haven't felt this attracted to anyone in a long time. I know to be cautious, but I am beyond the warning. I smile a faraway smile as I think about him on my beach. "Summertime" dances through my mind.

The freeze inside me is melting. It was, no doubt, a defense mechanism to ward off the horrors of work. Somehow it had crept into every aspect of my life. But it didn't keep away the nightmares. No, be honest, Katey, the freeze is more than that. It started long before then.

I was six years old when my father died, and I began to guard against abandonment. I cannot count the times I allowed myself to fortify against intimacy. I didn't want to feel the devastating feeling of loss ever again. I don't want to feel that kind of vulnerability, either.

Why this seeming disarmament toward Joseph? I felt a change occurring in the last weeks I was away, more so since I returned home. I longed for friendships, and maybe even a romance while still at Ruthie's Bar. There was not a chance of a romance for me in Nebraska, not since I was an outsider. And now this handsome, intelligent, intriguing man is melting my heart. I shut my eyes to remember his smile, his voice, his aftershave.

The ringing phone wakes me. The sun is bright and the clock on the wall reveals I am lucky that it is Saturday or I would have been late to work.

"Do you have plans for this morning?" Karen asks, wanting to come by in an hour.

My bed is still made since I fell asleep on the sofa. I calculate that I can be presentable within an hour. "Sure, a visit will be nice."

Quickly, I make a pot of coffee and take a shower. By the time Karen arrives I look like I have been up for hours. She wouldn't have cared, but I want to put some distance from my reputation as a night owl. The realization of a deliberate change in my attitude is curious, but exploring it will have to wait.

~~~

"Good morning, Kathryn. Guess what Maggie found out —" Karen stops suddenly. "Kathryn?" Her voice spreads to a wide-eyed whisper, "Tell me all about him. Leave nothing out."

By my widening smile at hearing her words, there is no hiding that she has read me well. Karen wants to know about this mystery man. I find her interest in me personally very different from how I remember her.

"His name is Joseph," I begin. "All I can say is my heart is way ahead of where our relationship is." I confide in a whisper, "I think his heart might be there too."

Karen smiles a warm, knowing smile. It feels awkward. We move away from talking about my feelings toward Joseph.

She looks out the patio door at the ocean across the street. "Did you know I grew up two blocks from here?"

So this is her beach. It is no wonder she often found her way here to read documents from work. That explains why she gravitates to the other side of the pier when given the choice.

"No, I didn't know."

"If you want to go for a walk, I'll show you which house it is." She offers an excuse to walk on the beach.

After we pass the pier, we walk up to the street and view the house.

"My parents are away visiting my brother and his wife. I house-sit and bring paperwork to read at the beach."

I smile because I have seen her working on the beach.

~~~

We walk back, soaking in the ambiance of the shore. It is a different world from being inland. It's odd how humans adapt to a specific environment and aren't quite at home anywhere else.

It isn't until later that I realize Karen never told me what Maggie found out. Joseph must have been such a shock that she forgot about Maggie.

The previous night with Joseph is still intriguingly running through my thoughts. My life is transforming in ways I had not anticipated. The memory of the Judge's letter is so remote I have all but dismissed it. I have someone new and more pleasant to think about—I have Joseph to fill my idle-time thoughts.

~~~

Life has a way of settling into a comfortable rhythm. Work is demanding because of the premeditated, deliberate way Mother Elizabeth expects us to think and perform. At the same time, it is invigorating to be openly creative and to work with an energetic staff, not to mention the tireless good sisters. Our families are beginning to respond to Spirit of Hope.

The children are laughing, maybe not as often as regular children laugh, but they are laughing. The expressions on the faces of the parents are beginning to relax. Their eyes look less scared now that they are not living from moment-to-moment with their little ones' hunger on their mind. To that extent and more, the program is showing signs of success.

Mother Elizabeth knows someone who knows someone at a plush Hollywood salon. Several of the hair-magicians-of-the-elite are coming to the convent this week to donate haircuts. It's a good idea. Everyone feels better when they look in the mirror and see someone attractive looking back at them.

Our clients will begin to see themselves differently as each piece of the program integrates their survival skills with successful experiences. With enough positive experiences, they will become strong again. Then they will interview for jobs with more confidence.

One of the sisters posts a haircut sign-up list on the bulletin board in the family room. Also, there is a notice of dates when trips to a dentist and health screening teams, all volunteers, of course, will be available.

Mother Elizabeth is taking care of the basics before approaching the issue of employment. However, she is not forcing any of these free services on our families. They have to take the initiative to set their own appointments and make their own decisions about the services they want or need.

Sister Theresa has posted a list of repairs needed around the property. This household of single women intends to keep the men busy and feeling useful until they find jobs. I am pleased to see they will not be left to sit idle, as they are given the opportunity to "work for food" so this doesn't feel like charity.

Even though working for food is not required, the projects provide finished results that are concrete and observable. It's obvious the sisters intend to rebuild the adults' self-esteem before sending them out into the world of work. Feeling useful is a good place to start. They are given many opportunities to re-establish their roles as adults and parents within this safe closed society. It will only be a matter of time before they will be encouraged to expand their roles into the outside world while living safely at Saint Mark's Spirit of Hope.

~~~

Maggie found Linda's middle name, but we run into one dead end after another. Has Linda left the state or married? We have no trail to follow.

As our schedules allow, we canvass Linda's high school classmates. We follow leads, only to end with nothing helpful. Linda hasn't maintained contact with anyone from her school days. She doesn't attend class reunions. The last two invitations were returned as undeliverable, so the reunion committee has taken her off of their mailing list.

We find no newspaper archives of a wedding announcement for Linda Jones. Maggie jokes that maybe Linda became a nun. Karen and Keith don't laugh. I catch my laugh, but it comes out as an odd faint sound. Unfortunately, they heard the sound, which causes the three of them to laugh at me. It breaks the tenseness of our duty to find Linda—a duty imposed upon us by her dead father. Damn him!

There is no help from Linda's mother's siblings. One of her aunts has advanced Alzheimer's disease and is in a nursing home. Another has died. The third has had no contact since Linda's high school graduation.

To my relief, we unanimously decide to put Linda on the back burner of our lives. Until she surfaces, we will have to wait for inspiration about where to search next. I mind the decision the least of us. The others are more reluctant to give up on Linda. I'm ready to spend my time in ways not related to Judge Jones.

The warm spring weather brings tourists to the beach. I still find time to have the beach to myself by varying my walking schedule to very early or very late—yes, early. All the people in my life are woven into a nice package. This is the least stressful and out-of-control I can remember my life in a very long time. I enjoy the peacefulness of these days.

~~~

Mr. Goldstein is more mentally alert from the stimulation at the Senior Center, and I like to think our friendship helps too. He is looking and acting younger.

He and his friend, Karl, go to Spirit of Hope to read stories to the children every Sunday afternoon. The reports are that the children love the voices Mr. Goldstein uses for each character while reading. I imagine him reading, then chuckling to himself.

Karen and I have become closer than I would have ever thought possible. Maggie and I make sure we find time to get together once a week to shop, lunch, visit, and sometimes to do things with Dave and Joseph. My life is a nice, tidy package. I couldn't be happier than I am right now.

Joseph and I have been seeing each other almost weekly for over a month. We have exercised restraint in our physical attraction to each other. I suppose that we both want this to last longer than the heat of passion.

On Memorial Weekend we drive the short distance to Malibu to visit the remodeled J. Paul Getty Villa, which has recently re-opened. The Villa is beautiful. The gardens are in bloom and the grounds are inviting.

What I will remember most about today is the walk up the seemingly hundred or so steps beside the Greek reflecting pool, under columns, and around statues of gods and goddesses. At the top of the steps, turning back to the west, we can see the blue Pacific stretch peacefully to the horizon and blend seamlessly with the sky. The breeze from the ocean cools us as we stand in silence holding hands at the top of the hillside paradise.

Later, Joseph wants to drive to Griffith Park Observatory to gaze at the night sky. No doubt it is an excuse to make the day last longer. We pick out the few constellations we know. I don't know that many and I am suspicious of some of the ones Joseph mentions. The dragon and Athena constellation can't be right. I know for certain that he is making up the leprechaun one. We laugh about it, and for a moment, when we look at each other, I think he is going to kiss me. He smiles warmly, then seems to change his mind about a kiss. We have kissed before, so I am not sure why not now. Even though I would have welcomed the kiss, it is still a romantic evening without it. The day has taken on the air of ancient Greece—her mythology was visible in statue form at the Villa and now in the night sky.

Joseph leans his head near mine while directing my vision toward yet another stellar cluster. As he does, he puts his left arm around my shoulder and pulls me toward him slightly while pointing his outstretched right arm toward the heavens.

My heart begins pounding as soon as Joseph touches me and pulls me closer to him. There is a stir of excitement inside me. Yet I want to be sure not to make more out of his action than is really there. I want the memories for the future, in the event this relationship doesn't develop further than what it is now. I want to savor every moment. As I lean into his touch, my heartbeat reaches a crescendo.

~~~

It has been a wonderful day. As I make a pot of coffee, I can tell Joseph doesn't want to leave. I want him to stay too. I put on music. Joseph offers his hand for a dance. We dance slowly in the small space between the sofa and the dining area of my apartment. Joseph is a wonderful dancer. In his arms I feel like I am floating on air. With his gentle touch, a stir of desire wells inside me. I close my eyes and melt into his arms. He smells good, and his hand on the small of my back feels good. He leans down and kisses my cheek near my ear in a snugly way that gives me chills. I stretch up to reach his mouth with a kiss. Our selection of music is perfect. Everything is perfect.

It is getting late as we move toward the door. Hesitantly, he goes out into the night air. He turns back to me and puts his arm around my waist, gently pulling me toward him. I stretch up to put my arms around his neck as he leans down to kiss me goodnight. The stir inside me longs for him to stay—my resolve weakens. I say nothing as I watch him go away into the night. The taste of his kiss is still on my lips.

~~~

~ CHAPTER 9 ~

The Obvious Truth

One Saturday a month, Karen provides therapeutic group activities for the children at St. Mark's. On one of our beach walks, she reports her little "patients" are a refreshing diversion from a steady diet of abused children. It also allows her back in the therapist chair and away from administrative duties.

Silently, I agree with Karen. I have had enough of child abuse cases for a lifetime, maybe two lifetimes. Children are amazingly resilient, but adults who work with abused children have to develop ways to deal with the intense emotions silently directed toward abusers. Personally, I am delighted to be away from child abuse investigations. Spirit of Hope is brings out the best in each of us.

~~~

Mother Elizabeth has a talent for rounding up free services for our families. No one in their right mind would get in the way of Mother Elizabeth and her little army of nuns when they are on a mission.

It wouldn't surprise me that she is aware her volunteers and benefactors benefit as much from giving as the recipients benefit from receiving. It's that mutual give and take that gives meaning to what we do and who we are.

This is certainly true of Mr. Goldstein and me. I hadn't expected any depth to our relationship when I began including him in my walks. Now I look forward to seeing him more than he can know. I couldn't have imagined what richness he would bring to my life. It doesn't seem the same when he is gone on overnight excursions with his Senior Center friends, as he is today.

~~~

On a solitary walk along the beach, I stop to watch an artist drawing sketches of seagulls with the surf spewing into the air near them. I have seen her at the beach on and off over the years, but have never officially met her. Her work on display at the library is quite good. Something about the way she captures the water and the beach impresses upon me that she has an understanding with the beach others cannot hope to have. She must have grown up here. There is no other explanation for her ability to get it right like she does.

I stand a slight distance away and I watch her work. Just as I am about to move on, she speaks, apparently aware of my presence all along.

"Are you an artist?" she asks without looking away from her canvas.

"Oh, no! No. I'm not." I gasp with surprise at the question. "But I do admire your work." I move closer to look at her painting.

She smiles in response to the compliment. "Are you from here?" she asks. She had been looking back and forth from the water to the painting while she spoke, but now she looks at me for the first time.

"I grew up in Huntington Beach." I motion over my shoulder in the direction of Huntington Beach. "But I moved here years ago. Are you from here?"

"All my life," she laughs.

"I've seen your work at the library. I love how you make the feathers on the seagulls ripple in the breeze."

She smiles again as she dabs grayish-white paint on the water's edge.

It is amazing to watch her work.

"I own the art gallery on Main Street."

"I've been there. It's a nice shop."

"Do you work downtown?"

"No, in L.A. at Saint Mark's program for homeless families."

She smiles. "I helped Sister Bridget paint the mural for the playroom."

"Ahhh, it's wonderful."

"You know Sister Elizabeth Craig, then?" She stops painting for a moment, putting her brush at rest, then turns directly toward me.

"Yes, I know her," I reply as I realize for the first time that Karen and Mother Elizabeth have the same last name. I don't think of nuns as having last names. Their first name is always "Sister" and another name or two—but no last name. That's not exactly true about their first name being "Sister." It is only their title, but the part about rarely using their last name is true.

I am becoming suspicious, very suspicious, about Karen and Mother Elizabeth's shared last name—and how I came to be employed at Spirit of Hope. It was easy to get the job.

The conversation goes on a few more minutes. The artist attended grade school with Elizabeth and knew her younger sister, Karen. That confirms my suspicions the shared names between the two are not a coincidence.

Walking along the beach toward home I am still amazed, Mother Elizabeth is Karen's Sister-sister. Wow! Imagine having your sister turn out to be a nun.

This new information explains a lot. Things seem to fit together, especially the thing about organizing papers into neat piles that both Karen and Mother Elizabeth do. When she asked me to take Sister to the airport "on my way home," it explains why Mother Elizabeth did not ask where I live.

At the time I thought she just assumed I would want to do it in the way nuns do not expect anyone to say, "No." Or Mother Elizabeth could have looked through the staff addresses and found that the airport was nearly on my way home. Who knows?

There may be no connection to any of it, but it sure seems connected. Of course that is how she obtained a first-rate child psychologist to volunteer with the Spirit of Hope children. And my employment? Did Karen pull strings with her Sister-sister? That explains the file full of papers on Mother Elizabeth's desk at my interview.

I hope that I landed the job on my own merit. I guess it doesn't really matter. Things are working out in my life much to my satisfaction. This is an interesting twist of events, yet it makes no difference in the overall scheme of things.

Thinking about my long-awaited contentment with life makes me think of Linda Jones. I had forgotten about her after we ran into one dead end after another. Now I have a sense of needing to find her. The instinct is only a guess that something is wrong, but I think I should do what I can to see if I can help her. Now that I know running away doesn't cure the pain, I know it won't for her either.

Judge Jones, for whatever reason, asked me to tell her he was sorry. Mr. Goldstein rightly said I need to do that. If I can help her, then I should. I believe delivering the letter is part of the healing process for all of us touched by her father. In this, the choice is not mine to make. I must find her. After that, what she does with the letter and its message is part of her life's journey. The problem is I have no idea where to search next.

~~~

Much to old-fashioned Irish luck, Linda attends her first class reunion ever. It is the fifteenth reunion. Maybe it is just a nice round numbers that compelled her to attend. Or maybe it is her time to come home. Whatever the reason, she came to the reunion on the three-day 4th of July weekend.

One of her school friends, Melissa, kept Keith's business card from when he asked her about Linda. She notified Keith that she had permission to give him Linda's address. "Linda went home, suddenly, after the first day of the reunion," Melissa adds.

This seems a little too easy to me, but maybe Linda is ready to be found. Maybe she doesn't know she has been lost. Maybe it is no different than me returning from Nebraska without warning. It is just time to get on with life, a better life.

On Monday, Maggie, Keith, Karen, and I meet for lunch. It is like the old days when we worked together. Keith tells us that Linda lives in the Bay Area. She is married to Todd Whitmore.

"Todd Whitmore?" I asked surprised. "Todd Whitmore whose father is Governor Whitmore and his mother is actress Angela Whitmore? That Todd Whitmore?" We must have missed the wedding in the newspaper archives.

"Yes, that's the one," Keith answers.

The first family aside, we all agree we should make face-to-face contact, to put the letter directly in her hand. Keith is unavailable for an out-of-town trip anytime soon, as he is under a subpoena for a lengthy jury trial starting next week.

Before anyone can say anything else, Maggie "suggests" that I go—alone.

"Oh, I don't know about me going." My voice fails to disguise my uncertainty. "What do you think he might have been sorry about?" I ask the same tired question again.

"It could have been any one of a hundred things," Maggie answers. "Whatever it is, you can do this, Kate. I know you can."

Karen helps more than Maggie. "The obvious thing is the suicide, but it is hard to tell what was on his mind when he wrote that letter of yours." Karen is staffing this like it is an active case—and maybe it still is, at least, for us.

"No, it's not *my* letter."

Keith says nothing. His silence does not mean he isn't paying attention to our conversation. He's astute. I was fortunate to have been assigned to work with him. Keith taught me more about child abuse investigations than any of the graduate classes I took.

"Suppose it is the suicide, what does Kate do?" Maggie asks as an atonement for volunteering me for the trip.

Karen briefs the interventions on the most likely scenarios as I listen with urgency. I don't like going into this blind. If the letter triggers a crisis situation, I will have to handle it until I can get help. Since I haven't done crisis intervention for a while, going solo makes me uneasy. Not to mention, I will be in a city where I don't have professional contacts or favors to call in. These guys are only a phone call away, but isn't the same thing.

I wish Karen would go in my place. She is clearly the best qualified to handle any reaction Linda might have to the letter. The boxed-in feeling of this ordeal makes me uncomfortable. Once again, I have Judge Jones to thank for bringing this unwanted disruption into my life.

Maggie reaffirms her belief that I am the one—the only one—to make the trip. The truth is we all know that I have to do this. Maybe it's because the Judge sent the letter to me. I know I must make the trip north, alone, whether I want to go or not. We all want this finished. Clearly, this is mine to end.

It is amazing how often really intelligent people can pool their energy and come up with a terrifically lame idea. We decide I should wait to call Linda until I am in San Francisco. It never occurs to us that she might not be home when I arrive. All I am concerned with is the possibility of a copycat suicide from this unknown woman. There is no way for me to anticipate how she will react to the letter from her father.

It is decided. I fly to San Francisco tomorrow after work and deliver the letter. I am reasonably confident that I didn't get to vote on this timetable.

Maggie says, "You're going before you have time to back out."

I think she is kidding, but I am more than a little annoyed they are pushing me so hard. Before I can protest formally, Maggie is on her cell phone making my flight reservations with her mom, a travel agent.

She says, "You will leave on the first flight after work tomorrow."

Not that I am a good sport, but I pull my credit card out of my wallet and hand it to her to pay for the ticket. They bought the transcript. They waited patiently for me to return and open the letter. The least I can do is pay for the flight to San Francisco.

~~~

The time passes quickly at work. Soon I am pulling into the parking garage at LAX. I spend the flight to the Bay Area reviewing Karen's advice regarding hypothetical responses to my arrival and the letter from Judge Jones, now five years old. I desperately try not to forget anything Karen said.

When the runway appears beneath the plane, I settle down, check my apprehension, and clear my thoughts. Even after all the years spent away from investigations, instinctively the clear, focused discipline returns . I welcome the familiar feeling of confidence as I walk into this unknown situation.

I hail a taxi at the San Francisco airport. The driver drives up and down the hills and across a bridge. Clearly, I have no idea where I am. On previous trips to the Bay Area I hadn't paid much attention to our wanderings, since I was with people who knew the lay of the land. It is probably best for Linda this way, but I would feel better if I was on home turf.

When the taxi pulls onto her street, I make the call to Linda's house from my cell phone. She's home and willing to see me after I explain my connection to Detective Knight.

Linda cannot possibly know about the letter, since Keith and I didn't mention it to Melissa. I can't help thinking Linda isn't prepared for the visit she is about to have. I feel sorry for her, but the truth is she wouldn't have had any more warning if her father had mailed the letter directly to her.

~~~

The taxi comes to a stop across from Linda's house. There is the usual damp chill in the air, but no fog. At the top of the steps of the stylish, historical Bay Area-style building, the door opens almost as soon as my finger leaves the doorbell. The first thing I notice is that Linda is attractive and dressed nicely. She has a sophisticated air of upper class about her demeanor. There is a sense of grace about her.

The room is tastefully decorated and shows the residents are well-traveled and well-educated. There is an unmistakable sense of old money in the Whitmore furnishings.

Linda brings coffee in a polished silver serving set, reminding me this is a formal visit. Protocol. There are rules of etiquette to follow, but I am not sure they will fit the occasion for very long.

She offers coffee and I am relieved to have it. She pours herself a cup and sits on the sofa with me. After explaining who I am and how I came to be at her door, I remove the letter from my purse and hand it to her.

As Linda accepts the letter from me she asks, "Why did my father send this to you?"

"We have no idea why. My cases usually weren't docketed in his court." I offer the last information as proof I truly didn't know her father.

"We?" she questions, looking up from the letter in her hands.

I explain the letter went to Keith, to Karen, then Maggie, and finally to me. "The delay is because I moved out of state for five years. I didn't know the letter existed."

Linda still doesn't understand why her father sent the letter to me, since he knew where she was. They spoke on the phone and went out for dinner when he came to San Francisco.

Frankly, I admit I don't understand either. I mention the name similarity with her mother's. She looks a little sad when I say her mother's name, but she quickly regains her composure. Linda thought over the name similarity for what seemed longer than it probably was. Finally she agrees, "It is one possible explanation, but who knows? He wasn't well."

Considering his state of mind at the time, he could have meant anything when he wrote it. I won't go into that detail unless she asks. We leave the topic of why me and move on. His motive is apparently to be left unsolved. It probably doesn't matter now anyway.

"I wish my husband was here," she says softly. She shifts her position and leans forward as she looks at the letter in her hands. "Todd is in Paris for another week."

I suggest she can wait and read it with her husband when he returns, but Linda insists that it isn't necessary to wait. She is resigned to go forward.

As she fingers the letter she whispers pleasantly, "Thank you for bringing this to me."

Linda is proper, she could have easily convinced an observer that she was about to read my favorite omelet recipe. I am ashamed that I didn't eagerly make the trip.

Linda unfolds the letter and silently reads it. On the outward appearance she looks perfectly calm. I know better. I don't understand the message, but I know the letter must be heaped in emotion. Especially considering that her father wrote to her as one of his last actions before committing suicide.

When Linda finishes reading the page, she glances toward me. Her eyes begin to fill with tears. Incredibly, she keeps the tears from spilling over and down her cheeks. She looks deeply hurt. I want to comfort her, but manage to check my desire. My sixth sense tells me it is not the time to intervene.

"Thank you," she says in a nearly clear voice.

"Do you know what it means?"

She nods affirmatively. She understands. She looks at me again, but this time a tear slips loose and trickles down her face. Another tear follows closely behind the first one. She makes no attempt to hide her tears. Simply, silence lingers.

I know not to touch her. A touch could rally her strength to hold back everything waging war to break free. What I have learned in doing investigations was "Questions result in answers; well-timed questions produce information." It is premature to ask Linda questions. It is premature to touch her.

Following my instincts I say softly, "Linda, no more secrets."

Linda looks at the letter for what seems like five minutes, though it couldn't have been more than one. Her hands shake slightly, so slightly that it is barely apparent and could easily have been missed by someone not watching for her reaction.

She looks straight through the letter and the floor. She begins to slowly relate the time after her mother died as feeling alone in "confused darkness." Her father threw himself into work. She was raised primarily by domestic help. Linda pauses and looks at me to see if I understand.

Yes, I understand. Even though I was only six years old, I remember what it was like after my father died. A child losing a parent can't be described to someone who has never been through it. They can guess what it's like. They may even think they understand, but they can't possibly comprehend the loss.

I nod my head, just slightly, to indicate that I understand. The feelings of abandonment are strong, even when the person leaves because of a terminal illness. Suicide must be worse. The person chose to abandon their child.

She takes a deep breath and slowly, softly begins her real story of her father's sexual advances. I offer an encouraging, yet slight nod when she chooses to look at me, but I say nothing. I won't disturb the moment for her. She is not only telling about what happened. In her mind she is going back in time and reliving the moments and emotions attached to the memory.

It would be easy to touch her hand or say something to ease her pain, and bring her back to the present. I have heard this story before and it would be so easy not to hear it again. It would be easy to stop her and protect myself under the disguise of consoling her. I do nothing, except listen attentively. I am back in the role of child abuse social worker, even though she is not my client.

Linda continues to relate the graphic details of her father's behavior, her feelings of desperation and shame, and her struggles to survive each day.

Her eyes dim as she relives the experiences in her memory and every fiber of her being, except her voice, moving far away from her living room to the child she once was—a sex slave with no mother to save her.

I feel myself slip into her story. I know there is more to it than words can express. There are things about sexual abuse that elude expression in words. Years of experience and training taught me to recognize the feelings that defy language—I listen for the clinical markers. Sadly, I find them. She is speaking from personal experience, no doubt about it—she didn't make this up.

I believed her from the beginning. There is a sense of truth in the telling of it, but now I have clinical verification. A person can't make up this story, in this way, and get the feel of it right. She is telling the truth.

"It escalated into frightening sexual involvement," she continues in the matter-of-fact, numb way incest victims relay what had happened to them. "I had nowhere to turn; he was a prominent man—I was alone." Her voice wavers with the weight of the memories. Her voice is a knife piercing my chest.

Linda draws a deep breath that has a little quiver in it. She tells about the day she approached the school counselor under the guise she wanted to talk about her mother's death. The counselor had been flirting with the vice principal when Linda came into her office. She was disinterested in listening to Linda's pain. After that reception, Linda didn't bother revealing her real problem to the counselor—her father's incest. Until now she had told no one. She had buried it so deeply that she had blocked the memory.

Each time I heard this story it was the same, and yet distinctly different. The story is told to a very few people, if ever told at all. It still lives on inside of her.

I dreaded cases that were covered by the media, reports which were insensitive and poorly done. On one of my longest days at work, I heard three of these stories' first telling. How does a person deal with that? I can't explain the emotions I feel stirring in me as Linda relates what happened to her.

Linda's face has an out-of-place smile as she continues, "You know what is funny about that?"

I shake my head. "No, what's funny?"

Her smile disappears, "When I went to the class reunion this summer, that same counselor came to our table and started talking to me like we were friends."

I hear the hurt in her trembling whisper.

"She was trying to impress Todd. It never occurred to her how gravely she had let me down the day I went to talk with her. The incest continued for three more years—the counselor could have ended it, if she had only listened and intervened. But she wasn't interested."

Linda's tears well up in her eyes again. "I couldn't take it any longer. I desperately wanted someone to make him stop. It had taken weeks to gather the courage to talk to her about him. And she couldn't be bothered. Three more years–" Tears fill her eyes and roll down her cheeks. She wraps her arms around herself as her body begins to sob.

Now it's time. I reach my hand around her shoulder and ease her into my arms. It's a few seconds more before I feel her weight relax onto me and her sobbing increase. She has let go. It is all coming out. I can hear the pain as she cries for help.

The counselor's original lancing blow was eighteen years ago. Damn fool. I'm angrily aware that the pain this woman caused Linda again this summer is still a fresh wound.

I know full well the system, as well as the professionals, were capable of letting her down, even if she had told anyone what was happening. It would have been a media nightmare if the story broke. It is unfortunate the system doesn't always work correctly, especially when a prominent person is the offender. Society doesn't want to hear that persons in a position of public trust have violated that trust, especially when it has been violated in this way.

Several hours pass as Linda talks about her feelings of guilt and responsibility for the situation occurring at home. The confusion she felt compounded her need to keep the secret and emotionally withdraw.

In her case, the outward over-achievement in academics and extracurricular activities was her smoke screen to keep the secret hidden from others. Linda worked hard to convince everyone, including herself, that everything was fine, couldn't be better.

Eventually, Linda confronted her father. There was no scene, no admission of guilt, or responsibility—nothing. Linda says she went into therapy after she was in college at Stanford. Even though the therapy helped her to intellectually cope with her mother's death, she had buried the memories of her father's abuse by then. Until the reunion this summer, those memories had not resurfaced.

Linda thinks the letter is about the sexual abuse. She isn't sure of the meaning of the rest. Another tear rolls down her face. She gently wipes it with a tissue from her pocket.

I hope the letter is enough to help her begin to process the relationship with her father and the unresolved emotions she carries with her. I hope it will act like a long overdue admission of his guilt. I hope she will be able to accept that what happened was not, and could never have been, her fault.

Tears build up inside me, but I don't tell her about her father letting the alleged perpetrators walk. I realize if he had admitted they were guilty, he would have had to face his own guilt. I am beginning to understand what happened in court.

Finally, I realize why he sent the letter to me. I had testified flawlessly in that last case. I testified well enough for him to know that I understood sexual abuse. We had hammered home the point that it was a parent's duty to protect his child, not rape her. I made it impossible for him to ignore what he had done to Linda.

Still, he didn't understand soon enough. He let that sick bastard go rape and murder his little daughter. It took the death of my little client for Judge Jones to finally realize what he had done to his own daughter and what he was doing through his power as a judge.

Apparently he chose me to be with Linda when she read the letter, otherwise he could have mailed it directly to her. If he had sent the letter to Karen, she might have assigned it to someone else to handle since I was gone. By sending the letter to Keith, my former partner, Judge Jones must have figured the letter would somehow get to me. It had nothing to do with his wife's name and mine being the same. It had to do with me. He was sending the quintessential social worker by special delivery.

His apology, though simple, seems to be a starting place for the healing to begin. Now maybe she can put the abuse in perspective and get much-needed help.

She looks up again to meet my eyes with hers. "It is good you came, Kathryn."

I smile warmly at Linda and touch her hand. Yes, it was worth the inconvenience the letter caused to deliver it. After everything that has happened, she deserves the special effort of this trip. Finally, her father did one small, correct thing when he wrote the letter and sent it in care of Keith.

Linda and I talk for another hour. I encourage her to make an appointment for therapy and suggest a few things to look for in her selection of a therapist.

I say things I can say at this juncture to reinforce that it was not her fault that this horrible thing happened to her. I want to make sure she really is coping well enough to be left alone tonight. I ask that she consider spending the night with friends or having a friend stay with her.

She says thanks, but she will be fine. I think she will be fine, but it won't happen overnight.

Before I leave, I tell her I am sorry this happened to her and assure her again it was not her fault that it did. I admit that after the incident with the school counselor, it made sense to think the next person would let her down. I want her to know she deserves many apologies—from her father, from the counselor, and from me as a representative of a horribly flawed system within our society.

I give her Karen's business card, since I don't have any of my own. On the back, I add my number and encourage her to call either of us— at any time. It's important for her to know this time someone "official" is listening and there are people she can turn to who will listen and believe her. I am listening, Karen will listen, and her therapist will listen. The expression in her eyes moves me when I tell her she is not alone with her secret any longer.

Just before leaving, I ask Linda's permission to tell Karen, Maggie, and Keith the meaning of the letter.

She has a faraway look for a moment, then quietly agrees. The secret has lost its power over her life. Maybe it has lost its power over all of us. I hope so. I need to believe this will soon be finished.

During the taxi ride to the airport I think about Linda. Hopefully, she will find a qualified therapist. This isn't over for her yet. Even the letter will take time to resolve. I whisper a brief prayer she will get the help she needs to do more than survive what her father did to her. I hope she can begin to thrive—not just make it through the day.

The usual airport bustle has quieted. There aren't many people at the gate waiting for the last flight to L.A. I am glad to have time alone to think about the lives the Judge touched. It's sad his crime was the very thing allowing others to continue to perpetuate their crimes. He must have been in full-blown denial to be capable of what he did. There can be no other explanation, other than he was sick and didn't get help.

A shudder goes through me at the thought of how Judge Jones' own crime lead to the brutal death of the sweet little girl in my last case for CPS. I wonder if he saw the police photos of her little dead body. I hope so. I hope they gave him nightmares —the really bad ones, ones that woke him up in a sweaty panic. It's mean, I know, but I'm angry.

I'm not sure that Karen will tell the staff the real reason why their cases failed in Judge Jones' court. He sentenced himself to death. What would be the point of saying anything now?

~~~

At LAX Maggie is standing with the few people meeting the flight as I come down the stairs from the gates. She explains she is here, "In the event I have to pick up the pieces after your meeting with Linda."

I reassure her, I am fine.

Maggie looks at me intensely, wanting answers. I signal to wait until we're outside, so our conversation won't be overheard. In the parking garage, I tell her everything. We stand leaning against my car in silence for a long while. I wait for Maggie to make the first move.

"It is good he apologized, that's the first step for her."

My tone is more critical than hers and my thoughts aren't as well contained.

"I agree. It's important to her recovery. Linda must fully internalize the knowledge that the responsibility was not hers.

And that he finally had remorse for what he did to her. But it is not enough, not nearly enough. How do we stop these rapists? These, these bastards who rape kids?"

Maggie shakes her head and offers to drive. Dave must have dropped her off at the terminal. I'm glad that I had taught her to drive a stick shift. Willingly, I hand her the car keys. I am spent.

I am justifiably angry that we let people do this to children. Rape is sick. I always saw the children. I had never seen an adult still living with all the pain and damage. The longevity of the abuse disturbs me.

Once inside the car Maggie confides, "I'm relieved he admitted his guilt."

"It would have been better if he had done it sooner or started with grief therapy and worked into discussing his physical feelings for his daughter. Especially if he had gone for help and never raped her in the first place." I can only speculate why he didn't get help. It could have simply been his pride that caused so much harm to so many, beginning with Linda. "But you're right. I had to find Linda."

The intimate details of Linda's story play over again in my mind. My mind's eye constructs an image from Linda's words and the expression on her face as she spoke them. It is like the old days; my mind is preparing to write case notes, a court report, and eventually testify. But this time none of that will be necessary. So why can't I turn off the instinct?

The distraction of arriving home is a welcomed relief from our discussion and my thoughts. I cannot think about Judge Jones any longer. I am too drained to fight the anger those thoughts bring.

~~~

Maggie has Karen's mothering look on her face. It makes me feel uneasy as I fumble with the door key. I know she is up to something.

"Kate, do you think," Maggie begins, her eyes widening with her words, "well, I was wondering if your testimony finally made Judge Jones grasp what he had done to Linda?"

"I doubt it. Linda confronted him years before that." I appreciate her gesture to give me credit. I'm not willing to admit

I agree with her assessment. Though I think the case is what led him to commit suicide, I do not want credit for any part of it. I want to finally be done with Judge Jones. I don't want to say aloud that I may have played a role in his death.

Maggie sets her jaw and looks at me as if she is debating whether to argue with me or let it ride.

"He didn't admit it before. Why would an unrelated case make him repent, especially considering his ruling?" I ask, hoping she has an answer. It's unkind, but I hope he suffered over the death of my little client.

Tossing my jacket on the sofa, I head straight to make coffee and breakfast. Not to be distracted, Maggie waves off the offer of toast.

"Kate, ask Karen to let you read the transcript—you were good, very good, practically perfect."

"Oh, Maggie, don't say that. I don't want the guilt of contributing to Judge Jones' suicide because of my testimony," I plead. I am too tired— emotionally and physically—to keep from being honest with her.

Until now I haven't told anyone that the moment I heard about his suicide I did fear my testimony made him realize what he had done. That I pushed him into a corner and over the edge when his error was confirmed by the bloody pictures and the grand jury. I didn't know he was a "perp," but he had to see his responsibility in the little girl's death.

"No, Kate. When you hold up a mirror, you aren't responsible for what the other person sees in it. All of the guilt is Judge Jones'. Eventually, even he knew it."

She reaches to touch my wrist as she speaks.

I don't want to be touched. I escape to interrupt the coffee and fill our cups under the drip. I know she isn't going to let me walk away from the past just yet. But I want to run from it. I don't want to think about this anymore.

We talk for a long while, interspersed with silence. Whether I want to or not, we have to process our thoughts. She insists on it. At least that is something we do well together—staff cases. But this isn't a case, this intimately involves us and I can't be objective about my anger.

In retrospect, there had been a few signs of an abuser in the Judge's behavior. He flexed his power to keep his secret hidden. We know we couldn't have been expected to notice the clues with such limited contact with him, but still I think we should have—at least I should have seen it.

Even if we had suspicions, the statutes do not provide for witch hunts. Without someone outside our agency reporting him, an investigation wouldn't have been initiated solely on hunches.

Eventually, with enough coffee in my system, I collect my thoughts and order them to respond in the manner a seasoned professional should. We are attempting to give each other a sense of absolution through our conversation. I'm not sure it's really working. We express feeling ignorant and inadequate for letting him deceive us. We were supposed to be better than that, smarter than that. I was supposed to be smarter. I was supposed to be the expert.

By the time we finish the pot of coffee, I am able to drag myself to the shower. I am more emotionally drained than tired. It is a good kind of tired to be rid of Judge Jones' secret. But still I wish I had never heard of him.

I stand in the shower hoping the warm spray will wash away the years of pain caused by the Judge's horrible secret and corresponding rulings. I think about the pain of the last five years of isolation. I am overwhelmed by the senseless waste of the little girl's life; Linda's stolen innocence; the anguish Karen, Maggie, and the department staff went through; and the pain that I carried with me. I lean against the cool, wet tiles, sobbing quietly as the water pours over me.

I don't know how long I stood in the shower before I slid down in a heap and rested my head on my arm on the edge of the tub.

I think of the years I spent numbed in Nebraska. I think of what Judge Jones stole from me. As inconsequential as my pain is to the pain Linda felt, I am still overcome with it, and I sob uncontrollably as the warm water showers down upon me.

Finally, there are no more tears. I put a cool cloth over my eyes, hoping it will erase the redness from them before I face Maggie again.

When I emerge from my refuge, I find Maggie has moved to the patio. I refill my coffee cup and join her. If she does notice I have been crying, she says nothing. Apparently she realizes now is not the time to probe my fragile feelings.

I wonder about her inner response to resolving the Judge's letter. I think about consoling Maggie, though she shows no signs of needing my counsel. I think about my duty to her as the lead staff on this case. But I know, at this moment, I am not really able to deal with her emotions in addition to mine.

She doesn't seem to need my strength. It is a good thing, since I don't feel strong. Maybe I'm not a very good friend right now, but I barely have enough strength to hold myself together, there isn't enough of me for any more than that.

"Dave and I left my car here last night. Listen, You look tired. Get some sleep. I'll pick you up in a couple of hours."

"Sure? Okay," I answer.

"I'll go with you to tell Karen—partners to the end," she adds.

"Yes, to the end."

It is strange to say out loud that this nightmare is ended. The feelings of completion have not come with the spoken words. "Partners to the end." I was never really alone, if I had only realized it. Nebraska was an unnecessary detour to get to this point.

~~~

Wrapped in my robe, I crawl into bed and marvel at the mess Judge Jones made of life. We know Karen and Keith will be eager to hear about my trip. Undoubtedly, they will be distracted from work until they hear the outcome of meeting Linda. The last few hours of waiting must have been harder than all the previous years.

It is finally time to end this. Maggie and I go together to find Karen and Keith. It has been a long road to San Francisco.

When we walk through the doors, Karen is in the reception area leaning over the receptionist's shoulder. They both are looking intensely at the computer monitor. Karen looks up as we approach the desk. Of course, she knows why we are here. She seems to be trying to read our expressions, so that she will be prepared for what we have to say.

Before we can speak, Karen directs us, "Let's go to my office."

Once inside her office Karen telephones Keith to see if he is able to join us. He is on his way to court in a case where there was a change in venue, so Karen leaves a message on his voicemail for him to call when he comes back.

Maggie listens while I tell Karen the Judge's secret. Karen suddenly puts her hand over her mouth to ensure her self-control as she catches her breath before she can gasp. Her other hand has gone to her stomach. This is that sickening that she could vomit.

She checks her emotions almost immediately. I think in that brief instance, she is thinking the same thing I thought: How could we have missed this? We should have seen it—somehow. It's hard to watch her go through what Maggie and I have just gone through.

I choose not to respond to her initial reaction. Karen will verbalize it when she is ready—or deal with it privately on her own terms. I continue to describe Linda's reaction to my visit and to her father's apology.

The three of us process the information in the familiarity of established procedure. This time we do it for us. There is nothing we can do about Judge Jones. He made sure of it with one simple bullet.

When she hears the school counselor's role in Linda's silence, Karen slowly shakes her head in response.

"Something has to be done about this. Those people are our first line of defense in saving these kids and stopping this madness." The look on her face makes tears well in my eyes.

At last Karen's frustration shows. "How could we have been so blind?" She isn't assigning blame, but maybe assuming it.

"We saw him in a limited setting. We couldn't have known," Maggie counters Karen's assumption of guilt. She takes a step closer, softly touching Karen's shoulder as an invitation to be held. Karen pivots into Maggie's arms.

"Karen, it wasn't your fault," I insist, nearly reaching to touch her— but I catch myself. Touchy-feely stuff is Maggie's department, not mine.

When it is all said and done, we have to be careful how we deal with our guilt. This won't be over if we don't find absolution.

Before we leave her office, Karen calls Linda. She says what I had said last night, only with a more expert twist to it. Karen ends the conversation by reiterating, "I am sorry he raped you. I am sorry you had no safe place to go." Karen's tone of voice is warm and healing as she continues, "Linda, you didn't deserve what happened to you. It wasn't your fault. You did nothing wrong. You didn't cause this to happen to you."

She suggests to Linda, "If you don't have a therapist in mind, I will give you the name of two who are good. Use my name when you call for an appointment." Karen listens to the phone quietly then says, "Maybe it will help bring closure for you."

In a way, Karen is healing all of us as she reaches out to Linda. We desperately need to know we have done everything we can for her. Maybe Linda will be able to move beyond being a survivor—beyond going through the motions of getting through the day, and really thrive.

With all of this behind me, I am ready for sleep. It was a short night. However, for now, I have to get to work.

~~~

It isn't a particularly busy day, but I am "dragging-butt" tired. My duties do not occupy me enough to keep me energized. I can't wait for a nap as soon as I return home. Hopefully there will be no more nightmares of the little girl. Maybe now she can rest in peace. Maybe we all can find peace.

By the end of work I am less interested in a nap. I am craving time on my beach. The waves will be full of surfers. I don't mind the surfers. At most they leave their packs where they can see them from the water. There is an unwritten code among the beach people: No one bothers a surfer's backpack left unattended.

The next thing to consider is whether I want to bother with the tourists or to drive to another, more secluded beach. No, I am too tired to drive the 405 again this time of day, or to deal with stoplights if I hop over to PCH.

To be alone, I walk to the end of the pier and have no one between me and the ocean. I can get lost in the swirling water near the pylons. Or I can walk the beach a safe distance from the masses, or even dare to walk silently among them.

When I arrive home, I change clothes and walk to the beach. I stand at the water's edge just beyond the reach of the breaking waves. The fine misty spray blesses me (in a Catholic sort of way) and bathes away the grime of Judge Jones' memory. With each crescendo of the waves, I take a step back from the incoming tide.

And so it goes, a series of waves blessing me with the Pacific's "holy water," while the rising tide slowly pushes me back into the real world with every step backward, on and on, until the tide pushes me to the mark left on the beach from the previous high tide.

The spray nudges me like a mother gently prodding a child to move toward the classroom door on the first day of school or in the wings nudging her hesitant offspring on stage for the first piano recital. The waves push me to go home and sleep—it will be all right.

~~~

~ CHAPTER 10 ~

Comfort Returns

The August sun bakes the sand. It is too hot to walk shoeless on the beach, unless at the water's edge. The beach is filled with tourists taking the last days of summer to play in the ocean. Standing ankle deep in the water, I watch the children play in the waves. For some unexplainable reason I don't mind sharing the beach with the crowd of strangers, not that I could keep them away if I wanted. But I notice the change in my attitude.

My life is sufficiently settled to stop the nightmares now that Judge Jones is truly dead. I haven't forgotten any of the cases, but they do not haunt me like they have for years. I am beginning to get perspective on who was really at fault for these horrible cases slipping through the court. It was not us—it was not me. It was the abusers, the perps, and Judge Jones.

Things seem to lull into a comfortable routine again. Work is a joy, especially now that the Judge no longer interferes in my life from the grave.

Several of the Spirit of Hope men have found work, maybe not as CEOs of profit-sharing corporations, but it's steady work with the possibility of some advancement. For the families and staff, there is an air of hope surrounding their employment.

When someone finds work the Sisters throw an employment party complete with all of the festivities, and the ceremonious presentation of a new lunch box to take to their new job. Some people wouldn't get excited about a new lunch box, but to these men it is a trophy of what they have endured—and endured successfully. Even though they had every justification to think life was a stacked deck, they took the risk to come to Spirit of Hope, and it paid dividends.

The program at St. Mark's is providing more and more services. Volunteers are appearing miraculously when a need is identified. Mother Elizabeth never ceases to amaze me with her resourcefulness, her inner strength, and her compassion. She possesses a spirit of hope and she shares it just by being herself. The woman is contagious.

Most of all, I like to watch her with the families, especially with the children. This morning she was in the family room sitting on the floor surrounded by children. The skirt of her habit was gathered in balloon-like mounds close to her, and she was demonstrating the finer points of playing jacks. The whole affair was quite a sight to see. Mother held the children spellbound. She is amazingly good at jacks and already has some of the kids able to do their "twosies." I leave unnoticed.

I long to find the sense of peace I see in Mother Elizabeth. The past has been put to rest, but I have not found peace with it, even though it ceases to haunt my sleeping. Each passing day seems to help a little. But a sense of harmony is still lacking. Nonetheless, I cannot find reason to complain.

There is a certain amount of pride connected to the fact that Spirit of Hope is the envy of all the social work directors in the city. It shows in the way the staff say where they work when we are at conferences. I feel it when I speak about Spirit of Hope. Even the pious nuns show an un-nun-like pride in the program and the success it is demonstrating.

To make good times even better, we are going to have a baby! The older sisters are busy crocheting, knitting, and sewing everything imaginable for the new baby. Mother Elizabeth thinks it is a good sign, "A sign from God," she said, to have a new life come during the first year of the program. I agree with her.

Sister Clare, one of the oldest and most reserved nuns, takes a special interest in the coming baby. Ever since the news of the baby, it is rare to see her without her yarn and knitting needles busily working, even while she fills in at the switchboard for Sister Theresa.

I like watching the interaction between Karen and her Sister-sister, Mother Elizabeth, as they discuss Spirit of Hope and the people who are the object of our hope. Karen advises Mother Elizabeth's staff how to involve all of the children in preparations for the new little life, especially since the baby is already getting a lot of attention and still months away. She also reminds us not to forget the adults' needs in our excitement.

It is important to keep in mind that everyone has needs for support. Everyone needs to recharge their inner strength. We must ensure our own needs are addressed in healthy ways, so we do not drain those around us with our whining or neediness.

Karen warns, "Life isn't a competition to see how much we can GET from each other. The trick is how much can we reach inside and pull from ourselves for others, and ourselves. In the end, the competition is only within us."

Mother Elizabeth adds, "Saint Francis said, 'Grant that I may not so much seek to be consoled as to console.'"

"Exactly," Karen confirms.

Karen and Mother Elizabeth's comments have a ring of truth about them. I take them to mean more than the conversation about the clients' needs and the coming of a baby. I take them to be larger than this place and this time.

Since my trip to San Francisco, I spend every minute I can on the beach. Mr. Goldstein is busy more often than not these days, but he joins me for walks when his schedule allows. Maggie joins me sometimes. It seems that she is also healing more completely since we understand the intricacies of the case. Joseph has been consumed most of the summer with a major criminal case. Almost nightly, I see him in sound bites on the local news ignoring the reporters as he exits the courthouse. I would like to see him in person, but, in a way, I need this time to allow the conversion that is occurring within me, as I continue to heal from the emotional trauma that drove me to Nebraska.

~~~

This weekend my mind is flooded with old images that finally fit together. Things that hadn't made sense are becoming clear to me. I have been acquitted of contributing to the little girl's death. It is as if some sort of transition is occurring within me. I just have to let it run its course and embrace the person I am becoming. Absolution is sweet.

As I walk along the beach, Karen waves for me to join her in her usual spot on the sand. She is talking with another woman. As I approach them I am surprised to see the woman with Karen is Mother Elizabeth. The possibility of meeting Mother Elizabeth on the beach has never occurred to me. They both have a good laugh at my expense when they figure out the confusion going through my mind.

I make them both admit the Lakers T-shirt, slacks, and sandals are quite different from the brown habit and veil Mother Elizabeth usually wears. They confess Mother borrowed the clothes from Karen. They fit fine, but the look isn't quite right. I smile at them. After all, who am I to decide the look isn't right? I find myself studying her hair. I don't know what I expected. Mother Elizabeth's hair is nearly the same color as Karen's, only cut shorter. It is a nice cut, though very different from having her head completely covered by a veil.

Her white arms and feet seem out of place on the beach where everyone else has some degree of brown to their skin. Mother Elizabeth reaches for the bottle of sunscreen in Karen's beach bag. She casually applies another layer of lotion to her arms and offers the bottle to me.

I have on sunscreen, but allow her to squirt a bit into my palm. It was a caring gesture, and I have tried to allow more of them after what Maggie said about me keeping people at a distance. It is difficult to be less self-reliant, though in the past self-reliance didn't work well, either.

Mother is at ease on the beach. I struggle to remember that she wasn't always a nun. I try not to laugh. After all, I was more out of place in Nebraska.

Accepting their invitation, I join these two sisters. At first, as I listen to them banter back and forth to get the rhythm of the conversation, something gives me the sense that they had been having a sister-to-sister, heart-to-heart talk about a more serious topic before I arrived. They move the conversation to memories of sitting in this spot as children, then to the present. Mother gets up and walks to the water's edge. She removes her sandals and gets her feet wet. Karen and I watch her enjoy the waves, sandals in hand, full of abandon. I relax into the moment.

Karen says she met Linda the last time she was in San Francisco. She thinks Linda is going to be fine, better than fine. The cryptic letter was the admission she needed. First she was a victim, but when she told her story, she became a survivor. She is no longer a survivor. She is whatever is beyond that. I have never heard a word that suits going beyond surviving. Perhaps it is a higher plane of thriving. I like to think of it as a living symphony. All I know is surviving isn't quite enough, even though sometimes that is the best we have. We seek thriving for ourselves and our clients.

Mother Elizabeth returns with a handful of shells to take home to the children. She smiles contentedly. I get terribly sentimental about having these two women in my life, but I don't mention it. If Maggie were here, it would be perfect.

The sun, the beach, and the company get the best of us. We discuss how good life is going for each of us. Karen mentions that life is an enigma.

Her comment makes me think about how I used to call her "Mother Superior," and claim she must have been a nun in a previous life, when in reality it is her sister who is the nun. Still, I bet Karen was a nun in another life. Without considering my audience, I mindlessly ask, "Do you believe in reincarnation?"

I'm not sure the Church approves of such talk. I wish I hadn't asked about reincarnation without thinking about my audience and checking the question until some other time with some other person.

Typically, Karen asks back, "Why do you ask?"

Smiling, I say, "Oh, I don't know, no particular reason, I have always wondered." There is no way I am going to admit to them what I had been thinking about her previous life.

Mother Elizabeth studies me a minute, then answers, "I don't really know, Kathryn, but I plan to get my money's worth out of each day in the event I only get one shot at life."

We laugh. Obviously, she isn't being theological. The thought of this panhandling nun getting her "money's worth" is hilarious. For her, most things in life are free. Who among us can refuse any of her charitable requests? Not even God, I think. Besides, for people like her there is probably an express route to heaven when they die—no toll, of course.

~~~

After an hour of visiting, I leave Karen and Mother Elizabeth and walk down the beach, past the pier to my favorite spot. I sit watching the waves break while thinking about the importance of the beach in my life. I think about Maggie, Karen, Mr. Goldstein, Joseph, and now Mother Elizabeth on my beach. We grew up near the ocean. We know her moods, and as much as anyone can, we understand them. The beach is the place we go throughout the ebb and flow of our lives.

It seems strange how easily Joseph accepts my beach, especially since his world is very different from mine. He doesn't share the attachment, but he accepts it. On the evenings when he takes time out from his trial preparation to come over, he usually finds me sitting, watching the Pacific, or walking along the beach. There is something about the sand and the ocean that enhances the mood required for authentic conversation.

Watching the water rise and fall mesmerizes me. I watch the gulls hover on the breeze then land to peck at shells, accessing the meal inside with the usual amount of bickering over ownership of the food.

A smile comes over my face when I see Joseph approaching. Right on cue. I draw a deep breath as he sits down in the sand beside me. The way he settles close, I feel confident he feels the same toward me, but our feelings are the one thing we haven't discussed. I can't believe he still gives me chills when he is near me. And, oh, when we kiss, I melt in his arms.

~~~

Life goes on comfortably through October. Things are much better than I could have hoped they would be. The summer is gone, and with it the tourists. As winter approaches the beach seems peaceful. I am more satisfied with life than I remember ever being before. This year I am not dreading winter. Maggie and I spent a weekend on Catalina Island without the guys, for girl time. Good friends, good work, and good, good times with Joseph—what else is there?

~~~

Joseph is still a mystery in my life. After all these months I think of him, on and off, during most of my waking hours. I thought infatuation might have burned out with the departing of the summer sun. Yet he remains my knight in shining armor.

Our relationship is becoming more romantic. We are no longer casually dating. He is more than someone to fill an empty space in my life. It has nothing to do with hormones or the infamous biological clock driving me to connect with someone.

I adore him as a person and want to be near him for its own merit. Together, I feel richer than I am alone. I am happier because he came into my life. I am beginning to entertain the notion of actually being in love. I love his laugh. I love—him!

The best thing, though, is the smile that erupts on his face when I walk into the room unexpectedly. I have noticed that smile more than once. Not only do I think I love him, I feel loved.

Thanksgiving is coming in a few weeks. Emily, my cousin, has mailed out the family newsletter telling who is planning to attend Thanksgiving dinner and the latest news we have submitted for her to share with everyone. After I read each article about trips taken, new additions to the family, and the usual updates about everyone, their spouses and children, and sometimes their grandchildren, I study the photos of the people I haven't seen since my return. Everyone looks much as I would expect. It is comforting to know that no matter how my life spins out of control, these people are a constant.

My family always has Thanksgiving dinner together—my vast, extended family. I consider taking Joseph to meet my family. I have never taken a boyfriend to meet them before. But Joseph is special in a way no one else has been. I want to share them with him.

My family will notice this change in my behavior and understand the implications of bringing Joseph to dinner. I have discussed him at length with my cousin Ilene. Her knowing grin when she meets him is sure to confirm anyone's suspicions.

My mother's family is a little difficult to describe. The sense of belonging and acceptance is something I have never felt anywhere else. I never think about having a paternal family.

The Stewart family resemblances are strong. It's comfortable to look up and see familiar faces across the table laughing and telling stories, heavily embellished stories. I see Grandmother's smile and Grandfather's mischievous eyes in the faces around me. Without a doubt, that connectedness has sustained all of us through many difficult life experiences.

Long before I was born, Thanksgiving dinner was moved to the local park, because It takes three large turkeys to feed everyone. I have twenty-seven first cousins. Together they have sixty-three children, so far, in addition to aunts, uncles, and everyone's spouses. There isn't room for all of us at any of our homes. Why rent a hall? Nothing beats a day at the park. After all, it is a long-standing tradition. No one with any sensibilities would break a tradition that holds such bonding power.

When one of us goes our own way for a while, we are always welcomed home with no questions asked. This family is an accepting group. This will be my year to prove that.

I know they will like Joseph, simply because I love him. That alone will be good enough for them.

Should I tell Joseph this is no ordinary family dinner, or will that scare him away? Before the first round of horseshoes is finished, I'm sure he will feel at home. I know it will be fine, but how can he know that? How can I explain it? What we have as a family isn't that common these days. Joseph will just have to come and see for himself.

I make a quick phone call to Maggie. "Maggie, the newsletter is here," I say dramatically.

"Oh! I'll be right there!" She laughs.

"Actually, I was thinking about lunch."

Maggie practically reads the entire newsletter out loud while I prepare our meal. She studies the photos and asks questions to reacquaint herself with everyone since she saw them last.

"I love your family. I actually considered going to the park the first year you were gone just to see if you would show up," she says, not intending to invoke the guilt that suddenly surges through me.

"Sorry! I didn't come back!" I joke, not admitting how I feel.

"Well, I am glad you finally did!"

"Me too," I admit softly.

During lunch I broach the topic of taking Joseph to the family dinner this year. In the typical girlfriend style, Maggie comes to my rescue with her definite opinion.

"Take him. He'll love it—and them. But don't tell him how big your family is, you might scare him. It scared Dave at first. After all, this is no ordinary family dinner."

"Okay." I laugh. I can't imagine anyone being scared of my family. It's not like we are part of the Irish Mafia or anything.

"I wouldn't know how to begin to explain your family to him anyway. He will just have to go and see for himself." She laughs warmly. "It will be fine, Kate," she says with a reassuring pat on my hand.

Maggie is right. I'm complicating things with unnecessary worry. Okay then, it's decided. I will let him experience the moments as they unfold.

I wish Maggie and Dave could come. My family would be happy to see her again. But they have plans to spend Thanksgiving at Lake Tahoe. They are flying up with friends for a long weekend of skiing. Sounds fun, but cold. It's not my kind of holiday.

Maggie and I vow to get together soon after she returns to L.A. I promise to tell her how Joseph reacts to the day. The last thing Maggie says to me is, "Let your family work their magic on him. And don't worry—it will be fine." We hug goodbye. "Tell your family 'Hello' for me."

"I will. Plan on coming next year."

I smile, thinking about bringing him with me. It would be so easy to imagine a life with him as part of my family. But I dare not entertain those thoughts, since neither of us has said "I love you" out loud.

The next time Joseph and I are walking along the beach I ask, "Do you have plans for Thanksgiving?"

"No, no, I don't," he says thoughtfully. "Do you want to make some?" he asks, turning his head in my direction.

I smile. "Sure, I have an idea, but let me surprise you."

~~~

Thanksgiving morning the picnic basket is packed and waiting by the door when Joseph arrives. I hope I don't have a ridiculous grin on my face. But I am excited enough to grin like the cat that ate the canary.

"What do you have here?" he makes a joking grimace as he lifts the basket up and down a couple of times before putting it back in its place. "It feels like enough food to feed an army," he comments as he gives me a hello kiss.

Little does he know — "One never knows how much food we'll need. Maybe we will be stuck on the freeway all morning and need a snack," I tease back with a laugh, and I stop him just as he is reaching for something to sample from the basket.

He laughs as he turns to the door, giving me a dramatic, cavalier wave to go out first. We stop abruptly. We almost forgot the picnic basket. He picks up the basket and carries it to the car, mumbling about being hungry as he pretends to attempt a peek inside again.

As we drive to the park I begin to feel a little guilty that I had not been forthcoming with Joseph about the size of my family. Giving in to guilt, I tell him, "My family might be a little larger than the average family."

He nods as he says, "Yes, Catholic."

I have forgotten he is an Irish Protestant. After all, he rarely mentions the fighting in Ireland that brought him to the States after his grandmother insisted on sending him to a boarding school. His mother gave in to her mother-in-law's insistence to send him out of harm's way and keep him from joining the fight.

He doesn't seem to mind that I am Catholic. Joseph makes such a funny face along with his comment about Catholics that I let out an uncommonly loud giggle. I am surprised by the sound, but it eases my apprehension.

It is, true to California style, a wonderful day. The weather is perfect. We arrive at the park early, before most of the crowd. The usual hugs and kisses ensue, then the introductions.

Arriving early allows Joseph to meet people in small groups as the family begins to congregate. Each new arrival deposits food at the food table, then greets everyone. Volleyball and horseshoe games are getting underway and someone invites Joseph to join in. He does. The little kids love him and hang on his every word.

Old family stories are retold to pass them on to the next generation, with new exaggerations added. We laugh, hug, and look at photos of family members living around the world. Most of us, though, make the annual migration home for Thanksgiving dinner to renew our bond.

After lunch, visiting takes center stage. I usually table-hop. After I see how comfortable Joseph is, I relax and enjoy visiting on my own.

We pose for photos, then the games begin again. Out of the corner of my eye, I notice two aunts sitting at a table visiting. It looks like—yes, they are discussing Joseph. I know how these women think. My aunts and uncles moved in to fill the gaps in my life caused by my parents' death. These two are grinning with a look of approval regarding Joseph, nodding their heads affirmatively as they watch him play horseshoes. I smile back when they notice I am watching them.

Growing up, there were too many of us to ever get away with anything mischievous. The women in this family are experts regarding the antics of massive numbers of children. They can tell what any one of us is up to, just by looking at us. I know they can tell I love Joseph. It pleases me they approve of him.

The day passes too quickly. It seems, as it does every year, no one wants to be the first to leave. We stand near the parking area for one last dose of family before we reluctantly depart.

Joseph says he genuinely enjoyed the day. Most people don't like going to their own family gatherings, much less someone else's family functions. I'm happy he had a good time.

I can't wait to get home and give Maggie a quick phone call. Actually, I can't wait for her to get back to town for a very long talk. I can't wait to tell my best friend everything, absolutely everything. Things are perfect. Who could have imagined a few years ago that my life would be so perfect now? I have come a long way this year.

Joseph doesn't stay long after he helps me unpack the picnic basket and put things away. He is tired from all of the fun. I understand. Besides, I am ready for a solitary walk on the beach after the big meal, but more importantly I want to call Maggie and tell her about Joseph's approval rating.

After Joseph leaves I look for the Tahoe number that Maggie left. It is late and I can't think where I put it. I decide to have a cup of coffee and savor the day. I'll find the number in a minute. Knowing Maggie, she will call me to find out how it went once she gets a minute. I smile, pleased with the way things are going for me this first year home.

~~~

~ CHAPTER 11 ~

Consumed by Fog

Sitting down was a mistake. I don't feel like going for a walk tonight. In a little over an hour, just as I am thinking about getting ready for bed, I hear frantic knocking at my door. Someone, not Mr. Goldstein.

I ask who it is through the locked door.

"It is Joseph!" says the voice from the other side.

Joseph nearly runs over me when I open the door. He glances at my television as he brushes past me without a word of explanation. I rarely watch television unless Joseph is in the news or an old movie is playing that isn't on DVD yet. Why would he expect the TV to be on tonight? Joseph heads straight for the remote and turns on the set.

By the look on his face I can tell something is wrong, terribly wrong. Just as he begins to search the channels, the phone rings. I move for the phone while watching Joseph's peculiar behavior.

Karen is calling. Karen and I may have stayed up all night, one time, discussing a mysterious letter from a dead judge. However, she does not call me late at night, not ever. It seems strange when she asks if I am alone. What does that matter?

Suspicions run through my mind when she asks to speak with Joseph after she learns he has just arrived. This is very uncharacteristic of her—of them. I have a horrible feeling about Joseph and Karen's odd behavior.

Joseph takes the phone. I try not to eavesdrop. Yet, I can't help but move closer to him while he is speaking with Karen.

"Yes, I heard it too," Joseph is saying to Karen. "That's why I came—to be with Katey."

I can only hear one side of the conversation, so I am still in the dark regarding this sudden spin of activity in my home.

"No, I don't think she does," he continues, quickly glancing at me as he speaks, then flashing a hurried half smile when our eyes meet. He gives me the phone and returns his attention to the television set.

"Hello, Karen. What's up?" I ask hesitantly as I walk to the window to mindlessly look across the street in the direction of the ocean while we talk.

"Sit down, Kathryn. I wish I could be there with you, dear." Karen's voice is serious and strained. "This may be nothing, but I wanted to tell you before you heard it on the news."

Automatically, I turn to look in the direction of the television. Joseph is still searching the channels.

"A news report just came on, Kathryn. A small plane went down near Tahoe this morning," she says.

I gasp as I sit down. Stunned. Frozen. Barely breathing.

"They aren't releasing names." She takes a deep breath. "The 'weather' came in without warning. Have you heard from Maggie?" I can hear the urgency in her voice.

"No, not yet." I cradle the phone to my shoulder while looking through my purse for the paper with Maggie's Tahoe phone number on it. "I am expecting a call, since I haven't called her. Actually, I thought it might be her calling now."

Karen's voice is not her usual capable, confident tone. Joseph has finally settled on the edge of a chair. I watch him glued to the TV while I listen to Karen. She is deeply worried about Maggie, and Joseph is worried about Dave. Neither have come right out and said they think Maggie and Dave were on the plane that went down, but it doesn't take a rocket scientist to tell they do.

I wrap my arms around myself for comfort. I catch the look on Joseph's face and hear Karen's tone of sadness. I realize I have to be the strong one this time. Acknowledging my feelings is a luxury right now. Karen and Joseph need me. Well, maybe it isn't me they need, but I am the one here.

"It could be another plane. When Maggie and Dave hear about it, they will know we are worried and call one of us," I fumble for words. "If they did go down, it doesn't mean they were killed." As soon as I say it, I wish I hadn't. Of course they could be dead.

Karen gasps, then finishes our conversation quickly.

My words haven't come out as comforting as I had hoped. I am upset and embarrassed for saying something stupid.

We can only wait for information that will give us a clue to who is in the missing plane. It is easy to worry. Surely it's not their plane that went down. There must have been others going to Tahoe for the extended weekend to feed their ski addiction. No, it's probably not them. Probably not.

Joseph finds a local station running the television news report. The reporter says, "...due to the severity of the sudden storm, the search planes couldn't get airborne..." It's a blizzard more than a snowstorm.

Each report we catch says much the same thing. I know we aren't likely to hear anything before morning, unless Maggie calls to tell us it wasn't their plane. There is nothing to do but wait. It is late now. In the morning we can call her brother Frank to see if he heard from his sister or Dave. It will be a long night for us.

Joseph wants to stay the night. We have never spent the night together, intimately, even though we have shared many late nights talking on the beach. I offer him my bed since I am just as comfortable sleeping on the sofa—as I do more nights than I am willing to admit.

This night is not a restful night. I toss and turn. I fling the sofa pillows onto the floor. A strange dream comes into my tormented sleep.

I awake with a start, covered in sweat. When I fall back to sleep the dream begins again in the tunnel and runs its course exactly as the first time. I can't say how many times the dream occurs. Each time I am more and more restless.

When I awake between dream cycles, I can hear Joseph in my bed making restless sounds. I could go to him and offer comfort, but I know what might follow would be for all the wrong reasons. So I restlessly stay on the sofa.

~~~

In the morning the newscast says the weather has cleared enough to get the rescue underway. I feel relieved, but only a little. They don't say where the downed flight originated. They don't mention whether the plane locator beacon is sending signals. What kind of news report is this? I wish for more information, but the reports are sketchy. I need to satisfy my investigative nature, but they offer no relief. I have to wait.

On the outside chance Maggie and Dave stayed home, I call their apartment. Joseph shoots a look in my direction like I am wasting my time. No one answers the phone. I suppose it was a waste of time to call, but I had to give it a try. In my heart I know it is unlikely they had only stepped out. I suspect they have gone on their trip as planned.

Finally, I find the Tahoe phone number Maggie gave me. It was on the kitchen counter and Joseph had set the picnic basket on it. If the basket hadn't been in my way, it might have sat there all day before I moved it. Before I tell Joseph that I have found the phone number to the ski lodge, I take my cell phone out on the patio when he is in the bathroom. The call doesn't go through. The phone lines must be down due to the storm or jammed with calls. I don't know which, as there was only a phone company recording on the line. The point is that I can't get through.

I try her cell phone, thinking that it won't matter if the lines are down if I call her cell. I try Maggie's cell phone, then Dave's. I try the Tahoe number again. Nothing works, and my anxiety rises with each attempt.

~~~

Karen and I call each other every couple of hours. We keep the calls brief. We are afraid to tie up our phones, but we need to hear each other's voice. I try not to say anything I have not thoroughly thought through, like before. One major brainless remark is enough to keep me aware of how vulnerable we all are. I call Frank, but he doesn't answer. We have to wait. That is the hard part—waiting.

My instincts tell me to run to my beach for comfort. But I only look at it from my window—afraid to leave the phone. The hours tick by slowly. I wish Karen was here, rather than home alone.

Karen is divorced. She has lived alone for four years now. Her children are away at college back East somewhere. This isn't a good time to be alone, even if she is used to it. I am glad for Joseph's company.

The local station runs the news briefs too seldom. It doesn't seem right that the regular programming is on, but apparently there is nothing new for them to report about the downed plane.

The day ticks along slowly. Joseph and I have trouble finding enthusiasm for meals or conversation. We sit around stunned. We pace. We take deep breaths.
We fear the worst. There is no hope of hiding our fear from each other, but we don't mention it so it can't become real.

~~~

Later in the afternoon Karen calls to say Mother Elizabeth came over to be with her for a while. I feel only the slightest relief in that knowledge. We are each still alone with our thoughts.

I hope, if it is Maggie and Dave's plane, that they were able to put on their ski clothes and stay warm. I don't know if they had skis or planned to rent them. If they have skis with them, maybe at least one of them can ski out for help, although I know it is unlikely no one was hurt when the plane went down. At the very least the plane would have hit trees in the descent.

I am immobilized. I feel powerless. I desperately try to think of something that will console us—something to grasp and hold. Maybe the pilot had been able to land on one of the small, remote landing strips up there, somewhere, even an abandoned one. It isn't likely to have a tower, and if the plane was damaged—or even if not—they couldn't take off again with the snow on the runway. But they could be safely on the ground waiting to be found. My mind torments me as it races through possible scenarios. Realistically, I know these are not plausible options, though this time I keep my thoughts to myself.

~~~

Joseph goes home for clean clothes. He had a choice of either going home or wrapping up in a sheet while I do his laundry. My robe will not fit him. Besides, when he saw it, he declined to wear it—quite emphatically. I'm restless with him gone. It shouldn't take this long for him to get back. I'm more restless as each minute advances.

As evening approaches in L.A., it is already dark in the mountains. The news reports the search has been suspended for the night. I am uncontrollably worried about them. The whole incident makes me extremely sad, and panic fills my insides.

I cannot stand that it has been forty-eight hours without a walk on my beach to find some sort of consolation. Yet I cannot leave. I urge the phone to ring, but it won't comply with my wishes. I even try to bargain with God. There is no indication that worked, either.

We are grasping at anything that might tell us Maggie, Dave, and their friends have arrived safely in Tahoe.

While he was gone, Joseph checked his machine at home and his voicemail at the office. There were no messages.

Karen calls, but she has heard nothing.

I call Frank, but he is still not home.

We have nothing to go on.

The long periods of silence are thick. It is obvious our minds are racing. Out of desperation, I say that people have been known to survive for several days in a downed plane

Joseph looks at me, horrified—probably wishing he hadn't returned. It would be safer for him at his house without me and my mouth.

Instantly I wish I had kept my thoughts to myself. But it is said, and I can't take it back. I didn't learn from my first spoken blunder yesterday. I really feel incapable of getting through this successfully. I have no idea of a plan, but I would pay any ransom to have one.

~~~

Morning arrives after another restless night's sleep. It is Saturday of what seems to be the longest Thanksgiving weekend of my life. We poke at our breakfast with our forks. We hardly speak. The fog is in, covering both the view of my beach and our moods.

The news reports another winter storm in the mountains near Tahoe, hampering the search efforts further. There is little chance of a rescue today. Until the plane is located, it's dangerous to send rescuers into the forest. The area is too vast to search from the ground.

The day ticks by slowly. Night comes again and brings with it another tormented sleep.

~~~

Sunday morning arrives. A thick fog still covers everything. We can't see the patio beyond the window. The television reporter excitedly reports clear skies in the mountains. We look out the window at the fog. We look at each other in disbelief and amazement that the mountain weather has cleared. We become alert and hopeful that the search will produce our friends. By now we believe it is their plane or we would have heard from them, but we don't acknowledge our beliefs aloud.

Reporters from affiliate stations are in Tahoe reporting live from in front of a crackling fireplace or outside of the lodge to show the amount of snow mounded by the doorway. Their voices are excited, but they have nothing new to report. The plane has been down since Thursday morning, and that is not good. Not good at all.

~~~

Karen comes in the afternoon. She couldn't stand the isolation any longer. Mother Elizabeth had been only able to stay a few hours, and that seems like months ago. It took her over two hours to make the twenty-minute trip to my apartment. The fog has not lifted. She took surface roads to avoid the dangers of the freeway in the poor visibility. She is obviously a wreck from the trip and probably wished she had stayed home. She looks as if she hasn't slept since Thursday. I can't think of words to comfort her, but being together is better than being alone. Maybe words of comfort will eventually come.

It's Sunday afternoon when the news reports the emergency locator beacon has been faintly detected south-southwest of Tahoe in a steep
isolated canyon. By late afternoon the reporters indicate the officials are fairly sure they have located where the plane went down. The plane is buried in snow, but they have a fix on the beacon, and trees have recently been knocked down where the plane should be. They aren't seeing any evidence of a fire or explosion. The news is only partly reassuring.

Rescuers are having trouble getting a ground crew into the canyon, because earlier winter storms had already made the trails impassable. The record snowfall coupled with the steep terrain, and the extremely dense forest is making them scurry for a rescue plan. The underbrush is too dense for snowmobiles. Parachuting into the ravine is impossible because of the dense trees and gusty canyon winds.

A reporter announces that San Francisco's U.S. Coast Guard sent a Dolphin helicopter and crew to provide additional support. "The four-person rescue team will be lowered by a cable apparatus from the Coast Guard chopper, similar to a rescue at sea, since the only access is from above. They are hoping to get into the canyon as close to the crash site as they can, then snowshoe to the plane."

The report continues that the Coast Guard will have to air-evacuate the people up from the surface, but first they will have to be moved to the pick-up area. The window of opportunity to get everyone off the ground is small. Of course, there are no rolling waves to contend with, but the rotor wash will whip the snow off the trees, decreasing visibility for the workers in the air and on the ground.

Another television station says the rescue is not going well because of the velocity of the wind gusts, not to mention the fact that by the time the sun falls behind the mountain, it will already be dark on the ground in the canyon below.

None of the stations have reports about the passengers. We have to wait. The news crews can't get near the crash site, so they still report from Tahoe, limiting their information, which is often replaced with speculation. We can't tell the bits of truth from media fiction.

My imagination and emotions run out of control with the information we have and the parts that are missing. For the most part we cling to silence. I fear I will say something moronic out of the dullness of desperation.

I have given up bargaining with God. Karen, Joseph, and I are exhausted from the emotional intensity of waiting, and it shows on our faces. They rely on me for meals. I don't have the strength to do any more than sandwiches and snacks. It doesn't matter—we aren't hungry.

Karen laments she needs to get to the beach. It's welcome news to me. There is an unexplainable bond between us and the Pacific. The beach is the comfort of coming home. The closer we are to it the better, especially today.

I urge Karen to follow her instincts and come walk on the beach with me. Joseph supports my efforts and encourages her.

He volunteers to stay by the phone. She gives in after only a tenuous protest. I think she knows we are right about the walk.

I am not sure any of us have the strength we are going to need. There is no way I am emotionally ready to give up on Maggie being found alive. She is the best part of me.

Our friendship developed deeply from seeing things that cannot be shared with people outside the circle of investigators. Maybe it isn't that as much as the haunting nightmares that came from the work we do, the unspeakable horror we share. At any rate, there is something private we share that others cannot know, and we rarely mention, but it bonds us together.

Karen and I pick our way to the street corner marked with only the stop light's alternating glowing red ball above our head in the fog. We inch across the sand, listening to the sound of the breakers to judge our distance from the ocean. Karen and I walk carefully in the murkiness. We stay close, not wanting to become separated in the fog. I have never seen fog this dense so late in the day in this part of California. It should have burned off hours ago, but the sun did not shine today.

In a strange way, the fog shrouds us from the outside world. Unable to see the waves before they hit the beach, we are occasionally showered unexpectedly with spray when they break, even though we hear them coming.

We pause for a moment, standing silently, listening to the waves, occasionally feeling the mist thrown toward us by the backwash. The rhythmical sound is like a mother's voice to her infant child in the dark.

We are standing near to each other. I can see Karen slightly tip her face downward. When she lifts her head tears roll down her face. I can't see them, but I see her hand move to wipe them away.

She takes an audible deep breath and begins to walk in the direction of the pier. There is nothing to do, but silently walk with her. I can't imagine how to console her. When she is ready to share whatever thoughts she chooses to share, I can only hope the necessary words come.

We are nearly at the pier when she finally whispers, "I am not sure I am ready for this."

Her whispered comment begins a reckoning of our reality. With it, I realize Karen hasn't resolved the past. Her voice tells the burden of her responsibilities and all of the pain and loss that comes with it: our murdered child, my leaving, the Judge, and a million other cases and staff problems that I know nothing about.

More than any of us, Karen must have blamed herself for the murdered child. After all, she was the senior staff member involved, and, as supervisor, the buck stopped with her. The retrospective reviews, the second-guessing—none of it has helped ease her burden of guilt or the raw emotions left behind.

People outside CPS can't possibly understand. Sometimes it is just one person standing between a child and an abuser until the system begins to work, if it works at all.

Multiply my caseload by all of the staff's cases, and the budget, and the legislature, and the public—and the court. All of this has been harder on her than I realized, harder than she allowed us to see. She isn't ready to lose another staff person. Unlike losing me, this time is forever. Unfortunately, that looks like how it will turn out.

"I am not sure there is a way to be ready for this," I answer.

She turns toward me, close enough to see her face in the thick fog. Tears are rolling down her cheeks in a steady trail. She is not sobbing, but she is no longer able to hold back the tears. Maybe it is just time and she has no choice.

Without thought of my own comfort level, I reach for her hand. Karen silently squeezes my hand in response. Maybe she is looking for an excuse to let go of her strong exterior and quit warring with her vulnerable side. I intend for my touch to be that invitation.

Slowly she talks about feeling she let her staff down by allowing us to think it is our sole responsibility to save the children in our cases.

Karen hesitates for a moment, slightly tightens her hold on my hand and says, "I never told Maggie what I should have." Karen's voice trembles and goes silent.

"You can tell me. I'm here," I say softly.

Karen lets out a breath that becomes a sigh. She begins. She discusses at great length her horror about the murdered child in my last case. The sound of her voice weeps. She speaks quietly of other murdered children that slipped through the cracks in the system. Just like Maggie and I felt, Karen still feels she should have seen what was going on with Judge Jones and others—the cops, social workers, mandatory reporters—anyone who left gaps in the system. She has forgotten none of the children who died in this social war. Not one.

People who choose this profession are not the type of people who turn off the responsibilities at the end of the day. There is a decisive innate sense of responsibility attached to advocating for those who cannot advocate for themselves. There's a sense of guardianship involved in this type of social work. We have a deep-running responsibility to do what is right while residing in a corner of society that has gone all wrong. To think otherwise would be a lie.

She knows her staff were sent into harm's way. She worries she pushed us too much, that she didn't notice in time when we were in trouble, that she couldn't do enough to heal us.

I'm not sure what to say or if I should say anything. If I accidentally invalidate her feelings, the conversation is over. Who knows when she will be ready or able to let go of her self-imposed guilt again—if ever?

There is no doubt our emotions are on the edge, a raw edge. There is nothing I can do to fix the plane crash. I don't know what to say to ease her guilt about what we go through at work.

If the system is going to work, it will have to be accountable. We can only do so much on our own. But the changes that are occurring now are too late for a horrifyingly large number of children. We are human, so this appalling sickness in society wounds us deeply.

All that I can say is, "I'm here."

Karen clears her throat and says, almost in a desperate whisper, "There are so many things I need to tell Maggie." Her voice breaks, she turns toward me, grabbing my arm above the elbow and holding on desperately tight.

"Now I may never see her again. I may never get to tell her I was wrong about so many things, about our duty, the cases, the system—about everything. Oh, God! Why did I wait so long?"

Karen is pleading with her Creator for a second chance with Maggie.

She is quietly sobbing.

I wish I could tell her honestly that she would have that chance. By now, I don't even think God can give it to her. The best I can do is to gently place my hand on hers. I feel her lean toward me in response to the touch.

"Maggie knew, we all knew. It's all right."

Karen begins crying softly audibly now. I don't know what more she wanted to say, but she is unable to speak. Her shoulders start shaking violently. She sinks down to the sand, her face in her hands— uncontrollably sobbing, louder now.

I sink to the sand beside her. The knees of my jeans quickly soak through as I kneel near her in the damp sand with my arm around her shoulder. I want to say something—the right something—but I have no idea what else to say.

I don't think absolution is enough for Karen today. She needs more.

Children's Services social workers are a different breed of social worker than all of the rest. Not necessarily better—just different. As alone as we sometimes feel, we are a family, a unit, a community (not unlike the nuns), and we hurt terribly when one of us is in trouble. Maggie is in trouble. So is Karen. I whisper a prayer for wisdom.

I don't know if my prayer has been answered or not, but I have to intervene. I gently pull her against my shoulder.

"Maggie already knows," I say because I think it is true. "She knows —we all know. It is all right. We are alright, Karen," I say and gently I move her hair out of her eyes and ease my arms tighter around her.

She melts into my arms, sobbing uncontrollably, unashamed. From somewhere I gain the strength to hold her and comfort her. Not the physical strength to support her weight, but the inner strength to shoulder some of the weight she has been carrying on our behalf.

I speak for all of us in the department. On some level, even when the case blew up in our faces, we knew none of it was her fault. I probably should say the things I had been taught are the things to be said, but I have to go beyond the mechanics of this. No one, not even she, could have predicted the outcome or prevented Judge Jones' rulings, especially considering what we know now. I doubt we could have made a difference in time to save the little girl, even if we knew about the Judge then.

The nature of the system leaves social workers powerless. We know others are relying on us, which adds to the weight of the situation. We fight to overcome the immobilizing force. Most of the time we succeed. We never forget the times we don't.

I continue to follow my heart as I console Karen. I talk softly about everything I know to be Maggie's true feelings and beliefs, about all of the things Maggie would want me to tell Karen on her behalf. I apologize for my behavior, absolving her of everything. Karen could not have prevented what happened to me, nor was it her responsibility to do so. We need to carry our own weight.

She did nothing wrong. She had omitted nothing that would have made a difference. None of this, not the murdered child, or the Judge, is her fault. If only she could understand that we don't blame her for what went wrong, especially Maggie. Maggie admired her.

If anything, Karen strengthened us. She gave us the training needed to improve our skills and save more children than ever before. We are better professionals and better people because she came into our lives. No, she is not at fault. I do not blame her. Maggie does not blame her. No one blames her, and she must not blame herself for anything that has happened.

Karen's sobbing continues. There are years of weight on her shoulders, years for her to reconcile—to heal. Her strength and position within the welfare system had isolated her to keep all of the problems to herself. I knew she lived alone, but I had mistakenly thought Keith shared some of the weight, supervisor-to-supervisor. Apparently that was not the case.

Even the strong need a place where they can rest from being strong. When I worked for her, I didn't realize a friendship between us could be possible. None of that matters now. Or maybe everything matters. Maggie loves her—we all do.

Karen stops crying and sits quietly. Then she gets up, spent, almost in a daze, and starts walking back toward my apartment.

Even in the obscurity of the fog it is clear that she is emotionally exhausted. I catch up and hold her weight as I did with Mr. Goldstein, with my arm around her shoulder. I can only hope this walk has helped her begin the healing process, the process she guided her staff to find, but hadn't found herself.

As soon as we open the door and see Joseph's face we know he has heard something, and that it is not good news. They have called off the rescue due to the darkness and the bitter cold. But that makes no sense. They were arriving at the crash site when we went to the beach, and it was expected to take hours to fly them to the hospital and go back for the rescuers.

My imagination is uncontrollably running amuck, I say nothing.

"The news reports said there are no survivors from the plane crash," Joseph says softly. "Everyone was killed instantly when the plane crashed into the mountain."

He has tears in his eyes as he speaks. His voice is filled with overwhelming grief, though he gives a failed attempt to hide it behind a weak smile.

"Have they released the names yet?" I ask cautiously as I move Karen and myself to be near him.

They don't have to release the names. We have a feeling that Maggie and Dave were on that plane. They aren't coming home. We will never see them again. I will never hear Maggie's laugh as she torments me about something she thinks I am totally wrong about, then offers coffee to make peace so I will forgive her.

"No, they are in the process of contacting the families now," Joseph replies, still trying to be strong for us all.

Karen says, "Maggie carried her department I.D. in her wallet. Maybe the rescue workers will call the department if someone sees the card."

She calls the social worker on call to see if there have been any calls about Maggie. But there has been no call. Karen is frantically in denial. "Good, no calls. It might not be them," she tells us.

She knows it's them, but isn't ready to admit it.

Desperately searching for hope, Karen calls her voicemail to check for messages, and her home answering machine. There is no reason there will be a call at either of these message centers, but she had to try anyway.

Karen looks at the floor as she listens to her messages. When she finishes, she looks at us. Her eyes are hollow with disappointment. There is no message from Maggie. It doesn't matter if the authorities call or not. We know.

We huddle together trying to hear from the phone receiver as I call Frank, Maggie's brother. His wife answers the phone. She says Frank has just hung up from talking with the rescue command center. He is on the way to his parents' house in Monrovia to tell them about Maggie and Dave. Elda, Frank's wife, confirms our worst fears. It had been Maggie and Dave's plane that crashed. Now it's official.

My chest tightens, I can't breathe. My heart is pounding in my ears now that the words have been spoken. I gather my manners and ask if there is anything we can do. Elda declines the offer. Before I hang up the phone, I offer our condolences.

With my comments, the horrible truth is confirmed for Karen and Joseph. They've moved even closer together as they listen to my side of the phone conversation. Now they are holding on to each others' hand like they will die if they let go.

Slowly I sit down in the chair by the phone. Joseph and I just stare at each other like zombies. His eyes that were full of pain minutes ago are blank, now that we know for certain that our friends are dead.

Karen moves her other hand to Joseph's arm, as if holding his hand isn't enough to keep her on her feet. Joseph puts his free arm around her shoulder, and, rotating her toward him, he pulls her close to him with both arms holding her secure.

She is sobbing quietly into his chest. When her sobbing subsides momentarily, Joseph steers her to the sofa and eases her down. She complies with his assistance without a hint of strength of her own.

We can't speak. Words are nowhere to be found. Our throats are tight. The tears roll down our faces. We sob with the desire to cry out in sorrow, but not the strength to do so.

I move to sit on the other side of Karen. She begins to shiver, partly from the damp, but mostly from the loss of Maggie. I put one arm around her shoulder and reach across in front of her to hold onto Joseph's leg just above his knee.

Joseph reaches out and touches my hand softly, then firmly. The three of us sit there and sob nearly inaudibly, huddled together on the sofa—hanging on to each other.

I don't know how long we sat crying. The fog shuts out the rest of the world beyond the windows. We are horribly alone. There is no Hollywood movie music to go with this moment. Our world is silently empty.

~~~

~ CHAPTER 12 ~

Requiem

There is no denying that I miss Maggie terribly. Sometimes I actually physically ache on the inside. We had a bond that occurs only once every now and again. Maybe, just maybe, only once in a lifetime.

We knew things too. With one glance across our desks, we knew how each other's cases were going by the look in our revealing eyes. Even after I had been away, we still had that connection.

I shut my eyes, reliving a montage of memories involving Maggie. I can hear her laugh, but I can't recall an image of her face. During the five years in Nebraska I remembered every detail about Maggie's look. Now I can't see her in my memory, and it scares me.

I bolt up and begin pulling boxes out of the closet, dumping their contents on the floor and rifling through them for a photo of Maggie. "No, not that box," over and over again until I find the box from college. Leaving the mess on the floor, I seize the photos of Maggie and collapse on the sofa. I study her image carefully. I can't believe she is gone. My fingertips touch her image softly.

It was reckless for them to fly in such a small plane, in the mountains, in the winter. What had they been thinking? I don't dare allow myself to be angry with her—but if they had survived the crash, I would have given her a severe scolding.

Because Maggie and Dave have so many mutual friends, both families agree their funerals should be combined. As I think about the upcoming funerals, I imagine the attendance will be enormous. There would be two families in addition to twice the friends. All of the publicity about the crash will bring people out of the woodwork, including the media-grabbing politicians. I saw what happened at the funerals for the others in the plane; it was awful. I can't begin to imagine this production.

Until now I have made it a point-of-rule to avoid funerals. There was something about seeing my father in the casket that

I could never quite shake from my memory. I would not have gone to my mother's funeral if there had been any way to avoid it. There was no avoiding it. I went. Likewise, I will attend Maggie and Dave's funeral. But I will attend no others, no others.

~~~

I plan to wear the black dress that Maggie helped me select for some function that is far removed from my memory now. Maggie really liked the dress, and it looks good with my mother's pearls. I am as ready as I can be for this cultural requirement.

Karen, Keith, Joseph, and I ride together. None of us have the strength to go alone. Karen and I are in the back. I reach for her hand on the seat between us. Staring out the car window, I don't remember much about the drive to Monrovia. Everything seems a blur until we walk through the church doors and it hits me in the face. It's real.

The funeral begins. Keith and Joseph aren't Catholic, so they sit through the ceremony rather than genuflect and kneel as the Catholics do. Karen and I stand, sit, kneel, and recite the congregational responses. It is a very nice Mass. Father gave a nice homily. That is what they always say after a funeral, "Father gave a nice homily."

Maggie and I had conversations about the predictability of Mass. It calmed us after our work in a very unpredictable world. Maybe in a way it shielded us—for an hour—from the evil contra-culture that was forced upon us by its very existence.

Still, seeing their caskets side by side with matching ornate palls draped over them is not at all comforting to me. Who says funerals are to comfort the survivors? My knees are aching from the kneeler. The incense fills the air, making me dizzy and sick to my stomach with its thick, sweet smell. My chest hurts from missing Maggie, and I can hardly breathe because of the empty stabbing pain of her loss.

After the grave side service we walk aimlessly to the car. It is hard to say goodbye to Maggie and Dave. We are a mess. We ride in silence as Joseph drives Karen and Keith back to their cars. Then he drives to his office where I left my car. He said he isn't going to stay longer than it takes to look through his messages. He doesn't feel like working.

Maggie would have been pleased with her Mass. The singing from behind us, in the choir loft, sounded like angels from heaven. I turn the radio on, then turn it off again, and drive myself home in silence. Even my mind is empty, aching.

Karen said she might come by later. I don't really expect to see her. It is going to be an unproductive day. There isn't energy for even the most mundane tasks. After I change into something comfortable I sit on the sofa with my feet on the coffee table and a cup of coffee in my hand.

About the time I finish my first cup Karen is at my door. She waves off the offer of coffee, but I go for a refill. She stands just inside the door like a zombie until I return from the kitchen and gesture her to a chair. She makes no attempt to remove her coat when she sits down. Karen is pale and expressionless.

"Father gave a nice homily," I comment.

She nods her head slightly in agreement.

"The music was nice, too."

"Let's go to the beach," Karen says and rises.

Quickly I set down my cup, grab a coat and keys, and catch up with Karen, who is already out the door.

~~~

The ocean is rough from a tropical winter storm coming from the west coast of Mexico. The waves pound the beach with a thunderous booming that resounds in my chest. It is like a war zone and the coast is being bombarded with thousands of rounds. The ocean beats the Earth angrily, just the way I want to drop to my knees and pound my fists into the sand, full of grief.

For the longest time we say nothing, there isn't much to say. We smile an uneasy smile from time to time, but words don't come. Eventually, she tells me Linda followed the story about the downed plane in the media, as did most everyone else in the state. Because of Karen's contact, Linda asked if the lost social worker was one of hers.

"Linda and Todd made a sizable contribution to a statewide child abuse prevention coalition in Maggie and Dave's names."

"That's very thoughtful," I comment. "How is Linda?"

"Linda is doing as well as one might expect. It has only been a few months, and she still struggles. She did start therapy."

They must have had quite a conversation. It really doesn't surprise me that Karen would have kept in touch with Linda.

"Todd and his parents have been supportive of her. Linda has testified to the State Legislature about child abuse prevention and treatment funding." Karen smiles for the first time I've seen since before Thanksgiving. "The governor appointed Linda to the coalition's board."

It seems a little soon for Linda to be doing these things when she has personal wounds that need healing, but I reserve comment. It is nice to know our efforts to find Linda paid dividends by involving her and her celebrity in-laws in child abuse prevention efforts.

Karen shows me the "thank you" note she is sending to Linda and Todd. Maggie would approve of the donation—at least that is what Karen wrote. More importantly, Karen sincerely communicated deeply felt appreciation for Linda and Todd's thoughtfulness.

My fingertips run over the ivory-colored embossed card like it's a connection with Maggie. I stop when I notice Karen watching me. She says nothing when I return the card to her trembling hand, but I watch her fingers follow the same path as mine had. Everything, even the slightest things, connect us to Maggie, and to each other.

~~~

Joseph, Karen, and I help each other through the grieving process as best as we can—but life and work get in our way sometimes. There's a piece of the process we have to do on our own. I have done very little to reconcile her death in my mind. I don't really know where to begin, and I am not sure I want to whisk away the emotions tied to Maggie. I don't want the grief, but I want everything else. Is that possible?

Maggie and Dave are buried beside each other. In the weeks that follow their funeral I often stop by Rose Hills Cemetery on my way home from work to spend time with Maggie. I believe the essence of Maggie is not in the grave, but I sit and talk with her anyway. And, I wander to the beach as often as possible.

Slowly, very slowly, I am coming to accept the reality of the plane crash. Death is a part of life and we are not necessarily expected to comprehend it. I am glad for our years of friendship. These last eleven months have been very special. In some ways I am glad I went away, so when I returned we stopped taking our friendship for granted. Now I am glad we put so much effort into these last few months. She is a permanent ingredient to the wholeness of my being.

~~~

Several weeks after the funeral Frank brings two boxes to me. Maggie had kept a diary since she was in junior high school. Frank says he knows she never intended for him to read them, but he couldn't bring himself to throw them away.

After discussing it with his parents, they agree he should give them to me. He says he feels certain Maggie would approve of the idea. He shoves the boxes toward me rather abruptly.

I'm humbled with the thought, though it seems like an intrusion into her privacy.

Sensing my hesitation as I accept one of the boxes into my arms, Frank asks, "Did Maggie ever punch you?"

"What?" I reply as I struggle to readjust my hold on the box. "No, of course not," I say with a puzzled tone as I set the box on the table.

Frank sets his box on top of the other one.

"The first time I teased Maggie that I was going to read her diaries she punched me." He grins slightly with the memory. "She punched me so hard that I knew better than to ever think about reading them again."

Frank reaches into the box on top, handing me one of the diaries.

"Thank you, Frank. I will take good care of them for her," I say taking the book from his trembling hand.

He begins to cry.

I hold him tight with my arms around his shoulders and Maggie's diary clasped in my hands behind his back. My eyes and heart are begging to cry, but I insist they wait until Frank leaves.

Many times since Frank gave me Maggie's diaries I sit and hold one of them tightly to my chest. Holding her diary feels like a link to her. Her family was thoughtful to give them to me, and it brings tears to my eyes every time I think of it. I hope Maggie would have approved, somehow I think she might.

Eventually I find the courage to open her diary. When I see her familiar handwriting, I am not sure if I should or can read her entries. I snap the book shut and lay it on the coffee table. I stare at it from a safe distance, and I sip my coffee.

After a long painful silence within me, I set my cup down and pick up the diary. I open it again, then quickly shut it. I clasp my hands around the diary, lean my head down on the book with my chin resting on its edge, and shut my eyes. My chest hurts from missing Maggie. My eyes are begging to cry.

After a few minutes, I take a deep breath, then open her diary again. Deliberately, I turn to the entry of the day I returned to L.A. I wondered what Maggie thought of the day that I stopped by the office unannounced. She never really commented about my abrupt return. Maggie simply wrote,

Kate has come home. I am glad.

I sit staring at the page for some time, trying to imagine that day from her perspective. I had expected her to write more than that. I become lost in the moment of it and time passes more easily. I read the entry again.

In the evenings while I wait for Mr. Goldstein to arrive for our walk, I begin to venture to other places in her diary—looking for insights into my friend. Some days Maggie wrote a great deal. Other days she didn't make an entry at all. I begin to read her diary at length when I miss her the most.

She wrote fondly of Karen. I consider sharing those entries with Karen as part of her peace-finding process. For now, Karen is keeping busy with her new diversion, the California Child Abuse Prevention Coalition (Cal-CAP). Linda submitted Karen's name to her father-in-law, the governor, for appointment to the Cal-CAP Board. Regardless of the nobility of her diversion, Karen will eventually have to return her attention to the loss of Maggie and finish grieving.

~~~

To shake up my life even more, Joseph is going home for a couple of months over the holidays. The timing for his trip is

~173~

incredibly lousy. He asks me to go with him, but work will not allow me to go right now, even for a short visit. Besides, I don't feel up to meeting a lot of new people in an unknown country. Joseph offers to change his plans, but I urge him to go home and see his family. After all, the ticket was bought months ago. Somehow life has to continue. We should stick to our plans and move forward.

Moreover, after losing his best friend, the trip will comfort him in ways I cannot. He needs Ireland. It is his beach, his place of solace and healing.

Luckily for me, Joseph's flight is scheduled at a time when I can take him to the airport. At least we have that much.

While we wait for his flight and after Joseph exchanges his U.S. dollars, we go to the duty-free shop for gifts for his family. Finally, he disappears from sight as he boards the plane. I watch the runway long after his plane enters the sky and vanishes.

Leaving LAX I brave the torrents of traffic, I instinctually make my way home, too numb with loneliness to mind the wait as the traffic stalls to a standstill on the 405 heading south.

When I arrive home I am painfully aware of the void caused by watching Joseph leave. I sit down to write an email to him. It takes several drafts to get past a sappy-sounding message. It isn't perfect, but I want some sort of connection with him.

The email helped, but is not enough. I take Maggie's diary with me to sit in the sand and listen to the ocean sounds on the deserted winter beach.

My dearest Diary; There are moments in life beyond words, beyond emotion. Only the silence around me fills my breath, and gives me life. For lingering moments, everything stands still, as if frozen in time. There is no violence or laughter, only silence beyond the sounds of my breathing. I shut my eyes, not wanting to disturb the moment and hurl myself crashing into the world again. My soul desires peace and quiet, without thoughts disturbing it.

Karen and I see little of each other in the weeks that follow the funeral. I planned to spend time with her, but found myself spending time alone. I make several failed attempts to finish my Christmas shopping, but I lack the initiative to maneuver the masses. I decide the only solution is to survive this holiday duty as best I can. Sending Christmas cards will have to wait until next year. I just need time to get up to speed again. Shopping and everything else will eventually get done.

I look forward to walks with Mr. Goldstein when his social calendar will allow the time. To think less than a year ago he had trouble walking across the street and down the beach to the water. Now he has a social calendar.

Mr. Goldstein deliberately directs our conversation to Maggie. At first I resist the discussions, but they are healing once I trust him.

Many nights I sit for hours, feet propped up, drinking coffee and reading Maggie's diaries. Sometimes I read only one entry, then re-read it several times. Sometimes I read a month's worth. Most of the time I pick up the book and read where it falls open.

I am learning so much about the depth and breadth of my friend. I am learning some things about myself, too, as I read Maggie's insights into the complexities of life.

Tonight I leaf randomly through the pages of Maggie's diary— reading whatever catches my eye.

...Life is good, not necessarily easy, but good.

Yes. Rather simplistic, though, I hope that it is true. I need it to be true. I hope Maggie knew what she was talking about when she wrote this. I want something to hold on to that will make me feel secure, even for a minute, to see me through this time of mourning.

My dearest Diary: Sometimes I wonder if there is a better way to make life decisions; is there some simple formula to seeking clarity? Is there a guideline to one's destiny—optimal destiny?

Are we—am I—close to being all that I can be? Is this all there is or are there other depths of who we are—yet undiscovered?

Staring at the page as I run my fingertips across the handwriting, I understand the quest, and crave a sense of clarity for myself. I wish Maggie and I had more time to have these discussions when she was alive. I am envious of her diary for knowing her so well.

My dearest Diary: It is days like this that I understand the true value of friends. Friendship is an amazing thing. No one can tolerate too many needy people in their life. But the give and take in real friendship occurring over the years is a wonderfully fulfilling experience. Hurry home, Kate.

"Maggie, I'm sorry I left without a word. I am sorry I wasn't a better friend," I whisper to her diary, wishing for a reply. Sometimes it is almost as if she does reply.

I am not sure if I feel better or worse. I think about our friendship, the many cases at work that flung us into a dark and evil world, a world we fought to keep from totally eradicating our humanity. I know what she meant about needy people and about friendship, true meaningful friendship. I understand her entries in a way that I think no one else can. I really miss her, but feel blessed for the time we had together.

Often Maggie's diary does not elaborate on the external things that occurred to bring her insight—only the results.

My dearest Diary: Lately I have been reminded of both the frailty and strength of the human spirit. What exactly constitutes the human spirit? "Choice." I think that we "choose" to be strong, we "choose" to succeed, we 'choose' to triumph over the adversities of life. Even on our own, alone, we choose how to face life on our terms: in an honorable fashion or to whimper and whine, feeling sorry for ourselves every time there is a bump in the road.

The simple truth is others can't fill that "place" within that allows—no, compels us—to continue forward on our personal sojourn. I believe each of us possesses the power to face adversity with dignity—to stand alone and walk through the tempest, and emerge—perhaps wounded—but not broken. Clearly, the choice is ours to make.

After months of agonizing entries about the dead child, the graphic police photos that showed only a glimpse of the horror the child went through, and the horrible guilt of not being able to stop the murderer from abusing again, there was a long silence in her diaries.

Since I was the primary on the case, I hadn't realized Maggie felt the same guilt as I felt about being unable to protect the little girl. The difference between us was that my silence was from a distance which lasted five years.

A few months later, without saying what happened to her or inside of her, Maggie finally wrote again.

My dearest Diary: Please believe it was not my intention to neglect you. My apologies. I have discovered something about myself —I am very strong through adversity, though not as good with 'good' times. Things are going well now, but I find myself tentative in trusting that things are, indeed, well.

I suppose I don't want to be blindsided again by my childlike trust in the goodness of life. I will strive to relax and learn to trust in God during good times, as I do in tough times. Though I suppose it is easy to trust in God when there is nowhere else to turn.

Somehow Maggie found peace. Did it have something to do with God or something to do with her? I wish she had written the details of her recovery, leaving a map for me to follow.

Maggie and I never mentioned our personal spirituality. I wish now that we had. The next entry was written a week later.

My dearest Diary: We are laughing again at work. I see the creative side in each of us starting to emerge from the dark night. We must consume it and be willing to be consumed by it.

Though I don't know what prompted her comments, I find them strangely enlightening and comforting. They give me hope.

I tell myself I will read one more entry tonight, then go to bed. My inner spirit is in need of consoling words.

My dearest Diary: It isn't how long one lives, it is how wide that really matters.

Right on cue, Maggie's words are exactly on point, as if she was here to deliver them herself. I want to believe Maggie's life was not cut short, that it was as long as it was meant to be. Her words make it seem a little less like her future had been robbed.

In time I will reconcile Maggie's death. After all, I have managed all of the other deaths in my life.

With that I lay her diary on the coffee table and go to bed. Tomorrow is another day, and I am too tired to contemplate the wisdom of the universe any further tonight.

~~~

~ CHAPTER 13 ~

The Celebration of Miracles

The good sisters are planning a Christmas pageant with the Spirit of Hope families. I love Christmastime, but I haven't been able to get into the mood since the little girl was murdered. I thought this first Christmas home would be different, but it is even more difficult with Maggie gone. I am barely able to get my shopping done, and that was only because Ilene pushed me to get it done or I might have missed it all together.

Hopefully, the activities at Spirit of Hope will provide a suitable diversion from my grief. Sister Clare let it slip that she is praying for "our" baby to arrive in time to play the starring role in the Christmas pageant. True to what I have come to expect, I, too, believe our baby will be born in time for Christmas, not only because that is the due date, but because the nuns want it that way.

I am beginning to think even God, with His infinite wisdom, thinks twice before refusing these sisters anything they request. If He did refuse them even the slightest of their desires, I see no evidence of it. It seems there is a steady flow of well-timed miracles around here.

Sister Clare is frequently heard going to the chapel. Because of her limp there is a distinctive clicking sound from her dangling rosary, swaying on her belt as she walks. Whenever I see—or hear—her heading in the direction of chapel, I can't help smiling. I think to myself, though I would never admit it out loud, "Look out, God, Sister Clare is looking for you."

The Christmas program is scheduled for two days before Christmas. In the meantime, children, their parents, and nuns are singing Christmas songs under their breath while they are busy with their daily routine. That is, all except Sister Mary Veronica, the music teacher, who believes one should "PRO-JECT" their voice at all times. And she does. Luckily, Sister Mary Veronica has a beautifully trained voice. It echoes throughout the building and down the hallways, adding to the Christmas feeling in the air.

The staff is willingly recruited as stagehands. Those who can sew are persuaded to bring their sewing machines and are pressed into service making costumes.

Others are delegated to Sister Bridget's work detail. She is busy making the scenery and is convinced anyone can paint under her watchful direction. To my surprise, she is quite handy with power tools and seems to have an endless supply of lumber.

All of the staff is expected to scavenge for props. Looking at the prop list, one would think this is a Broadway production.

I send Joseph a Christmas card and later another email. He never answered the first one, but I miss his toothy smile and twinkling eyes. The email doesn't return as undeliverable, so I have hope that he will respond this time. I am eager for any contact from him. Maybe I will hear from him at Christmas.

The other man in my life, Mr. Goldstein, has invited me to celebrate Hanukkah with him. While we are on our walks he helps me prepare by teaching me the prayers and responses for the celebration. I give my sincerest effort to the process because the goal is important to Mr. Goldstein, and to me.

He is a patient teacher and I am an eager student, even after it is painfully apparent that I am not necessarily adept at learning Hebrew. I want to at least memorize the prayer that seems to be his favorite or the most important to our celebration. He accepts my pronunciation attempts, if they are reasonably correct. I believe it pleases him that his young Irish-Catholic friend wants to make the effort.

It pleases me to be included in his celebration. We are family, now. Little does Mr. Goldstein know that I have become desperate and have the neighborhood rabbi helping me. It requires a group effort for me to be ready in time, but I am committed to do my part. Granted, it will take a miracle.

~~~

Whenever possible I walk along the beach listening to the tape of Hebrew prayers Rabbi Karol made for me. I repeat the words over and over, struggling to master them. All I can do is give my best effort, the rest is up to God, providing Sister Clare allows Him time for projects other than "her" baby.

Before long my footsteps in the sand are matching the rhythm of the waves and the sound of the prayers in my earphones.

Baruch atah Adonai
Eloheinu melech ha-olam
Asher kideshanu b'mitzvotav
Vitzivanu
L'hadlik ner shel Chanukkah
(Praised are You,
Our God, Ruler of the universe...)

I am pleased the words are beginning to sound familiar and I'm beginning to master the pronunciation. I am immensely pleased with the gift of sharing I can give Mr. Goldstein, the gift he has given to me countless times.

~~~

In the evenings I to curl up on the sofa with coffee and Maggie's diaries. With the hopefulness of the season, I scan the diaries' pages with a willingness to learn more—more about Maggie, more about me in the process, and more about the human condition in general.

I find I have gravitated to reading only from the diaries covering the five years I was away. Sometimes I include that last, highly visible investigation Maggie and I did together up to my return to California, nearly a year ago.

For some reason I can't bring myself to read the entries from this year, except the entry of the day I returned. I have some catching up to do before I read this year's pages. I recognize that I fear reading her last entry. For now, instinct is guiding me to read her entries of the lost past.

Maggie's mood fluctuated during the end of the investigation. I know, in retrospect, that my mood did too. As it became increasingly clear in court that Judge Jones was biased in his denial or acceptance of motions, evidence, and testimony, especially my testimony, she writes:

My dearest Diary: I am grieving the wasted years. Damn them all, and damn my stupidity!

~181~

Maggie continues to write through the nights and days of darkness until she writes herself into the light. Within weeks, her writing indicates she began again to reconcile her pain in intermittent intervals. I wish for her sense of clarity and ability to look within myself and within life. I wish I had better insight during those days. I wish that I had been stronger.

Her writing amazes me. I cling to it. There seems to be something there for me in each entry, even if I don't see it the first time I read it. I need her and she is here from beyond the grave.

My dearest Diary: Flashes of insight come unexpectedly, at random moments, but, in truth, I think there is always "insight" dimly looming in the shadow of our consciousness. I feel unsophisticated when I'm betrayed, yet betrayal may be the greatest teacher. I think there are many distractions in life and the hardest thing any of us does is see the big picture, then focus on the narrow bit that is our path to travel. When we try to catch it all and hold it all, we lose our balance and struggle to right ourselves and stay on track. It is letting go of the distractions that frees us to be who we are in our innermost being.

I have an unquenchable desire to read Maggie's diaries. On the weekends I take them to the beach and sit reading. I almost think the light of day helps me understand her writings more than anything else, though coffee and the beach help too.

But it is at night her words are most able to speak to my spirit. Even though her resolution of the guilt we silently shared was a fleeting remedy, I would have learned that reality sooner if I had read her entries in the order they were written. For now, I am committed to my method of reading randomly and seeing how her writing touches me at the moment.

My thoughts take me back in time to before I threw my keys on Karen's desk. I can remember the frustration of those last days in the department. I can identify with Maggie's thoughts the first few days after we learned of the little girl's death.

At the time, and for years later, I shared similar feelings of uncontrollable hopelessness and inexplicable feelings of despair. Maggie found the strength to be honest about those feelings. Perhaps in time I will, too.

My dearest Diary: ...As for myself, I dream up projects and goals to give myself a sense of purpose—but I don't really feel it. I am just trying to survive for now and hope there is a future, and that it is far better than this.

Even now I fight the memories of those days when Maggie and I struggled to make sense of things. While I was tossing my keys on Karen's desk, Maggie found a brief moment of clarity. I am thankful Maggie decided to write something specific this time.

My dearest Diary: Dave says I am too circumspect. That is why things bother me so deeply. ...I have been attempting to pray more and think less.

As I try to make sense of my confused and yet unresolved emotions from the past and the loss of Maggie, I find my mood beginning to pace Maggie's secret thoughts in her diary.

My dearest Diary: There seem to be several new insights on the horizon, though they are still unfocused. In addition to whatever reflections those insights spawn, I still must remain motivated to stay the course. There is the lure of intoxication in enjoying the emergence of "peace." But it has been slow in coming and long overdue. The drunkenness should not take too much of my time, yet I want to pause and appreciate my new birth. After all, I have suffered the wait. And, oh, it has been such a long and lonely wait.

I'm sorry that my actions left both of us alone with our pain and guilt. At least she had her diary and Dave. For a while she must have expected to hear from me. My remorse is useless.

I desperately want to mimic what she did to heal, if there is any possible way to do so. I wish she wrote more of the internal workings of her thoughts, not just the outcome of them. I know, though, there are no easy answers.

It was nearly three years after I went to Nebraska when Maggie finally wrote:

My dearest Diary: I have come to the end of some sort of self-imposed penance. With a certain amount of contentment, I find no burning emotions to express. Though not everything is as I would hope, I cannot bring myself to be dissatisfied with life.

I frantically search preceding entries for what brought Maggie's absolution. I want the same for myself. But there is no key to unlock the secrets. I have only the slightest hope that I will find the inner peace she found.

My dearest Diary: It is comical how different life looks in the light of day. We expend a great deal of energy getting things physically in order—then, to avoid inner boredom, we crave the spontaneity of the moment, though we are afraid to risk the uncertainty it holds.

In life, spontaneity cannot come from chaos. There must be some sort of order about the workings of the universe for life to make sense. I hate it when I feel the unresolved turmoil running rampant inside of me. I thought I was making progress until Maggie died. That grief has stirred everything inside me into a whirlwind.

The coffee tastes particularly good tonight, so I make another half pot. I sit for a while sipping it, and I hold her diary on my lap—closed. I am not thinking anything in particular, simply holding my link to Maggie.

After a while, I lean forward and slide the diary onto the coffee table in front of me. It isn't the end of the book, but I feel finished with it. Perhaps I am beginning to understand. I decide to put away all of Maggie's diaries. For now I must move on with my own life. I must find my own absolution.

~~~

My full attention turns to Mr. Goldstein and our Hanukkah celebration. As I prepare for this celebration, I review in my mind as many of the details as I can remember from my research. I continue to practice the prayers in Hebrew.

The first day of Hanukkah arrives. It takes me awhile to go through my closet to select just the right outfit to wear. With a selection in each hand, I position myself before the mirror and alternate the choices in front of me to see which seems right. I decide I don't like either of them, toss them on the foot of my bed, and start the process all over again. I settle on a nice navy-blue suit—Maggie always said navy is one of my good colors.

This is one time there is no such thing as being fashionably late. Since the celebration must begin at sunset, I have checked the paper for the predicted time for today and have paced myself accordingly.

I ring Mr. Goldstein's doorbell, grinning with excitement and holding his gift. I try unsuccessfully to calm myself, but when Mr. Goldstein answers the door my grin explodes.

Mr. Goldstein attempts to be more formal—or maybe it is reverent, but I can see the excitement in his eyes. He is dressed for the occasion and looks handsome in his emeritus suit. He smiles warmly as he holds out his hand and says, "Katerina, please come in, come in."

Unsure of exactly what to do, I hand him the gift wrapped in blue-and-silver paper. As I enter his apartment I smell the wonderful aroma of the potato pancakes he made.

"I used Sylvia's recipe," he says, glancing at her photograph then back, "We always cooked together for Hanukkah."

I smile warmly and say, "I miss her too."

Before I arrived he had cleared the little table by the window and covered it with a beautifully hand-decorated cloth. I can't help running my fingertips over the raised threads of the embroidery design.

Mr. Goldstein moves the menorah and the shamash from a side table and notices that I am admiring the stitching on the tablecloth. He touches the threads and says, "Sylvia stitched this during her long recovery in hospital after we were liberated from the camp. Everything we had was taken. We didn't know where our families were or if they were alive." His eyes redden.

He pauses to regain his composure then begins again. "She said, 'Abraham, it is a miracle we are alive. We will celebrate the miracle of Hanukkah with a new tablecloth this year. It is a new beginning,' and she kept stitching without saying another word about our imprisonment," he says, then falls silent.

We move close together near the table to watch out the window for the last of the setting sun to disappear into the Pacific across the street. Then Mr. Goldstein begins. His voice is rich and clear.

> Baruch atah Adonai
> Eloheinu melech ha-olam
> Asher kideshanu b'mitzvotav

Vitzivanu
L'hadlik ner shel Chanukkah...

Thus began our celebration of eight days of light and of the miracles in our lives.

After spending the evening with Mr. Goldstein, it seems a natural transition to sit on my sofa with my feet propped on the coffee table and reflect on the evening—and the events of the past year. "Life is good; not necessarily easy, but good," Maggie wrote. I smile.

For all of us—in uniquely private ways—it has been a year of transitions, a year of loss, a year of healing, and of struggling to find inner strength.

I miss Maggie, but she is gone and isn't coming back. I need to concentrate on the people who are here. Karen has taken up the torch of the California Child Abuse Prevention Coalition and moving it into a viable force in Southern California, as it is up north. She is so driven in her commitment that I sometimes wonder if it is a release of her expertise and energy—or a consuming diversion from dealing with Maggie's death.

~~~

Karen's department is scheduled to host the Coalition's December roaming meeting. Karen has invited Linda to stay an additional day after the meeting and attend the Spirit of Hope Christmas Pageant.

Since Linda's public disclosure of her abusive childhood, she has become the Governor's ambassador of California's children. He calls the coalition "guardians of our children."

Savvy politicians and marketing firms have adopted the Governor's battle cry, "for our children." The solution to every debate about violence, drugs, hate crimes, homelessness, abuse, and even the ongoing energy crisis comes down to doing what is "right for our children."

It's not that I disagree with these issues, it's that as a society we have a long way to go to protect our children. It is everyone's duty to care and intervene. I believe when we take care of the tiniest members of our world, all of us will be better people, and richer for having made the effort to keep our children safe.

~~~

It is obvious Karen is proud of her sister, Mother Elizabeth, and her contribution to alleviating the homeless situation. Karen wrote articles about Spirit of Hope for social work and child psychology journals and a feature for the Sunday newspaper insert.

Because of those articles, even the media has taken notice of Spirit of Hope. Saint Mark's switchboard is inundated with calls begging to make referrals or for interviews with Mother Elizabeth, and on occasion to make donations of Christmas gifts for the families. A decorated tree arrived yesterday, to the children's delight.

Governor Whitmore is encouraged with the possibility of a real plan to help California's homeless families. He and Mother Elizabeth have become close allies. Mother Elizabeth made it clear in her public comments that she hopes the governor will find funds for duplicating Spirit of Hope in other cities in the state.

I suspect it is more than coincidence that Karen wants to introduce Linda to Mother Elizabeth. As for Linda, she fills her life with her role as "the children's ambassador." Karen reports Linda enthusiastically accepted her invitation to the Christmas pageant.

December 21st, right on schedule, the "Spirit of Hope" baby arrives. She is beautiful, with big eyes and blushing cheeks. Her parents name her Clare Elizabeth, for obvious reasons. Words are inadequate to describe Sister Clare's reaction to the baby and her name. Little Clare's birth gives all of us at Spirit of Hope a renewed sense of hope.

Watching Sister Clare hold baby Clare might be described as a spiritual experience. Sister Clare chuckles under her breath when baby Clare squints and squirms before making new-baby sounds as she snuggles and settles for a nap in the nun's arms.

Little Clare had perfectly timed her arrival. She came home from the hospital in time for dress rehearsal, not that she needs to rehearse being the most beautiful baby in the universe.

Later, one of the other children asked if she was the new Baby Jesus. Only a child would accept Jesus as a boy or a girl.

Little Clare's parents are cast as Mary and Joseph. Father Herber is the narrator, and his rich, deep voice is perfect. The homeless choir opens the program with Handel's "Hallelujah." It is marvelously professional sounding.

Little Clare Elizabeth stretches, as if on cue, reaching a tiny hand out of her blanket so everyone can see that she is a real baby. When she moves, the congregation catches their breath. The sound of the audience caught off guard takes advantage of the marvelous acoustics in the church, sending chills through me—and probably others, too.

Mother Elizabeth's eyes fill to the brim with tears during the opening moments of the Christmas pageant. The tears stay in their place. Her face is beaming with excitement and pride. She looks as serene and holy as the statues in the alcoves in the hallways. I feel as if I have been deeply touched, transformed.

Karen is sitting next to me. I glance in her direction to see if she has seen her Sister-sister's response. Karen is looking in Mother Elizabeth's direction and smiling. Apparently Karen has seen her too.

Linda and her husband are sitting on the other side of Karen. They seem lost in the drama of the play. This night puts the rest of the year into its proper perspective, at least for the moment.

Life is good; not always easy, but good.

Karen's daughters are home from college, so, of course, I don't plan to see her today. I could go to Spirit of Hope and watch everyone open the gifts that one of the Indian casinos donated, but instead I spend time at "Vinney's" (Saint Vincent de Paul) Mission helping serve Christmas dinner to other homeless people.

After lunch I walk along the beach with Mr. Goldstein. Since he is Jewish, there is no risk of intruding on his Christmas plans.

The ocean is strangely still. The sky and the water are the same tint of gold as the sand. I have never seen anything like it. There are no waves. The water looks like a calm lake. Both Mr. Goldstein and I are surprised by the silence of the ocean. We walk to the pier to look down on the water and see its stillness from above.

Kathryn's Beach

The pier anchors the beach. That is where everything begins and ends, that is where the high and low tide is posted, that is where the Beach Patrol has their base station. And that is where I sometimes go to Ruby's diner at the end of the pier to eat and look out on the ocean without obstructions to the view.

There are no warnings posted to stay out of the water for any of the usual reasons, such as high bacteria count or an abundance of various water creatures that bite or sting. There are no waves, even small ones, breaking on the pier pylons. For that matter, there aren't any swells in the water that I can detect from our vantage point.

Mr. Goldstein remarks about the calm, peaceful feeling of the nearly deserted beach. We keep looking at the mirror-smooth water, then at each other in amazement, and back to the water.

All of the action is stopped. It is the strangest real-life thing I've ever seen. Mr. Goldstein agrees. It seems so silent without the sound of the waves crashing on the beach and against each other in the backwash.

For the first time, I notice the absence of the seagull sounds. I look around for the birds, but they are nowhere in sight. Even the sandpipers are gone. That probably means something. Maybe a tropical storm is coming, but I haven't heard of any typhoons in the Pacific during the previous week. Even so, it has never been like this before a storm.

"Wait here, I'm going home and get my camera," I tell Mr. Goldstein.

He nods in agreement. It is as if he is left to guard this mysterious mood, so that it won't slip away while I am gone.

~~~

Sometimes photos don't capture what we see with our eyes. This time I was lucky. The photos show nearly exactly what we saw. I had double prints developed. Mr. Goldstein tilts his head to get near his stack of photos at the correct angle for his bifocals. I study my copies. We comment on things in the pictures. It's amazing that we were there to experience such a phenomenon—a still ocean. I think it was a miracle or a sign of some sort.

~~~

~ CHAPTER 14 ~

A New Beginning

Joseph is still in Ireland. I think of him often, but I haven't heard from him. I won't admit it to anyone, but I am terribly hurt that he didn't at least send a Christmas card.

I consider hopping on a plane to spend New Year's Eve with him, but I decide to stay in L.A. I don't want to intrude on his visit home during the holidays.

Early in the afternoon, when it is New Year's Eve on his side of the globe, I think of him. With my freshly brewed cup of coffee I toast him and the New Year at what I believe to be precisely midnight in Ireland. Even having my feelings hurt doesn't keep him out of my thoughts. I am hopelessly in love with him.

~~~

Instead of a trip to Ireland, Karen and I plan to spend New Year's Eve together. Her girls are with their father for the second half of their holiday from the university.

Mr. Goldstein is at the Senior Center with his friends, although he thinks the party will use New York time and end early, so "those old people can be in bed by 9:00." He is so funny.

Our party isn't glamorous. We bring in the new year with carry-out Chinese food. The meal reminds me of our first dinner together after I returned home. It is almost as if the year has come full circle.

I can't help laughing when I read my fortune. "Now they tell me," I say as I hand the slip of paper to Karen.

She smiles when she reads it, but doesn't seem to see the same humor in it that I did.

> **Simplicity of character is the natural result of profound thought.**

"I guess the paradox just struck me funny," I lamely explain, but don't say it is the paradox with my life that is funny.

This year has been difficult in so many ways, but all of the details are left unsaid. I was on the right track when I allowed myself to be led home by instinct.

When will I learn not to try so hard to avoid the things about the past that caused me to question my self-worth, my abilities, and my emotions? I really must learn to trust my emotions—to trust me.

Maybe, just maybe, everything will find its own equilibrium if I don't fight it or push it forward before its time. Maybe there is a natural order to the universe. Sometimes I wonder what made me want to get my life back on track. Whatever it was, this has been quite a year. Though most of it was good, I would have to say I hope the new year will be less exciting. I'm ready for some peace and contentment, and maybe, for a while, a little less growth. Whether or not I have the answers doesn't seem to matter as much as it once did.

My thoughts return to the casual conversation at hand, as it always does on New Year's Eve, to what we did last New Year's Eve.

Karen reports she spent a quiet evening at home last year. However, the year before she attended an elegant party.

"I was tending bar in Nebraska," I say with a tongue-in-cheek grin.

Karen laughs.

But the words mean so much more to me than "tending bar." I came home.

I return her laugh with a smile. There is only one thing to do to make the coming year complete—we bundle up and walk to the beach.

The night is clear. The moon seems brighter than usual. The rushing waves are somewhat calm with a rhythm of serenity. We turn toward Karen's favorite place on the beach, reminding me of the day Mother Elizabeth was there, too, and the day we learned Maggie was dead.

"Do you believe there is an afterlife?" I ask, more seriously than before.

"Yes. I think I do, Katey. Do you?" she says thoughtfully, seriously.

"Yes," I agree willingly. "If not, then I will miss our beach, I will miss you, and I will miss me," I say, realizing it is true. I really do (finally) feel that way about myself again after all of these years of exile.

I have come a long way to think of myself in affectionate enough terms to miss me. Finally, I am beginning to find my own sense of peace. It seems we really are all going to be okay.

Karen nods in agreement, then smiles. "Life is full of contrasts, of paradox, like your fortune cookie."

"It isn't how long we live, it is how wide that really matters." I softly speak Maggie's words to our mutual friend.

The clock at the church chimes twelve strikes, indicating midnight. A new beginning.

"Happy New Year, Katey!" Karen says as she lifts her coffee.

"Yes, Happy New Year!" I laugh and I raise my coffee to join the toast.

~~~

~ Acknowledgments ~

My family, aunts and uncles, twenty-seven first cousins, their spouses, children grandchildren, and great grandchildren who really do gather for Thanksgiving dinner at a park in Southern California;

To the spirit of our grandfather, Arthur Thomas Stewart, and our grandmother, the love of his life, Minerva Jane Evans Stewart. She was matriarch of our clan, the goddess of wisdom, an example of inner strength, and more importantly the one who taught me to laugh in the face of adversity. Graciously, she left her family a rich legacy;

For research assistance, Chief Warrant Officer 3, Michael L. Tibbs, Sr., USCG, Baltimore, MD; Janice Laman Zitek, my sister-in-law; and David Shrimplin, my cousin.

Special thanks to Terrie Berg, my friend, who started this project when we were snowed in during an ice storm. She called and said she had nothing to read, so I wrote. Terri asked, "Then what happened?" wrote a chapter every night after the kids were in bed and emailed it to her. Without Terrie, there would be no Kathryn. My deepest gratitude is to Terri.

Special thanks to Joyce at Design by Joyce for support, advice, and a fantastic website at www.NadineLamanBooks.com.

Special thanks to Ilene Shrimplin Wood for unwavering support and assistance throughout this project.

Thanks for the comments, advice, and commitment:
Elynor Breiding; Tom Brown; Elda Clyma; Judy Craig; Ray Derby; Mary Ann Gabel, Sister Ann Cecile Guame, C.S.J; Father Alvin Herber, C.PP.S.; Asmaa Kadry; Keri Kahle; Karen LaMunyon; Shawn McKee; Beverly Po-t; Sister Rosemary Rader, O.S.B; Charlotte Stewart Saben; Judge Pauline Schwarm, Retired; Ruth Stewart Selee; Carlene Stewart Smith, and Neil Burton.

~~~

This is Kathryn's Beach

Dear Reader,
If you enjoyed this book, please tell your friends,
and write a review on GoodReads.com and Amazon.
Thank you, Nadine